jumping

jumping

A NOVEL

Jane Peranteau

HAMPTON ROADS

Cover design by Jim Warner
Interior designed by Frame25 Productions

Hampton Roads Publishing Company, Inc.
Charlottesville, VA 22906
Distributed by Red Wheel/Weiser, LLC
www.redwheelweiser.com

Sign up for our newsletter and special offers by going to
www.redwheelweiser.com/newsletter/.

ISBN: 978-1-57174-719-8

Library of Congress Cataloging-in-Publication Data available
upon request.

Printed in the United States of America.

EBM

10 9 8 7 6 5 4 3 2 1

Dedicated to Jake.

Contents

Introduction

She stands at the edge, where he stood. The wind whips her skirt around her legs, persuasive. She sways.

She has stood alone at this spot in her dreams for as long as she can remember, feeling the Void's call. It always feels familiar. In her dreams, she jumps. She falls and falls, twisting and turning, grabbing for a handhold, a ledge, anything, as panic grabs her breath. She never sees what's beyond this upending fall into darkness. She never touches bottom. All she's left with, when she jolts awake, gasping for air, fighting her sheets, is the taste and smell of her fear. She has it now.

What her dreams didn't have was the massively ancient presence that surrounds her now at the edge. It is as permeating and knowing as wind. It has found her and she will follow.

CHAPTER ONE

Babe Arrives in Town

HOW DID I GET HERE? For a moment I can't remember. I didn't walk, though I could have. It's only a little over three miles north of town. I drove the narrow dirt Forest Service road that branches off from the paved county road—the one that comes directly through town. It's afternoon, and things are a bit drowsy.

I parked on the edge of the Forest Service road and walked the half-mile to the Void, which is on public land. I walked through knee-high grass right up to it. I notice it doesn't feel drowsy at the edge of the Void. I stand at the edge, feeling the wind come up all of a sudden, its sound masking any other sound, as if I stand in the middle of a pause—just me and the wind. The energy of the Void is palpable, unmistakable. I can almost hear it hum. It's familiar, as if I remember it, though it's too unsettling to be comfortable. It feels like the first time I took mushrooms and the walls of my small off-campus apartment started to undulate, and I could see through the cat to what it carried, and I had a new understanding of reality after that.

I had to come here first, as any good reporter would, and I'm trying to remain the reporter, the recorder of facts, as I stand here looking in. I can't help but envision Duncan Robert falling, gravity causing him to pick up speed. I can feel the pull of gravity in the Void, especially here at the edge. It's dark in there, past the opening, with nothing to stop your fall.

It's been waiting for me. It knows I've wanted to know it. I know that's crazy, and it gives me the willies. I laugh at myself, but I can't escape the feeling. Probably everyone feels this way, I tell myself, when they're standing at the edge. Then I notice the light behind me has changed. More time has passed than I realized, and I'm not sure how that happened. The afternoon sun is dipping toward the horizon, the light through the woods getting dimmer, and I back away from the edge. I wouldn't want to be caught here in the dark. I turn and quickly follow the faint path back through the woods to my car.

As I drive the dirt road to the county road that takes me back to town, I think about how glad I am to be here, in this corner of the Northeast. I've been waiting for this for a long time. I grew up not far from this town of Dexter, New Hampshire, and had heard about the Void from the time I was a child. In school, I wrote essays about it and used it as an example whenever I got the chance, from physics to poetry to religion to philosophy. Could the Void illuminate the meaning of life? You had to go in to find out, I glibly said.

Later, as an adult, even as I was piecing together a writing career, the Void remained in some back corner of my mind. As I wended my way through the research and development of other stories—bald eagles raiding the town dump as they followed their migration pattern south, adolescents bullying each other via social media—it was there. I work freelance, as a stringer, for the county paper, which is close to 150 years old, for an editor who is almost as old. He is a business-minded liberal—two things that make interesting bedfellows. His name is Henry Carey, and he's been in the newspaper business for almost four decades. He shows no sign of giving it up soon, either, but seems to hold onto it all the more ferociously the older he gets. Usually, his interests align in ways that suit my interests, which is why I continue to stay on as a stringer, for minimal and sporadic wages.

I know, too, that he is just about as interested in the Void as I am, though maybe for different reasons. That business-minded side of him knows that Void stories sell papers—fear, danger, mystery—all contained within a very real geographic feature. That's all you need for a good horror story.

When I first heard about Duncan Robert's jump last year, I was dumbstruck. He went in. Much as I had written, thought, and talked about the Void, doing what he had done was un-thinkable to me. I was caught between immediate hero worship and viewing him as some kind of freak. I had to know more.

I wanted to start tracking the story immediately but I couldn't find a buyer. Editors were cautious. They wanted to see if it was a hoax, a lover's ploy, a simple suicide, or an accidental death, each of which would be covered differently, by a reporter with that particular agility with words. They've seen everything, so it's hard for them to believe an act is what it is, without an angle. They waited, and now it's the anniversary, a safer reason to do a story. My editor thought it was worth following up because there might be more than just an anniversary story here. We could be on the trail of something bigger. Duncan Robert hasn't been filed as a dead person yet. Someone might know something.

I came to town in the early spring, as soon as the roads were clear enough to chance it. Nothing was blooming yet—the cold still hadn't released its hold, but nothing was entirely frozen either. Everything was waiting, it seemed, for the weather to go one way or the other. It waited warily, knowing, as the poets say, spring could be the cruelest time. I felt the same. I was waiting for something, too, something that needed to occur in its own time and in its own way, and might even be cruel. All I could think about was the Void, and it was all I tried not to think about.

Henry, through a friend of a friend, found me a place to stay, for free. It is a small studio apartment above the one bank in town, and I like it, though I won't tell Henry that. The bank building has historical status, having been built in 1790, and is located in exactly the center of town. The best place to eat, Alpine Alley, is two blocks south; the laundromat is across the street; the one movie theatre is two blocks north; and in between is a bookstore, a clothing store, and a drug store. What more could anyone need? The apartment itself has high ceilings and huge windows in the front and in the back, with east-west exposure, affording great morning and afternoon light. It comes furnished, and I spread my World Market Indian and Asian throws over everything for atmosphere. My sister Kelly, the musician, would love it; its lack of a coordinated decorating theme would make my sister Marla, the mom, uncomfortable.

My sisters would, however, be united in their feelings about jumps into the Void. A responsible mother can't condone anyone jumping into the unknown, not on her watch, and a musician might appreciate the poetry inherent in a jump but would want to be around to put her guitar to that poetry. I'm their sister and they love me. They certainly wouldn't want me around the Void. They know the attraction it has for me. Since our parents died when we were in high school, we've watched out for each other, guarding the ties we do have. Void talk would just incite more caution.

Henry had come to be sure I had his thorough instructions, and for his own chance to be near the Void. "It's got all the elements of a good ghost story, Babe!" he exhorted, one more time.

"What?" I said, teasing him, but listening, too. He hadn't gotten where he'd gotten by being dumb, and I admired him for that. "What ghost story?"

"Well, the Void stands in really well for a haunted house, don't you think?" he said, pushing his point. "So we start out afraid. And you have the innocent idealist, Duncan

Robert, who decides to go in, looking to become the hero in his own life. We can identify with that, so we're scared for him. And we don't know what's happened to him, so there's lots of room for speculation, for asking ourselves what we can believe in, how far out on this branch we'll go. That's scary, too! You can't see this?" He's getting grouchy by the time he gets to his last point.

"Yes! Sort of," I say, because I can see his point. It is scary. It scares me. I know it scares Henry, too. That's why he wants to do this story. He knows scary sells. He's a big buyer of scary.

"So, you'll talk to the yokels, you'll talk to the family and friends, you'll get to the bottom of who this Duncan Robert is and why he'd jump. And meanwhile, you'll be finding out everything you can about this Void. Is it just a geologic phenomenon?" he asks.

"No!" he answers his own question before I can. "It holds some history in this town, so I imagine it's carrying more than just air and rocks."

"Is it seen as a magical place?" he asks. I know better than to try to answer. "Even a spiritual place? I wouldn't be surprised," he says sagely. "You know, there's a Native American community just north of town."

"Was your mother a witch?" I ask, just to rattle his cage. "Why are you convinced he didn't just jump to his death?"

"Because it's a Void!" he shouts, his face getting red. "Voids aren't about jumping to your death! There's got to be more to it than that." He paces to calm himself. "You just need to find the angle. I'm banking on you, Babe," he says, looking at me with his don't-cross-me look, "or I wouldn't be paying for all this."

I have to laugh. "Well, I'm not sure what you're paying for, Mister Man, since the place is free," I say, giving him my don't-cross-me look back. "And on what you do pay me, I can barely afford reporter notebooks."

"Don't whine to me. You're getting the standard rate," he growls, "and we don't even pay that to everybody. Not in these times. And don't forget, I found the place for you! A nice place, too."

"Okay, okay. I'll name my first story after you," I concede. I change the subject. "Have you been out to see it?"

He looks at me, not even having to ask. "Yeah."

"What did you think?"

"Spooky. Like it's alive, sleeping there in the sun, but not really sleeping. Waiting." He shakes his head. "You been out?"

"Not yet," I say. I don't want to tell him about my trip out there yet. I don't know how to talk about it to myself yet. "I thought I might go out there next week."

"Don't wait too long," he says, shaking his finger at me, "or everyone will already have told you how you feel about it."

That's one of his pet peeves—that reporters are regularly told their stories rather than discovering them for themselves. I know what he means. People are pretty opinionated about the Void. They would write this story for me, if I let them.

Henry pats me on the head on his way out of the apartment, his sign of misplaced affection. He's got three daughters, and he regularly forgets I'm not one of them. He can't help himself. I don't complain. There's lots of reporters who are either afraid of him or who actively dislike him. He's definitely a tough old sod, known for being merciless to those who miss deadlines or make excuses. He's old school. In his book, you just do the work. Period. I guess I don't disagree with that. Plus, I like the work. I'm pleased he's even interested in doing a far-out story like this one and letting me do it. I never thought such a day would come. So, no, I'm not complaining. He can pat me on the head all he wants.

I start by hanging out in the village—Alpine Alley, the post office, the library, the drug store. As I said, I'm a stringer, taking whatever stories are assigned to me, used to building them from whatever scraps of information I can scrounge. But at heart I'm a beat reporter, longing for my own assigned, well-known and well-loved territory, so I operate like a beat reporter. I love the routine of it and the gadgets and gear and creating old-style contact lists, all of which help to unearth a community. Us beat reporters start with trying to generate "the person on the street" reactions, attending community events, going where people gather—looking for what one reporter called "listening posts." I could go directly to community leaders—business people, elected officials, religious leaders— but because this story is about a community phenomenon over which they have no control, I'd rather hear it straight from the people first, without the "expert" opinion. I'll use a little electronic media, too, like blogs and email, and see what kind of response I get, but the town doesn't seem very technologically minded, so I'm not expecting much there.

People are generally friendly, but not everyone trusts me—I am, after all, "the press." A teller at the bank said, "What you're writing about is really sensationalism. It doesn't make us look good. We'd like to keep it private." But, still, they want to talk.

Most people's talk is pretty general—their opinions of Voids, of the jump and the town's reaction to it. So, I moved from the general to the specific and began to identify and talk to those who actually knew Duncan Robert. I found that those who knew him tell me all kinds of things, starting with what Duncan Robert looks like. They like doing this, because they like him and it makes them feel informed. I see a fair number of pictures, taken at town picnics, school events, and just regular school pictures. I stare at Duncan Robert—medium height and build, fair hair, hazel eyes, nice smile, dimples.

I learn he used to be a big green-chili-cheese burger fan and then became a vegetarian. That he preferred watching movies to watching television. I could build a somewhat interesting general sketch of him as a person but I couldn't feel I'd captured his essence. I remember reading that Charles Lindbergh slept with his bed next to the window, the window open, his head literally on the windowsill, or that Einstein didn't always wear socks, and you'd see his bare ankles as he walked briskly down the street in his suit. Things like that hint at something that might be profound, if you could just put your finger on it.

It was like that with Duncan Robert. Hints were plentiful, but essence not so much. As word got out about what I was doing, people I ran into anywhere shared their anecdotes, insights, or the thing that still haunted them. Duncan Robert slept outside every chance he got—often without benefit of tent or sleeping bag—in the woods and fields. He kept odd hours, and he was occasionally seen taking late-night walks alone. No one ever saw him eat very much at one sitting—the Alpine Alley waitresses said he usually left food on his plate. He kept to himself—most thought he preferred his own company, except perhaps in the case of Reggie, his best friend and girl friend. Blue was his favorite color; he even drove a '75 powder blue VW Rabbit he'd bought with his own money, earned from doing handyman jobs around town. Anyone he'd worked for said he was a hard worker and did a good job. He loved the Beatles, especially their early music—songs like "Imagine." His mother told me he had come to her when he was twelve and asked her if, as a child of the '60s, she'd ever heard of this group called "the Beatles." She tilted her head back in a wide-mouthed laugh in the telling of that. One woman, who'd gone to school with him and claimed she still harbored a crush, said he was a good kisser.

Lists and lists of casual observations and a series of photographs, versus the real story of someone. That's not enough for a legacy, let alone a decent article. I could describe him—his likes, his dislikes—but I couldn't tell you the whys of any of it, the what-made-him-tick. Or what made him jump.

Miles, his uncle, was still the best logical source for the story. He's a teacher of writing and argument at the community college in the next town over. He was the one who had been closest to Duncan Robert, everyone said, and the one most interested in making sense of the jump. As I talked to people, I learned almost as much about Miles as I did Duncan Robert. I learned that, to try to understand the why and how of the jump, Miles got as close to the Void as he could get without actually jumping in himself. He went to the Void's edge a lot because he considered Duncan Robert's act an argument for everyone jumping, and he worked hard to frame it that way. He talked to everybody about the Void. He tried to assess what the aftermath of the jump might be, especially for Duncan Robert, that would make it worthwhile, because, more than anything, he wanted it to have been worthwhile.

That's why he was willing to talk about it to just about anybody. He didn't care so much about what anyone else thought, but talking to them gave him the chance to wrestle with it again in the form of a different partner. The breadth and depth of it required a partner, if you were to gain any traction. So, I scheduled an appointment with him at his house in town, one evening after his classes had ended for the day.

I wanted a series of interviews with him, at his house for greater familiarity, so I approached him carefully, not wanting to scare off a member of Duncan Robert's own family. He lives in a small log house on the edge of the town, not far from the woods that hold the Void. Miles is about forty-five, almost ten years older than I am. He is just shy of six feet tall, of average build, with intense dark eyes framed by strongly arched brows and a shock of dark hair liberally streaked with gray. He struck me as having the face of a troubled artist. He came out his front door onto his large porch and shook my hand. He asked me my name. "Babe Bennett," I said, and he began talking even before he led the way to the large, old-fashioned swing suspended from the porch ceiling. We sat back on worn, comfortable cushions, and I took out my pad and pencil to try to keep up with his words.

His voice had a weight and seriousness to it, but allowed for hints of humor and uncertainty, too. In that first visit, he didn't tell me much I didn't already know or couldn't have gotten from public records, about Duncan Robert or about the facts of the jump. I could tell he had been over this ground many times in the intervening year, constructing an understanding of the basics in his mind, piece by piece.

"Duncan Robert was almost twenty-one when he jumped. We had his twenty-first birthday while he was in the Void," Miles told me. "He and I taught each other everything we know about hiking and backpacking and camping. Both of us were eager novices to start, but we didn't want anybody else teaching us." He stared off into the twilight.

"You know the kinds of conversations you have when you're out there in the woods, watching the campfire fade, and the night gather closer around you?" he asked, looking over at me.

I felt a slight chill on the back of my neck when he said that but said, "No. I'm a city girl myself."

He nodded. "Well, they're the best kind of conversations." I could feel how much Miles missed him.

"He taught me how to be his uncle, too," he said. "I wouldn't have known."

As an adjunct professor of English composition, Miles had undertaken the work of teaching scores of entering freshmen basic writing skills, over and over, for minimal pay and no health insurance or retirement. In my mind, that takes a special kind of endurance and tenacity, as well as some kind of basic optimism, to carry you. I heard that unwavering assurance under his words as he spoke of Duncan Robert and the jump.

During this time I also talked more to Silvia, Duncan Robert's mother and Miles's younger sister. I interviewed her at her job, over lunch, and occasionally in her home. She wanted to talk, too, to my great relief and excitement.

Even Abraham Lincoln said everything he knew he owed to his mother. I was struck by her resemblance to Miles. She has the same dark eyes and defined brows, accented by her long dark hair, which she wore in one braid down her back.

"All our lives," she said, "people have asked if we're twins. We're not—Miles is older than I am by a year and a half. We've always been close, and Miles has always played a big role in Duncan Robert's life, too."

She told me about Duncan Robert as he was growing up.

"Even when he was little, it seemed as if he knew more than he was saying. Though he said a lot!" she laughed. "He talked in whole paragraphs, long before he had the vocabulary for it. I hardly ever knew what he was saying." She smiled remembering it. "He could look at you as you talked as if he knew what you *weren't* saying, too. He laughed at any old thing and was curious about everything."

Silvia divorced Duncan Robert's father when Duncan Robert was three. She had never re-married, though I had heard some talk around town that she had a long-standing relationship with the seventy-year-old Vietnamese town sheriff, Michael Nguyen. She never validated this, but he had been great in handling the aftermath of the jump, she said, keeping it as quiet as he could, quelling any possible real investigation.

People feared calling the Void's energy by talking about it, but they thought Duncan Robert was going to jump. In those months of preparation, they saw the comings and goings, and they knew the character of Duncan Robert and his Uncle Miles. While they wondered if the jump might end in death, they never thought that was the intention. Michael talked with Miles and got the basis of the report that went into the official file. No one challenged it.

Silvia had been raised Catholic, and for almost twenty years has served as secretary to the Catholic church in town, keeping records of the congregation's membership and their tithing. She has a loyalty to her employer but seems fairly indifferent to the Church's teachings.

"Well, I've lived most of my life outside of the church's rules," she said, "because I haven't found them very helpful!" She laughed. "Let's see. I had sex before I married and am not about to ask forgiveness for that. I used birth control, because it suited my own situation, not the church's. And," she says with another laugh, "I divorced my husband, rather than hold him to a life that made him unhappy just to please the church. He's happier now, and I'm happier, too."

Clearly, Duncan Robert, not her faith, had been the center of her universe, and she loved him very much. "He was a good person," she said, looking out the church office window one day. "And he made me better." She didn't seem to think she would ever see him again, but she spoke of him willingly and even cheerfully. It had only been a year since his jump, and I think talking about him kept him alive for her.

But I still needed the story or stories that could carry the crux of Duncan Robert's life. I needed to get to the *why* of the jump.

CHAPTER TWO

Duncan Robert

So, in the quest for someone who could tell me what makes Duncan Robert tick, so far I had three candidates. First, Silvia, in her own words:

One

LIFE AFTER DEATH

When he was little, Duncan Robert was very close to his Grandma Ruth, his father's mother. He was her first grand-child, and she doted on him. And I mean doted. Grandma Ruth often took care of Duncan Robert, from the time he was born, to help me out. After his dad and I had divorced when Duncan Robert was three, I think Ruth tried to make up for what she saw as the abandonment by her son. She adored her grandson, so it was no hardship for her but a clear preference. So "doted," in my book, now means the activities of Grandma Ruth. She made whole coconut crème pies just for him, from the time he was five. She served him his favorite dinners on a tray in front of his favorite TV programs. She ironed his clothes, sheets, and even underwear. You're probably not old enough to remember when women did that. She taught him cribbage and they played endless games together. I don't know if she went so far as to let him win or not. He was first and foremost in her existence.

She died when Duncan Robert was 17, after a brief illness, and I believe he misses her to this day. How could he not?

He told me that Grandma Ruth had appeared to him the night before her death. She was in the hospital at the time, in a coma. "She came down the hall and sat at the foot of my bed," he said. "She told me she was leaving. She looked great. I've never seen her look better or happier."

I remember I turned and looked at him, feeling a chill creep up, starting at my legs. "At the foot of your bed?" I asked.

"Yes. She said she was on her way but just wanted me to know how much she had valued our closeness, how much it had meant to her. She said, 'And I want you to know you're never alone. We never are.' Then she got up to leave, giving me such a smile." He was smiling as he said it, gazing peacefully past the newspaper he was holding into the dining room beyond. I was paralyzed, afraid to look over my shoulder to follow his gaze, in case there was something there to look at. "Weren't you scared?" I asked, thinking of the dark house, everyone else unavailable in sleep, the vulnerability of bed. Of a dead woman showing up to tell you good bye.

"What would I be scared of?" he asked. "It was Grandma."

I stared at him in silence, still feeling scared in the broad daylight of the bright kitchen. I didn't try to explain to him that "scared" would be a sensible reaction. But this meant I had a son who saw ghosts, something I never expected. I could see the foot of his bed from my room at the opposite end of the short hallway. Was she going to come back, or was she really gone? What was a mother to do, a good mother?

She sat on the end of his bed and told him he was going to have a long and interesting life, and then she died the next day. He got comfort from the visit. In fact, he talked to his grandmother a lot, especially at night when he went to bed, discussing the events of his day with her. Duncan Robert and I talked of these things whenever someone in town died, too, wondering if they might get a visit from the deceased and

wondering if we should share our thoughts with them. Usu-
ally we decided not to.

"Couldn't the visits be created by his own imagination," I
asked, "driven by his need to maintain the connection?"

"You mean, him talking to himself? Sure, I thought of
that. I guess you'd have to hear him tell it." She smiles. "I could
be counted as biased, though."

"What does the story say to you about him, beyond the fact
that he sees ghosts?"

"That he has access to something I don't, to a world beyond
this one."

"That he's special?"

"Yes. And sure I want my child to be special. Maybe I
wouldn't have chosen this way, but he did."

The second story is a bit more revealing of Duncan
Robert's own belief system, and shows it in operation. It
was also told to me by his mother, though Miles knew of
it as well.

Two

BROKEN BONES

Duncan Robert had been helping his friend Dominic move out
of his house and into an apartment for the summer. Four of
them were going to share this apartment the summer before
their senior year in high school. All of them had at least part-
time jobs and were eager to be out of the nest. While carrying
a load of boxes, Duncan Robert tripped on a pile of lumber by
Dominic's back door, landing with his left forearm under him.
He didn't realize for a day or two that it was broken, not until
he went to his job as a waiter and tried to lift a full tray with
that arm. He found he couldn't lift anything. I met him at the
doctor's, since he was still under my insurance, and they x-rayed
and determined the outer bone, the ulna, had a clean break
right down the middle. They called it a 'nightstick fracture,'

an uncommon isolated ulnar shaft fracture. It happens to cops defending themselves against an overhead blow. "It's unlikely to heal in that area," the doctor said. "We'll need to do a rigid plate fixation to stabilize it so it can heal correctly. Let's put a cast on it while we're waiting to get the surgery scheduled in three or four days. We'll do a pre-surgery x-ray to make sure nothing has moved and do the surgery." Duncan Robert resisted the idea of surgery, and the doctor got a little angry. "Non-surgical treatments are prone to complications and associated with malunion and nonunion, with the break often recurring. That's a lot of unnecessary pain!" he sort of barked. Duncan Robert didn't argue, and the doctor put the cast on and we went home.

Duncan Robert was quiet and turned in soon after dinner that night. I stayed up doing some mending. Before I went to bed, I went down the hall to check on him, to see if his cast was causing him any trouble sleeping. As I walked down the dark hall to his door, I could see light coming from under it, brightening the hall. The light wasn't steady, it was colorful and it fluctuated. I remember thinking, "What in the world does he have going?" I was thinking video game or the small old television of his grandma's, though it's a black and white. I knocked gently and receiving no answer, I slowly opened the door to peek in. Colorful balls of light were traveling around the edges of the ceiling. Each was a different color, about eight inches in diameter, and traveling fast. I caught my breath and looked at his bed. He was lying quietly, eyes closed, his right hand over the cast on his left arm. "Duncan Robert!" I called to him. "What is going on?" He opened his eyes to look at me and said, "What?" Then he went back to sleep. I sat on the floor next to his bed until the lights stopped. It all felt very peaceful. He stayed asleep. I put my hand on his cast, and it was warm. I didn't know what to think. I went to bed.

The next morning, he had to leave for the restaurant, despite his arm. "I need the money, and there are still some things I can do." I asked him about the lights. He looked at me as if I was crazy. "I don't know about any lights. I just fell asleep holding the cast and thinking of healing. My arm feels great. I think it's healed." I gave him a kiss on his way out. "I guess we'll know Friday."

That Friday, the doctor was all set for surgery. He wanted Duncan Robert to check into the hospital that afternoon for surgery in the morning. All Duncan Robert said was, "Let's do the x-ray." They went into x-ray, and when they came out, the doctor was shaking his head. They had taken the cast off to do the x-ray, and Duncan Robert was rubbing his arm.

"It's healed," the doctor said quietly, looking at no one. "There's no sign of any break whatsoever. It's as if it never happened. I wouldn't believe it if I didn't have the first x-ray in front of me." He looked at Duncan Robert. "I asked him what happened, but he says he doesn't know. Do you?"

"I have no idea. I'm as surprised as you are."

"Well, somebody did something, because that fracture is gone. I'd like an explanation."

"I don't have one," I said and looked at Duncan Robert. He shrugged. "It healed."

And then we walked out.

She looked at me. "Don't ask. I don't know what it means. It's like seeing his grandma. There are things he does and knows that didn't come from me, so I don't know where they came from. Here's something with outside verification, and we still don't know what to do with it."

"What did Duncan Robert say?"

"Nothing! He's better at accepting these things, not having to endlessly worry over them. He did say, 'I knew I wasn't having surgery.'"

"I've heard of other spontaneous healings, though I don't hear of them often. Usually they're associated with a religious effort. I've never heard of this flashing light phenomenon."

"Well, imagine seeing it in the middle of the night, happening over your son's head. If it hadn't felt so benign, I might have gotten more upset. But it just didn't feel bad."

I was beginning to see a pattern emerge, of openness to alternate views of death and God. The parameters of a life that could permit a jump begin to materialize.

The third story is one that Miles told me. It involved Duncan Robert and Reggie, just after they'd finished high school, and a house-sitting job they had undertaken together in the next village over. Duncan Robert had been excited because they were sharing an adult responsibility for the care of a home, out of town, together. It was a new and empowering experience for him. They left town enthusiastic and determined to leave the place better than they found it so that they would be asked again.

"What happened in that house was a significant event for Duncan Robert," Miles said. "He recorded it as a story in his journal and re-wrote it over and over in his effort to settle the effect it had on him. That was probably my influence—to write it in order to understand it. He had me edit it for clarity, along with punctuation and spelling. He was compelled to tell it and to work to capture it exactly, and he further refined the details each time he re-wrote it."

When I heard Miles talk like this, I wondered if Duncan Robert was looking for a vocabulary that would be a faithful reflection of the alternative reality he experienced, even though he knew he was deflecting that reality as he did so, making it harder to believe. In other words, the better he captured it with his words, the better job he did of clarifying just how outlandish it was.

"It's a charming two-story cottage," Miles said. "I've visited several times. It was built in the late 1700s and is still pretty much the same as it has always been. Duncan Robert's story began the first morning of their weekend stay there, when he was in the upstairs bathroom, brushing his teeth."

Three

DUNCAN ROBERT'S JOURNAL

Toothbrush in my left hand, I reached over with my right hand to open the small casement window to the side of the small sink.

Pushing the window out, I looked down over the sill, expecting to see the large backyard vegetable garden.

Instead, I was looking out on a small, carefully manicured garden from another time and place, a time closer to the origins of the house. I could see flat green fields extending far beyond the boundaries of the garden. Within the garden, I could see people strolling, dressed in clothes from that other era, talking quietly as they stopped to examine the flowers and blooming shrubs that were there now. Closest to me were a man and woman, and the first thing that caught my attention was the woman's slowly twirling parasol. It was shaped like a small white gazebo with a tassel on top. It competed in size with the swaying side bustles of her skirt, which stopped just short of her ankles, leaving her small feet exposed. I followed the flat panel of the center of her dress up to the bodice, which was fitted tightly to her narrow frame, forming slight wrinkles at each rib. The print of her dress was small enough to be almost indiscernible, but looking closer I could detect violet-colored flowers edged in pale green.

Further up, I could see her neck and the lower half of her face, both powdered white, and her narrow tinted lips. As her lace-gloved hands shifted the parasol, I got a profile view of a tower of tight blonde curls topped by a tiny-brimmed straw hat, adorned with deep purple grapes, shiny red miniature raspberries, overlaid with a trailing of honey suckle vines that bobbed at her slightest movement. Fascinated by the combination of the hair and the hat, I wondered how both were attached—the hat to the hair, the hair to her head. My attention could not have left her if the man had not moved to take her arm, guiding her toward another display of flowers, and the couple stopped, now directly beneath my window.

Before I could do more than get a quick glance at the man's muted yellow waistcoat and matching knee-length pants, I froze. She was lifting her head to bring her slightly slanted blue eyes to mine. I turned my head and looked at her, through the opening between the small glass double doors of the casement window, my hands on the round knob handles, my toothbrush clasped tightly, toothpaste suds in my half-opened mouth, dribbling down to my blue and white striped Eddie Bauer paja-mas. I hung there, breathless, between worlds. Could she see me, I wondered, without comprehending how I could see her. She stopped, her lips slightly parted, her eyes not fully catching the sight of me.

Whether or not she saw me, I saw her. I saw directly into her eyes. I didn't think I could break my gaze away. She looked away first, turning to her partner, searching his face question-ingly. Still, I stood, toothpaste suds dripping down my chin, bare feet feeling the cold tiles of the bathroom in this world. A breeze through the window lifted the ends of my hair. I saw the same breeze gently move the tassel on top of her parasol. Both of them turned their faces up toward my window and then away. My eyes didn't connect with hers again. He held her arm, steer-ing her along the path. The parasol again hid her face from my view. I stood there a moment longer, watching them. I looked out at the larger scene, seeing a flock of birds rise from the far field and move low over it. Finally, I closed the window, leaning my head against it for a second, quieting my breath, wondering if I would open it again.

"When Duncan Robert did open the window again," Miles said, "all was normal outside, the usual vegetable garden there, along with the owner's cat, lying in wait for unsuspecting birds. Duncan Robert didn't know how to understand what he had seen or why he had seen it; all he could do was record it."

When I commented on the quality of Duncan Rob-ert's writing, Miles said, "Duncan Robert would never have considered himself a writer. He was just recording what he saw, like a court reporter would record what he heard. The incident changed Duncan Robert, though. The best way I can describe it is to say that it matured him in some way. He seemed more thoughtful, more introspective, even, than before."

I asked what Reggie had thought. He said, "Well, Reg-gie, like the rest of us, didn't know what to think. I know she had some other-worldly incidents herself over the years, but she wasn't given to talking about them. She didn't question or doubt Duncan Robert's experience, which I think must have meant a lot to him."

"I guess it's pretty elaborate for an hallucination," I said. "How would you explain it?"

"I have no idea. There are spiritual writers who call it a 'bleed through,' from one time and place to another. They say they've been written about for centuries—comparable to what people saw in crystal balls—pasts, futures, what-might-have-beens. I don't know the whys. I just think it says something about his sensitivity or his willingness to experience."

"Did he come to terms with it?"

"I think Duncan Robert understood the world and its possibilities and his place in it," Miles said. "I could see that. It was a world in which life didn't end, it just continued in another still-connected way, occasionally over-lapping with other times and places. It was a world that made more sense to him, an expansive world, without old, inhibiting rules that always told him who he should be, based on circumstance—that and no more. It was a world that he felt a recognized, valued part of. He wanted that kind of world, not a continually limiting one. He couldn't see how to create a life or future within such limits and didn't want to. I think this is what made the adventure of jumping possible."

That's what Miles calls it—the adventure of jumping. Like boarding a sailing ship in days of old, jumping seemed to make other things possible—for yourself and your world. In other words, maybe "the Void" meant something else to Duncan Robert than it does to most of us. Maybe he saw it as a portal to another place or time, because he knew such portals were possible. Maybe it seemed *right*. He might be jumping to some place *better*.

CHAPTER THREE

Jumping

I FELT I WAS narrowing in on the jump, but I would need Miles's help. I continued my interviews with him, on the porch of his little log house, which I had grown quite fond of. The house was so organic, so rooted to its spot and embraced by the trees and undergrowth around it, that it seemed like something out of a fairy tale. "That fits," I thought, "with a Void story." I found there was nothing I liked better than sitting on that porch, with a table in front of us, mapping out the Void and the jump, sipping Miles's good coffee, tasting his homemade cheese crackers with a slice of crisp, sweet apple.

So, one night not long after I had put together the three stories and sent them to my editor Henry, I sat on that porch with Miles and started reviewing things as they happened after the jump, since we knew as much as we were going to know about the jump itself (which is to say not much without hearing from Duncan Robert himself). First, I asked Miles about the immediate aftermath of the jump, for him and the other residents of the town, especially those who had been close to Duncan Robert.

"In the days following the jump, we were all a little dazed," Miles said, reflectively, "as if part of us had jumped, too. Silvia and Reggie were inseparable, wondering where he was and how he was faring. They dropped in to see me almost daily, but I had nothing to tell them. I knew no more than they did and I wasn't interested in speculating. I remember that Reggie and Silvia told me they visited the Void regularly, because it was the last place Duncan Robert had been. Sometimes they went together, sometimes separately. "Silvia often took flowers, dropping them carefully into the Void. It scared her less that way, I think, to treat it like a marked grave. And she knew he had liked flowers, just about any kind. She hoped he still did, wherever he was. It seems clear to me she believes he's not coming back, though she never mentions suicide.

"Reggie said she was more likely to sit near the edge of the Void and talk to him. She couldn't help herself. She wanted to be near him. She had tried sitting on the edge, even dangling her legs into the Void, but the sensation of tingling and tugging she would feel in her ankles and calves stopped her. She then spread out a blanket over the wild, un-mown grass and lay on it, either on her back, gazing at the sky, or on her stomach, gazing into the Void, for as long as she could stand it, before feeling as if she was somehow becoming the Void.

"In the beginning, she'd talk intensely to Duncan Robert, at times crying into the Void— you know, all the usual things, like 'why' and 'how could you' and 'what about me.' Later, Silvia said Reggie did more listening, and I think she found more comfort then. Not that she said she heard anything, just that she'd worked her way through her questions and had finished asking. Sometimes she'd even sleep there, on her blanket. I think she felt closer to him then. I say that because I did some of that, too, and that's how I felt. Then she moved away, to Idaho, I think."

"You never talked to her about what she thought happened to him?"

"No. It was too fresh for us to have much to say about that. We'd sit together, over here on my porch, for an evening, drawn together by the magnetism of the jump. I say 'magnetism' because we did feel pulled together by the fact of it, but we'd mainly just sit there, shut down by the immensity of it, the finality of it. We'd lost our words in the face of it. It occupied our heads endlessly, but it was like playing on an old pinball machine, where you pulled levers and watched balls carom around the course, willing them into their proper holes, if they'd go. Sometimes we'd lean against each other on the porch swing, communicating that way, feeling each other's emptiness. By the time we might have talked about it, she had left."

"What about everyone else?" I asked. "What were they doing, saying?"

"Well, you had the usual array of responses that we get with any happening in town, from a presidential election to a bar fight to a new movie at the Hillyard. Some criticized it, some wanted to pretend it hadn't happened, and a few tried to find the positive in it.

"Among the critical, most remained angry or annoyed about it. It was unseemly, even cowardly, they thought, to have jumped that way. Those who didn't want to talk about it left it as God's will. Some talked of it in relative terms, which is so common nowadays, saying it's everyone's own choice and there are no right or wrong choices.

"Those few who wanted to find the positive in it said he might be in a better place now, or wasn't it commendable that he'd had the courage of his own convictions. They were confused, too, because they weren't sure he'd chosen an acceptable way to get to that better place, and they weren't convinced courage was the determiner of his act. They wanted to believe 'everything is always okay,' but they knew a jump suggested otherwise. If I'd had to choose a group to belong to, I'd have been closest to that group."

"Why? You sound like you thought they were too Pollyanna."

"Because I knew him."

"What do you mean?"

"I believe the only reason he would have jumped would have been that he believed it was for a good purpose."

I pondered that a minute, then asked, "What about you, right after? What did you do?"

"I missed him terribly, as I imagine I would miss my own life after death. I was that lost. The jump, though we had planned for it, hit me unaware. Every night I paced a circle in my yard, from the front of the house to the back, from the back to the front, again and again, chain smoking. I wasn't a chain smoker, but I wanted an addiction, to dull the sense of there being no escape from it. One of my students said, after going through a recovery program, 'There's no substance that has addictive qualities. The need is in us.' He believed that and so do I. The need was in me. Sometimes I talked to myself, sometimes to him, sometimes to whatever power I thought was responsible for everything.

"At first, it hurt beyond expression, and I felt as if I walked without breathing, because breathing wasn't possible. I was like a lightning bug trapped in a jar—not enough air, nowhere to go and no way out, though you can see the world the way you left it, just beyond the transparent walls of your prison. I had lost all the things that mattered most—a friend, a confidant, a moral compass—and could do nothing about it. It was a while before I could begin to formulate my questions and a while after that before I started putting them down on paper, to organize them and see where I was.

"That's when I discovered I was angry."

"What?" I said, surprised to hear this from such a thoughtful, quiet man. "Angry? At whom? Or what?"

"At him!" he said, surprised at my surprise. "Isn't that textbook? One of the stages of grief? I talked to him, and he didn't talk back. No sign he was around. Just such a loneliness for him that it drove me to anger at his being gone. I'm not saying it was rational, for god's sake. I'm just saying I discovered I had it. And I was surprised, because I thought I understood all the reasons for his jumping and even *supported* him in doing it. I thought understanding it was my 'get out of jail free' card, as far as any suffering was concerned. But not so. Also, I consider myself a nice, peaceful guy, so it's not often I look at something like anger."

"What did you do with it?" I asked, wanting to know.

"I sat with it, for many nights running. That's advice from Duncan Robert's therapist, and he and I used to say there couldn't be any harder advice to follow." He saw the look on my face and said, "Yeah, he had a therapist for a while, to talk about what she called his 'free- floating anxiety.' You know, he tried just about everything, before he turned to the Void."

"Okay," I said, intrigued by his admission of his own vulnerabilities and failings. "Tell me about what happened to the anger."

"Well, I finally figured out that anger was the front man for the real ring leader of my emotions. The ring leader was fear—such a large fear that I would lose *myself* in the loss of *him*." He paused for a moment, studying me. I sat, uncomfortable, and let him. This kind of scrutiny often happens in interviews, and I know it's not really me they're studying. They're looking for a reflection of themselves in my expression, or lack of eye contact, or unease. So I held steady.

"I haven't loved that many people that deeply in my life, so I haven't experienced this kind of loss. I couldn't be sure of the ratio of its power to mine. I couldn't be sure I could survive the loss and go on." He coughed past the emotion in his voice, while brushing at his eyes. He laughed self-consciously. "I've become a weeper! Maybe that surprised me the most. I'm definitely in touch with my emotions, thanks to Duncan Robert!"

"So, how did you know you could survive it?" I asked, moved by this level of honesty.

"By realizing I had. One day I saw that I was surviving and knew that I could," he said, with a smile. "It was that simple."

I smiled back and said, "Thanks for sharing that."

"*De nada*," he said, looking down at his hands.

I laughed at that. "Sure. So, where are you with it now?"

"Well, jumping. I thought about jumping first. I don't mean I thought about going out there and jumping myself. I thought about his jumping—because it was Duncan Robert's essential act. I see jumping as an act of life—jumping rope, jumping into water, jumping into someone's arms, jumping from the frying pan into the fire, jumping for joy, even jumping from a plane.

"Often jumping involves some energy, at least a little excitement, a little (or a lot of) courage; and a change—from no movement to movement, from being in one place to being in another. Seeking that change is part of why we do it. It's like learning a new skill, doing what the bigger kids do, and finding the secret of belonging in that. You feel good because you could do it and you did do it."

I had to stop him and ask, "Are you trying to say that Duncan Robert's jump is like this? A normal, everyday, harmless jump that you're glad you did? A small risk with a big reward?"

"Well he did start with the normal, everyday act of jumping," he replied. "True, he was jumping into the Void, and true, we can only imagine Duncan Robert's actual jump. We're assuming that jumping into the Void would be scary. Agreed?" He waited for my nod, then continued.

"When I imagine it, I imagine that Duncan Robert would be so scared that he would immediately be brought to an intense state of awareness of himself, every inch of himself, as he experienced the initial sensation of free falling. He's probably more present to himself in that moment than he's ever been. He feels himself, inside and out, quickly. Emotionally, the excitement must be building to an incredible pitch. Could he sustain that? Who could keep hold of him- or herself in those moments? What can he do but let go? He's forced to. There's nothing to hold on to. Surrender to it, as they say.

"But wouldn't you go out of your mind? I've asked myself that many times. Or maybe you'd go in, to some still place in your mind that holds you at intense times like those. Maybe it would be like in other intense moments—car wrecks, battle, prolonged child birth, natural disasters—time would slow down, diminishing the scarier sensations, or some naturally protective mechanism would kick in, and you just wouldn't be present to or remember the whole thing.

"But maybe, for those few moments that he's profoundly aware of himself and the physical and emotional sensations of his situation, he's permeated by such a sense of wholeness, of connection to everything happening as it happens, that he transcends his fear. So fear isn't the only thing he feels. Maybe in that moment, when he knows it's all out of his hands anyway, like when we're on a roller coaster and it starts that great and long descent and we can't do anything but give ourselves over to it and scream and scream, he experiences a kind of gratitude for the Void and is even glad he's in it."

"Wait, wait," I said, not very professionally. "I can't follow this. I haven't spent a year thinking about it. You have to help me. How could he *possibly* be *glad*, plummeting into nothingness and completely out of control?"

"I don't *know* this. This is just where my thinking takes me sometimes. I try to stay positive. He could be thinking that if this is the way it's all going to end, better with a bang of a feeling than a whimper. Better to ride such an incredible high that you're thankful to have experienced this level of knowing and feeling of yourself.

"I think of those men who went beyond the charted courses, because somebody did, who sailed to what they thought was the edge of the Void, and came back less afraid and were willing to do it again. And some of those women who endured countless hours of childbirth and who could choose, *kept* having babies, with no assurance that they or the baby could manage it or would always survive it." Miles got up off the porch swing and paced as he talked.

"I can understand the act of child bearing as some kind of biological imperative, and you have relief when you act according to it," I said, "but, *glad*?"

"Well, what about that feeling—that excitement and aliveness he feels the moment he jumps and feels his feet leaving the ground, knowing he's made the commitment? Doesn't it sound like a kind of happiness? It does to me. The kind that's heart-poundingly, breath-shorteningly *real*? The kind you know is brief, and more precious because of that? The kind that makes you feel as if you've suddenly entered territory, in and outside of yourself, that you didn't know existed? And you like it?"

I saw his face lit by this discussion, from the inside, where his passion is, and I was moved. I know that his passion is driven by sadness and longing, too.

I was caught up for a moment in the force of his description. Then I said, "But we usually know the *ending* of those kinds of jumps. We have a parachute, or others have done it before us and survived, or we know it's supposed to be fun, not life threatening."

"Oh, he knows there might be a crash, into oblivion, or something worse, some pain and horror. He's taken a big risk here. He could die. But I'll tell you what I really believe, what I think made jumping possible for him, despite his knowing how it might end. I think the alternative scared him more." He turned from his pacing and looked at me intently, watchfully.

"Alternative? What alternative?"

"I think Duncan Robert had always been fascinated by the potential of what we can't or don't know and often bored by or disappointed in the reality of what we think we can and do know. You know, those commonly held beliefs we're all expected to use to navigate our lives by—untried, untested, unfounded by us, personally. Who you can and can't love, when, where and how; when, where and how to live; when, where and how to die. Maybe that's why he jumped—looking for the excitement of acting on his own decision, that sort of aliveness, before he died. Not just to purchase, through your own hard work and sweat equity, a facsimile of someone else's life, by the book. He looked for a way to live his life as his own."

He turned to lean his hands on the porch railing and stare out into the dark, watching as a car drove by on the road at the end of his drive. I thought about what he's said for a moment, trying to think how I can be clearer about my confusion. "Why do you think he felt that way, that he preferred jumping to the alternative?"

"Because he was restless. Because he said there had to be more. Because he kept finding ways to not follow the norm. He took a year off school, and everyone said he wouldn't return to finish, but he did. He hung out with the one guy in town with AIDS, even though everyone else seemed to think they'd catch it. He took in strays—cats, dogs, the occasional wounded bird. He seemed unable to settle for things the way they were. He kept his own hours, he wouldn't work a standard nine to five job, he wouldn't 'settle down,' he wouldn't pick the acceptable mate. Reggie being African American, that's definitely not the expected in these parts. Maybe he did find the best of a life, his 'something more,' in those first few moments in the Void."

I tried to get hold of this thought. "Are you speaking metaphorically, then?" I asked, "The idea of jumping as a vehicle for gaining 'something more'?"

"Look, this is all I've said so far: We know something about jumping, and it's not all bad. In life, we've all had some jumps of our own that were pretty good, that we're glad we did, and we'd do them again. Many of them were fun. We agree there's something unique about jumping, something that gives us our own experience, because the sensation of it can take us deeply inside ourselves, whether we're jumping rope, jumping out of a swing, bungee jumping, or even if we're jumping tandem."

"Jumping tandem?" I asked, not sure what that means.

"It's the only way I've jumped out of a plane, attached to the trainer," he said. He looked at me with a wry, sideways grin. "I'll admit it. I was too scared to jump alone, not sure I could handle emulating what Duncan Robert had done. It was an incredible experience. And I still felt the adrenaline rush for three days after. I did it to try to feel what Duncan Robert might have felt. And I learned, even though jumps have things in common, your jump is your jump," he said. He looked at me again and sighed. "And the big and scary ones can be profound."

"It's one of the easiest, most primary ways to know you're alive, to learn the parameters of your abilities and possibilities. If something or someone didn't provoke you, challenge you, tease you, push you into jumping, you would never have known that sensation of rushing into yourself, of meeting yourself so frankly, so openly. Maybe jumping should be an everyday activity? Even a required activity? Maybe if you haven't felt compelled to jump somewhere in your life, you haven't fully lived? That's what I think I think," he said with a laugh.

"I have no idea what I think!" I shouted, with a laugh, letting my pencil jump in the air and catching it. "I haven't thought about it!

"I can remember the first time I jumped rope," I remembered out loud to Miles, "with my sisters holding the ends of the rope, not sure I could navigate the timing and the sweep of the rope, not believing I was as smart and as quick as they were. I have to admit that I was pretty impressed with myself when I knew the rope had cleared the ground under my feet. Then I got my rhythm, and it felt easier. I forgot what a sense of accomplishment I got from that. What a rite of passage that was. I had forgotten."

He laughed and gave a little two-footed jump, shouting back, "That's what I'm talking about! You made your own jump! And we don't really forget our jumps. They leave their mark. What would it feel like to you if you jumped right now, Babe—right where you are, not into the Void or even out of a swing? You just jumped. Why can't we still do it?

"Nowadays, fun tends more and more to have to do with us watching someone else doing something that's supposed to be fun. Our fun is supposed to be watching or reading or manipulating something that someone else has created. And it's so tied up with time and work—it has to be allotted a certain hour or week or holiday at some special place or other. It's like they've taken our joy and given us pleasure instead—a pale substitute—and Duncan Robert felt that loss."

CHAPTER FOUR

The Void

The following night I couldn't sleep, as I lay and thought about everything I was learning about Duncan Robert's jump into the Void. The more I heard, the closer I felt to Miles and by extension to Duncan Robert, and the harder it got to write. It was becoming personal. I had no idea where to start when it came to writing about the Void now.

I lay in the dark, thinking of Duncan Robert at the jump, as he felt his feet leave the ground, getting that sensation of falling, tumbling, nothing to grab onto, leaving everything behind. Maybe calling for his mother, as they say dying soldiers do on the battlefield. This jumping into the Void is serious business. If he ever returned, which most people assumed he wouldn't, he'd be different.

Two sleepless nights later I couldn't ruminate on my own anymore and I headed back to Miles's little house, waiting for him to get home from the community college. I'd brought dinner, from Alpine Alley, to feel as if I was contributing something, not just taking. I wasn't quite ready to expose him to my cooking.

We sat out on his porch after dinner, sipping tea, staring into the darkness that ringed the porch and extended out to the road, where it was broken by the lone street light at the end of his drive. I thought about the difference in visiting the dark, as we do each night, from the safety of our own well-lit territory, versus jumping into darkness on its own terms, not knowing if we'd see light again. Finally I couldn't wait any longer. "What do we know about the Void?" I asked Miles, imagining he knows quite a bit.

"As you probably know," he said, and I heard the tone of the teacher for the first time, "the idea of the Void has been with us a long time. I've done a lot of reading on it, and discovered it's been a philosophical, literary, and religious notion since at least 300-400 BC, probably longer. It's a part of our spiritual and cultural heritage, no matter our religion. Aristotle and other Greeks like Democritus believed a Void was the space between things necessary for growth and movement," he paused and smiled and me. "The means by which we get from here to there—which is what Duncan Robert did.

"The ancient Chinese, about the same time, were formulating the basis of Taoism and Buddhism and noted the necessity of the Void, too, as the beginning of all being. They wanted to access it, to ignite being out of non-being. It's the basis of meditation, for example—to achieve a state of emptiness, making the mind a Void. We do that to prepare space for what can enter—to activate the space with our own spirit. Some say Christianity doesn't have a concept of the Void; some, like Thomas Merton, say it does."

He paused again before saying, "This is nothing Duncan Robert knew about. These are things I've learned about since."

Some of this was familiar to me, from my own readings over the years. I asked him, "So, is the Void really nothing, or is it more of a blank slate? And if it's nothing, why do we fear it?"

He was ready with answers. "Because it's empty, and emptiness scares us. We're afraid it really might exist, as a place, and we might end up there in the dark, all by ourselves. It's correlated with Black Holes and vortexes, and other dark places, too—places where unknown forces might take you and never return you, collapsing you or distorting you in some way. Its very name suggests it's de*void* of anything and everything, so you could expect no comfort there.

"And it's always there. We've seen to that. We seem to continually create the idea of it, tell stories of it, include it in our philosophical and religious discourse. We seem to *need* it. That's what I think. It's the collection place—the dump—for everything we don't want. We create it—by pulling our deepest fears together in one place, under one name, and then treating that mental construction like an actual place."

He stopped and looked at me intently. I held steady, not knowing if I'd ever get used to the power of those looks. "To Duncan Robert, a *life* could be an unacknowledged void—a place where we lived among our deepest fears, keeping them alive with our attention, our dread, our attachment—and we could be caught there forever by our own impassivity."

"Okay, wait now," I said, looking at what I've written. "A *life* as a void? Let me get this straight. What you're suggesting is that the Void—*the* Void on the outskirts of town—is imaginary? A thought construct? Isn't that like a metaphor? And haven't we all seen it with our own eyes?"

"Yes and no. You could look at it that way, something that may or may not have been imaginary, but becomes real with time. I mean, when anything collects that kind of ongoing energy, across space and time, there's got to be something to it. It's as if the energy, so focused, manifests something real. It is something we can see, but it's also a manifestation of a metaphor for emptiness, which we otherwise couldn't see. I think it's as real as we are. But I think it is empty—an empty dark place, until we fill it—with fears, with held breaths, with a jump. It's like fear—it's a concept, but it's as real as the human condition, right? What's more real than fear? Well, the Void is as real as fear. Can't thinking of the Void feel like thinking of anything we fear?"

Here we go again, I thought, trying to keep up, thinking about the reality of fear—though it's not a thing or a place. "So, over time, we've made it into this receptacle for fear—an adult version of the space that's under the bed? We enliven the Void, by filling it with our own fears? We bring it to life, make it what it is?"

"Yes," he laughed. "I guess you could say so. I think, in Duncan Robert's case, the act of jumping enlivened the Void. It was just lying there in the woods, until Duncan Robert jumped into it. Then it became something, for him. And his jump became something for everyone else.

"A Void calls for a jump—for someone to leave where they were and want to get to somewhere else. The jumper makes it what it is—a means to an end. Duncan Robert had to physically risk leaving earth for a moment, trusting he would land, finding a way to somewhere else."

"Why would we choose the Void, though, as a means of getting from *here* to wherever *there* is?" I asked, seeing myself standing at the edge of the Void again, in the fading afternoon sunlight. "Why would anyone jump into a dark hole in the ground?"

"Because there aren't that many places we can find to get us from *here* to *there*, and because I think it *enlivens* us to do so. It's all tied up together—the nature of the Void, the nature of the jump, the nature of us. Each calls out something in the other. A Void calls for a jump, a jump calls for a jumper, and we have to decide if we're a jumper. To be a jumper requires specific things of us—a certain focus, a certain energy or enthusiasm, a certain purpose. I think of those September 11th jumpers, choosing to jump versus choosing to wait for something to save them or choosing to succumb to the fire. I believe there's a certain triumph in a jump, no matter what happens, because it's a choice— a heroic choice. Those jumps became something powerful for us, too, images never to be forgotten. I know, I know. Not everyone would see it that way. These are my late-night thoughts."

I was so caught up in the discussion now, I hardly took time to jot down a note. "So when we jump into it, we create something—the Void becomes something. What does it become? And can a person ever come out of it? I mean, what does jumping into fear get us?" I'm stumbling over my own questions, excited to be talking about the Void to someone who knows it better than I do.

"I don't know," he said, shaking his head. "Look, if you think about it, you could argue that the Void doesn't last very long. How could it? You jump into it, it becomes known. Then it's not the Void anymore, because it's known. It's something else. So you have to keep jumping, not just one time. It's a life-long thing." The look on my face must have spooked him.

"Sorry. I'll stop. That's what comes from reading too much philosophy. The philosophers talk about the Void the most, but it stays theoretical, not like the one we have out in the woods here."

This talk of the Void makes me think of all of the talk of ascension, transformation, 2012, portals, etc., going on now in the "new age" world, which has made its way into mainstream media, too. It seems part of a continuum of definitions of dark, transformative places, from more to less real. "The Void seems to have more relevance than it has had in a while," I offered. "It seems less a place to avoid, than a place that has some kind of necessary part in the scheme of things?" I looked at him as he pondered my question. "Okay," I said to him, trying to go back to the question I started with. "I know where you stand on jumping. Where are you on Voids?"

"Well, I don't know," he said, leaving the safety of the swing to contemplate my question. "I'm not where I was when I started, I know that, but I don't know if I can define where I am now. Before, you're right, Voids were just scary places—like they still are for most of our own town's people."

"Yes. I'm like them," I told him. "I have the same worrying questions. I wonder why this town has a Void and others don't. Are you being punished somehow? Are you meant to do something with it? Honor it? Make some kind of sacrifices to it? Jump into it? Ignore it, for your own safety and well-being?" I pause for breath. These are questions I've had for a long time.

"You do ask questions, don't you?" he laughed. "Of course, I have those questions, too. None of them are easy to answer. So don't think I have all the answers! I don't know if other towns have Voids, but I don't believe this is the only one in the country. A town could have one, somewhere on its outskirts, and not know it, if no one stumbled on it. I think we know about ours because of the Tribe, on the outskirts of town, who've always known about it, from what I can tell. They don't particularly talk about it, but it's mentioned occasionally in the town records. The Tribe used to have ceremonies there, using it as a place to offer thanks to their ancestors, because it seemed to afford greater accessibility to those not in the here-and-now. They don't question why it's here. They just accept it."

"Yeah, they definitely don't seem interested in talking about it. I tried talking to a few people I saw around town, and they didn't seem to know what I was talking about."

"I've come to believe that—that we need Voids—even if I don't fully understand why," mused Miles. "It makes me appreciate the one we have in the woods in a different way—though I'm not sure 'appreciate' is the right word. Maybe 'respect' is better."

"Well, and it makes me wonder if the Void needs a name?" I laughed. "Wouldn't that make it warmer and friendlier? Maybe we could have a Void-naming contest." I'm only half-joking, wondering why no one has ever named this particular geographic feature, as they've named all others.

"Yeah, but then it might become known—known as a place for jumping, like some high bridges in this country. I can think of a couple of the more famous ones—the Golden Gate Bridge in San Francisco or the Gorge Bridge outside of the little town of Taos, New Mexico. About twenty people a year jump from the Golden Gate Bridge, and more than 150 have jumped from the Gorge Bridge since it was built in 1965. Would we want to try to police that? I wouldn't. I'd like to keep it the way it is."

I told him, "I can't figure out if I want it done away with or immortalized as a shrine."

"Yeah. Me either," he said honestly. "And a shrine to what?"

As I walked home from his place, beneath a shimmering lattice of stars, to my cozy little rooms above the bank, hoping my writing will do positive things for the town, I realized there wasn't another person in the world I could be having a conversation like this with. And I realized, too, that I can't think of a single conversation that's more worth having.

My dreams that night were all about falling. I have a little fear of heights, so falling dreams are the worst for me. First, I fell through the sky, as if I had jumped from a plane, something I would never do. I fell and fell, paralyzed with fear, unable to catch my breath to scream, but trying desperately to. Suddenly, I fell through a hole into darkness, as if I'd been swallowed. I knew I was falling towards something, something waiting for me down there, but I didn't know what, and I could do nothing about it—just fall. I tried to argue with it as I fell, yelling, "No! You have no right!" I woke in a sweat. I knew someone had been falling with me, just above me, just out of sight.

CHAPTER FIVE

Standing at the Void, Again

I HAVE TO GO BACK. I have to go and I have to stay at the edge until I figure this out. For the story, sure, but this is bigger. I know this. It has hold of me, has had hold of me since I was a kid. I managed to stand there for what felt like a quick minute when I first got to town. I fled then, spooked and disoriented knowing time sped by as I stood there, without my knowing. What will happen if I stay at the edge? *Will it possess me?* I think. I know it's irrational of me to think that, but if a Void isn't irrational, what is? Already most of my waking thoughts are about it, not to mention wherever I go at night, in dreams. Am I rational right now? Probably not. I'm using up too much of my rational energy avoiding the Void. My only hope to get any rational thinking back might be to go to the edge and reclaim it. Or lose it forever.

From the first time I heard about the Void—I must have been no more than six or seven and heard older kids trying to scare younger kids talking about it—I have been captivated. I knew those older kids were often full of it, but when I asked adults about it they couldn't give me a reasonable answer either. That really pricked up my ears and kept me thinking. "We aren't always meant to know the reasons why," they said. "Sometimes you just have to accept God's will." But I thought we *were* meant to know, which fueled a minor but steady passion about it over the years. But this was different, minor had become major, and passion had become compulsion.

So I know it's time to go, and one morning, after talking to Henry about what I've got so far, I decide to go. I don't tell him I'm going, I just agree as he tells me he likes what I have, and asks what else I plan to get. "You know, you should talk to all the officials—the police, the mayor— to see if what they say is different. The police always know what the real story is. They will have had some association with the Tribe, too," he tells me.

"Yeah," I say, absent mindedly.

"Babe," he says sharply, "are you paying attention to me?"

"Yeah," I lie. "I was writing it all down." We hang up after I reassure him a few more times how smart he is and what a big help he is. Does he really fall for that? I wonder. Well, it might be half true. I pick up my bag and my keys and head for my car out front. I drive north, to the Void. I'm there within ten minutes, walking through the clearing, through the dappled summer sunshine to the Void's edge, feeling a light breeze ruffle my gauze skirt, hearing insects buzz in the grass. I catch sight of a small black fox on the other side of the clearing, darting into the tree line. That makes me smile.

As I stand at the edge of the Void now, calmly gazing in, I realize, with some surprise, that I have always liked knowing it exists, with all its risks and possibilities. It's like knowing that the Very Large Array exists just outside of Socorro, New Mexico, one of my favorite places. It's a place scientists can listen to space, just in case. Somebody's on that job, ready to establish contact when it comes. I feel that way about the Void. It's pretty essential, in terms of meaning, like those listeners at the Very Large Array. Because some of us believe we're meant to know. And I'd like to write that story.

Just standing on the edge, I suddenly know some things now about the Void that I didn't know before. Being this close makes a difference in your understanding of things.

I'm waiting for him, Duncan Robert, to create the truth of the Void for us, I realize, by telling us what he found there. He can't do that because he created it for himself when he jumped. His act of jumping made it what it was. He brought himself to it, yes, but he brought his act of jumping to it, too. Any realizations he had were actualized by his jump. And his jump is his jump.

I stand there, feeling understanding fill me. I've always been drawn to people who've been through recovery programs successfully, of their own will or through interventions, because they seem to have been through something that transformed them in a really empowering way. They have a new quiet confidence about them, as if they couldn't be pushed. Yet they are humble, too. A jump feels to me like it might do the same thing. It might take you through a process that makes you more than you were, that releases some of the fear you've accumulated.

I feel, too, the presence of a truth here. I can't deny it. The Void is what it is. It's got its own "normal," separate from what we do or don't do, believe or don't believe. It doesn't require our belief, as the saying goes. I feel you can trust that, and I almost laugh out loud. I'm talking to myself about trusting a hole in the ground.

As I stand there, I'm aware that I'm still paralyzed by my fear of falling into it, of it swallowing me up for all eternity, of my no longer existing, no longer mattering, no longer seen or heard. My fear grows as I notice it. I feel I'm quickly losing my own sense of personal agency, and I start to feel helpless. A moment after that, my psychological and emotional sense of myself is reduced to that of a child. I'm overwhelmed by the power of the Void—its depth and darkness—and the powerlessness of me.

There's no arguing with that kind of presence. Either you have it or you don't. I don't, not in the face of the Void.

I have never felt so insignificant, so matter-less. I stand there as a cold realization dawns on me. I've never felt so insignificant *except* . . . except when I was a small child, and I would feel my father's hands on me. I'm shocked by the emergence of this felt memory, as I always am when it materializes unexpectedly, sparked by something outside of me.

Such a deep, long-held, closely guarded secret, one that doesn't belong in the daylight, brought out so quickly. But I'm also beginning to understand that this is what the Void is about—the truth, *your* truth. The truth of whatever dark secrets still hold you in their clutches, whatever secrets your power still serves, leaving you paralyzed, without strength to move or save yourself or protect yourself.

So, this is what the Void is about for me, I think. This is what I'd be jumping into. I feel myself shrink in stature and feel the wind buffet me. The wind is stronger than I am, too. I don't know if I can hold my footing on the edge, and there's nothing nearby to hold on to. Just the grass at my feet. I drop to my knees, insides quivering, and grab hold of it, twining my fingers deeply into it, feeling its roots hold me back. I anchor myself there, and it feels like the most natural thing in the world, just as jumping almost had a moment ago, to have the grass holding me safe, to feel in partnership with it. I breathe, realizing I haven't been breathing, not deeply, as I do now.

I've lived with an awareness of my abuse for a long time, managing as best I could. There had been a time when the damaged part of me had more passion for living than I did, directing my choices, determining my course. But I've had years of afternoon therapy and night-time support groups, I remind myself, and multitudes of books that helped me confront and overcome the horror of it to get to its core and remove its poison. I understand the abuse scenario and everyone's roles and responsibilities better, and I'm not entangled in the levels of guilt and shame I used to be. I'm nobody's victim anymore, and proud of it. Maybe I over-compensate for the years of feeling powerless by challenging the men in my life more than I should, but at least I almost always couch those challenges in my version of kindness. My proximity to the Void shows me all this about myself. It shows me the things I can celebrate about myself, and it occurs to me that my healing can move through my *heart* now, and not just be a *head* understanding.

I feel a kind of euphoria at this. It becomes clear to me now that no one jumps into the Void as a victim. It's not about that. If I jumped right now, I wouldn't be jumping still feeling like a victim. I don't! I'd be jumping to experience something else. You jump from a position of strength! It's not like suicide, in which you jump out of a sense of desperation, or because you can't go on. That's why you wouldn't pick the Void for suicide. I'm certain now that Duncan Robert had no intention of suicide whatsoever.

This kind of jumping is a whole different kind of act, but it's been hard for me, or people in the town, or his mother, or even Miles to see that because the Void seems empty, even nihilistic. Yes, you go into it alone, and you're leaving everything beloved behind—people, pets, places, things. But as I stand here, I *know* I don't feel alone. I've never loved all those people and things more. I'm crouched here at the edge with a sense of wonder and peace. Where has all that paralyzing fear gone?

And that's how Miles found me. I felt him before I turned on my knees and saw he was there, with a wad of my long, tie-dyed skirt gripped in his hands. I could tell by the look of stark fear on his face that he had been afraid I was going to jump. And, well, I almost did! It had felt like the most natural thing in the world. Miles calls this "the lure of the Void," he would tell me later. I hadn't known about this, but I certainly believe in it now. It doesn't happen to everyone, Miles says. It's only possible if you've made a kind of peace with your worst fears and they don't rule you.

"Your fears are your fears, hard won, every one of them" he would explain to me after, "but you have to get to the place where you no longer self-medicate against them, or lose whole days to them, or where you take them out and use them as weapons to wound or maim anyone around you. You know them, they know you, and everyone peacefully co-exists. They no longer assume they are in control. They just come out now and then to show you they still live there, and maybe always will."

"Sometimes you bring them out yourself, to remind yourself where you've found your strength. If you don't develop this kind of relationship with them, you just remain scared of them, and that's what you'd feel at the edge of the Void, scared. Because the Void strips you of all pretense, of anything that isn't the bare-bones, unadorned you. Titles, degrees, the color of your skin, the size of your bank account, how much you've suffered or how many you've made suffer—none of these things influence its accounting of you. Clearly, you can't fool it. And it doesn't want to fool you."

But now, as the immediate emotions of the moment start to even out, Miles and I sit there in the grass, on my skirt, catching our breath. The Void is *more* to me now, I think, and *less. More* in the sense that it seems to be a thinking, feeling entity capable of recognizing the authentic when it sees it. It's on the side of the good because it's on the side of truth. And it's *less* in the sense that, while no less formidable—in its presence, its depth, its darkness—it's less fearsome. It seems, well, reasonable taking whoever stands at its edge into consideration. In this way, the Void takes on a personality of its own—different from and far beyond the limited one assigned to it by current media influences, trends, hearsay and speculation, and so on. It's too big for a name, I realize with a laugh. I can't think of one that could encompass it.

Miles, brought out of his own reverie by my laugh, tells me my editor, Henry, called him. That's why he came.

"Henry? What did he say?" I ask, startled at this news.

"It went something like this," he says, trying to do a Henry Boston accent, "Holy Toledo! All of the talk of the Void—I knew where Babe was going to go. Yes, I suggested she hadda visit the Void, but I hadn't thought about her and jumping. Not right away. But it started to gnaw at me. So I had to call ya. I knew if *I* was thinking she might jump, the thought had crossed *her* mind. And I knew it would cross *your* mind, too, though maybe not soon enough. That meant it would cross the *reader's* mind, so we have a story to tell here!"

We're both laughing now—me, at his accent and his running of all the words together, in Henry's way. I think he's laughing because he's still feeling the relief of getting here and finding I hadn't jumped.

Miles says, "Henry said he knew you thought what you had so far was a non-story—so he thought you might jump, to find the rest of the story or create a story, like war correspondents wanting to go to Afghanistan or something."

Miles looks at me. "I thought you might jump, too." He smiles wryly. "So I come running over, to find you wobbling, hunched over on the edge." He pauses and looks down a moment. "I felt a bit responsible, you know, since I know that talking about the Void for a period of time can unleash a kind of physical fascination with it. And I knew you already had an intense interest in it, to build on." He looks up at me and smiles again, sheepishly this time. "That's why I grabbed a handful of your skirt, spread out behind there in the grass. It was the first thing I could reach." He pauses again, smoothing my skirt, and I let him organize his feelings, knowing this has all been kind of traumatic for him, certainly triggering memories of that other jump.

"When you turned to look at me," he says, and I remember looking directly into his eyes, and we were only inches apart, "the peace in your eyes released my fears, and that peace flooded me, and I felt at one with that peace and you." He pauses again, a bit choked up. I am, too.

"I instantly knew you'd thought about jumping but had decided against it. I knew you had had the same realizations about the Void I've had. It isn't a place for that kind of jumping." He studies my face. I calmly let him, not looking away from his gaze. It feels good to know him this way, through our knowing of the Void.

"That Henry's quite a talker," he says, after a moment, looking at me with a smile.

"Yeah, and all the while, I might have been jumping!" I say with a laugh, poking his arm. Miles laughs, too, catching at my hand, but then says, "He really cares about you."

"I know," I say, letting him hold my hand. "He has daughters, and he seems to forget I'm not one of them."

As we walk back to my car and his truck, Miles still has hold of my hand. I'm surprised Henry didn't ask about love interest, too, for the story, I think. He's asked me before, sure that women and men can't be in the close contact a good interview creates without some kind of spark being kindled. If Henry thought readers would want to follow a good love story—me pining after Duncan Robert, or Reggie and Duncan Robert, or Miles and me—well, Henry would be all for me taking that angle for the story. Maybe I'm a little in love with the Void, I think, laughing out loud. Hey, we can't ignore it. After all, it's what got us all together. Because I'm laughing, Miles laughs, too, and we swing our joined hands all the way back to the road.

CHAPTER SIX

The Return

ONE NIGHT, ONLY A few days later, I get a call.

I've just been working at typing up a summary of my experience with the Void. I'd spent half the evening on the phone with Henry, who still wants reassurance that I won't go anywhere near the Void again without telling him, and who is intensely curious about what I'm writing. After our years of working together, he knows better than to ask. I never know what I'm writing until I'm through. I've had more contact from Henry in the last few days than I've had in a month, so I know the calls are really his means of expressing his affection and concern for me. So, I'm distracted by Henry and trying to get back into my Void experience, when a voice reaches out from the Void itself. On the telephone.

"Hello? Is this Babe Bennett? This is Duncan Robert. I'm not disturbing you, am I?"

I drop the phone, then scrabble to pick it up.

"What?" I say, wondering if any of the town folk are engaged enough for a gag like this. The voice is calm, serious without being cold, and *respectful*, I think, after groping for the right word to capture what comes across the line.

"It's Duncan Robert," he repeats. "I'd like to talk to you about your recent experience with the Void and about my experience."

"What?" I say again, like an idiot, taken off guard by what he says. "How do you know about that?"

"Would you like an interview?" he asks, not answering my question. "There are some things I'd like to say, and I think you and Miles are ready to hear them now."

"Miles?" I say, seemingly only capable of monosyllables at the moment.

"Yes. We were waiting for you. Now that you're here, we can talk about it."

"It?" I say, continuing true to my new concise form of interacting, unable to break out of it.

"I don't want to become anybody's idol or guru, or even their reason. I don't want to be the reason anybody jumps," he says. "As you know, it's such a personal decision, a person has to arrive at it on his or her own. It's complicated, depending on what you're carrying." He pauses, waiting to see if I'll actually join the conversation. When I don't, he says, "The Void is always there. People will feel its call or not. They will make themselves ready or not. They cannot do it through me. I want to make that clear. But we can talk about that when you two get here."

That last part gets through to me, and I'm finally able to ask where and when he would like to meet. We agree that I'm to go to a place that's not far, the next day. Yes, I'm to bring Miles with me, he says, before I can double check. He seems to know that Miles doesn't have classes that day.

"What about Silvia?" I ask, suddenly remembering his mother and not wanting to leave her out of this.

"You don't need to worry about my mother," he tells me gently when I ask. "I've always been in touch with her." So that's why Silvia was able to talk about him with some ease and light heartedness, I think. She's known this whole time that he is okay. He gives a little chuckle. "I know, like any mother, she wants me to come back to life as it was, with her, and she hopes talking about me to others will help keep that possibility alive. She's saving my place. I don't begrudge her that."

Clearly, he's ready for the call to end, so I make sure he has my cell phone number and verify the time again, and we hang up, having wished each other a good evening.

I sit there, at my little desk in front of the window, staring out at the night street in front of the bank. Not a soul in sight. I feel completely alone with this news, and just about bursting with it. But before I can call Miles, I need to sort myself out and get centered. This call will have much more effect on him. Miles doesn't need hysterical babbling. He needs someone who can do for him what Duncan Robert just did for me—provide an anchor and a calm focus. I make myself a cup of peppermint tea, am calmed by the process, and sit down to make the call.

The first thing Miles says is, "Why didn't he call *me*?" The news hasn't made him speechless, as it did me.

"He said you two were waiting for me," I tell him, saying the first thing that comes to mind.

"He said we were . . . ?" That stops him for a while. He doesn't say any more.

I sit quietly for a few minutes, feeling my embarrassment, sipping my tea. I don't know what that statement means either, and I do not want to hazard a guess.

Finally, I speak into his silence, telling him the details of where and when. Apparently, he is silenced now, as I was. When he still doesn't respond, I ask, "Do you want to go?" I'm afraid for a moment that he doesn't.

"Yes," he says. "I'll drive." We agree he will pick me up the next morning, a little before 7:00. We hang up, without wishing each other a good evening.

I spend a pretty much sleepless night, after laying out what I'm going to wear, packing a snack bag, printing a MapQuest map, taking a shower, making sure I have my interview materials, wondering whether to take my miniature tape recorder, deciding to take it, trying to think of questions to ask, and writing in my journal. Mostly, worrying about Miles's state of mind is what keeps me awake.

The next morning, he picks me up in his old pick-up, with cups of hot tea and muffins from the café. I note that the pick-up looks just washed. He reminds me of my older sister, Marla, who always begins a trip by washing even an already-clean car. He notes how much stuff I've brought with me and smiles as he makes room for it behind the seats. I get in, and we look at each other for a moment.

"Hard to believe," he says.

"Yes," I agree.

He has tears in his eyes, which, unexpectedly, brings tears to mine. He extends his right hand to me. I put my right hand in his, and we shake, solemnly. I feel the warmth and strength of his hand before I let it go.

"Let's go," he says, and we pull away from the curb, the morning breeze freshening through the windows as we drive into it, the light spattering the seat between us as the sun travels through the trees. I can't help but feel good. I wouldn't want to be anywhere else, with anyone else, at this moment. That's a feeling I often have in his presence, I note. I wonder if Miles feels the same.

The town is about two hours north of our village, the appointed location is an attractive old hotel on the original town square. The town square is appealing, with grass, flowers, and a gazebo large enough for a band. It's ringed by huge, beautiful old beech trees that shade the square and the street.

We park diagonally in front of the hotel and stare up at it. It's eight stories high and a good example of Federalist architecture, I notice, with its fanlight over the door, narrow, symmetrical windows with shutters, and elliptical window in the gable at the top of a roof complete with balustrade. I recognize this from yet another article I researched on colonial architectural style and the hold it has on this part of the country. The hotel is a bit shabby, making its style a little less imposing and a little more welcoming. There's no cadre of well-pressed staff to greet us as we walk in, only a slightly worn down older woman behind the ornately carved mahogany and marble registration desk. She points us to the old-fashioned elevator, complete with wrought-iron gate.

We go up to his room, which is on the seventh floor, facing the square. The hall carpet is plush, but worn down the middle. The wallpaper is burgundy and grey broad stripes. The lighting is provided by old converted gaslight lamps on the walls, so it's dim. I realize that I'm cataloguing everything as I see it, an old habit to distract myself from my nervousness. We arrive at his door and stand there a moment, looking at each other. Miles smiles at me, takes a breath and lifts his hand to knock. The door opens before he can knock, and there Duncan Robert stands, looking larger than life—robust, fit, glowing with health. Light streams out into the hall from the large bank of windows that overlooks the square behind him. He and Miles look at each other a moment and then grip each other in a bear hug. Miles has tears in his eyes again, and in his voice. When they move away from each other, the tension has left Miles's face and a smile has taken over. He can't seem to stop smiling. His eyes don't leave Duncan Robert's face. Miles is just so glad to see him.

Duncan Robert greets me with a hug, too, and ushers us into the room, offering tea and muffins as we settle in. Miles sits on one end of the couch and I take the other. Duncan Robert sits in one of the two large, wing-back chairs across from us, sharing the coffee table between us. "Welcome," he says, with real warmth in his voice. "I thank you for coming."

I've put my notebook and freshly sharpened pencils on the table and I look at them, caught between starting to take notes and staring at him. This is something that will plague me the rest of the day. I'm mesmerized by him. I mean, he looks as everyone and his pictures described him—medium height, medium coloring, a medium sort of man—but he doesn't *feel* medium. He felt different. I don't know if I can put it into words, but he felt light and clean and clear. He felt happy and at peace. He felt strong and certain of himself. Even *loving* and *joyous*, though I'm afraid of how those words might sound if I put them in a story—unnatural or phony. Or at least they would have felt that way to me if I'd heard anyone else use them.

He reminds me of some of the good psychics I met doing a piece on psychics and ghosts for Henry. The real psychics looked at me in a way I've never been looked at by anyone—with a directness and openness that took everything in and *blessed* it, before anything was said. And I sure knew *everything* didn't deserve blessing. But they had such a strong sense of good will that they made you believe maybe everything did. While you were in their presence, they made you feel yourself differently, too.

He told us some things first, before he got into the story of his jump. First he talked about Reggie. She was the most significant person in his life then, and they were creating their lives together. He never doubted they would jump together. He remembered her response to his decision to jump. His description is intensely personal but ultimately less relevant to his jump, so I summarize it here from my notes, to give the reader a sense of Reggie, what she was to him, and her decision.

Reggie was one of ten kids, two of whom had been adopted out because her parents couldn't feed them all. Duncan Robert thinks this still happens, more than we know. Relatives came and made their choice, choosing her and her brother, and when she was twelve, she came from Alabama to live in New Hampshire. She and Duncan Robert met in middle school, arguing fiercely over whose turn it was to use the soccer equipment after school. His friends had backed off because she was black. He hadn't noticed. The question of right and wrong had his attention.

Over the years, they became inseparable and spent many hours on a blanket at the edge of the Void, talking and arguing, a favorite place because no one ever came there. They were gradually creating their future together, sure they'd be in each other's lives forever. As they moved through high school they grew aware that they were tired of the established order of things, restless and wanting adventure. He told her about his philosophical conversations with Miles, and gradually his talk shifted to the Void as their adventure. The Void scared her more than he knew, and she made strong arguments against jumping:

"It's crazy! We could be killing ourselves!"

Or, "It's not something black people do," she said one afternoon. "The Void is white people's stuff."

Or, "I don't see escaping into another world as the way to go. I think we're meant to deal with what's here."

And then one day, "It could be evil!"

That stopped them and made them both laugh. They stood there, near the edge of the Void, and laughed, knowing that their end was written in the laughing, because it meant they had nowhere else to argue to. There was a divide between them now because in her discovery that she couldn't jump, it was clear she would never understand how he could. She had been his biggest test. Once the question of her jumping no longer stood in his way, he was ready.

After the jump, they still stayed in touch from time to time, he said. If he still loves her, he didn't say, but I think he does. And always will. Maybe that's the romantic in me.

He paused at this point. I looked at him, and he looked at me and then at Miles. We knew he had to talk about the jump now, if he was going to. We could tell he'd been changed by it. He's not the person he was, as Miles would say. Miles later used words like *matured* and *steadier*, and *more at home in his own skin*. Duncan Robert's restlessness was gone. Everything I know about the Void and jumping is dancing around in my head, and now I'm trying to imagine Duncan Robert—his courage, his determination—facing down the Void. I'm literally perched on the edge of my seat, ready for his story to begin.

I write as the words fly out of him, describing the fall, the landing, and the return. I write fast and furious, without looking up, in a note-taker's trance, which veteran note-takers will recognize. Here are his words without further comment from me. I'd hardly know what to say anyway.

Duncan Robert:

Miles dropped me off that morning at the Void. Everything seemed the same as always. The light in the eastern sky was just beginning. The clearing was quiet. I walked through the damp, knee-high grass to the edge of the Void. I was nervous, hardly breathing. I was counting on the gravity at the edge of the Void for the final pull if I hesitated.

I stood at the edge, feeling the presence of the Void, and took a deep, shaky breath, breathing it in. The blood stirred in every corner of my body, and I felt something here bigger than my fear. It was an overwhelming eagerness for more, the same eagerness that had brought me to the edge. I knew this was the way.

I bent forward, arms outstretched, leaning into the Void, until I tipped, face forward into the fall, eyes open. It would have been a belly flop if there'd been a pool. In the first few minutes, I cried out for Reggie, because I wanted her to see this, too.

As I fell, fearing the ground was rushing up to meet me, certain I was making a jump I couldn't possibly return from, the exhilaration I felt still made me laugh out loud. I still feel it.

The fall, well, the fall is what you might think, if you've ever fallen. I think if falls are shorter, people remember less—about the fall, about what they were thinking or feeling. In a longer fall, though, you have time. You begin to notice things. Not right at first, though, because I didn't know how long this fall was going to be. At first, right after my feet left the ground, I could feel myself start to panic. I don't think I've ever done anything as final as that jump.

It's one thing to *talk* about and another to actually *do*. There was no taking it back, and I felt it in that moment. Einstein or some other physicist said the gravity force is strongest at the edge of a black hole. I can believe that. The force of it at the edge of the Void just took me.

I was in no way prepared for or expecting the helplessness. My heart raced up out of my chest and into my throat, and I couldn't catch my breath. I wanted to scream but only little gasps came out, like the sound a small child would make or someone in pain. I grabbed and twisted and turned, trying to get myself into some sort of protected position, until it became clear the force of the fall didn't allow for holding any position long. I never realized how much having our feet on the ground supported so many other things, like arms and neck and head—and stomach.

The walls of the tunnel moved past too quickly to look for hand or toe holds.

They seemed fairly smooth and unmarked in the beginning. I couldn't see what was down below me, either. It just was dark down there. I had no choice but to let the falling take me.

So, I fell.

Surprisingly, the tension and fear in me lessened pretty fast. That was the other thing I had no way of preparing for or expecting—how quickly we adapt, physically, emotionally, to whatever condition is thrust on us. I fell, and I accepted falling and the peace that seemed to come from not fighting it.

I fell, and my mind still worked, so I was conscious of the fall, and curious about it, too. How far would I fall? Would I be killed in the landing? When would it come? I knew the fall would end—I didn't believe this was the Void to nowhere. Then I noticed it wasn't pitch black and it wasn't freezing cold, two things I had expected. There was some sort of pale glow all around me, and it felt pleasantly cool in the tunnel, not cold, probably because of the air rushing by me that my falling body created. I was just falling now, at a reclining angle, with feet first.

I could see the walls were rock but not as unbroken as I'd originally thought. Now and then, I would see markings of some sort on the walls or I would fall past an opening, at times on both sides of my tunnel, and would get the sense there were other tunnels like mine, extending down. I'm pretty sure there were falling bodies in those tunnels, too, people and animals. It was a combination of hunch and sound. I heard no screams or calls; it was just the sense of wind-brushed, rushing solid masses, of varying sizes and shapes. I didn't know what to make of that. The openings came on too quickly and passed before I could think of calling out myself.

It sounds like a nightmare experience, as I tell it, but I can't say it was. Even though I was falling quickly, I felt suspended somehow, maybe because of my sense of falling and having an awareness of my fall, describing it to myself in my head as I went.

The truth is, falling added to my growing sense of excitement, which was different than my original panic-fueled resistance. Everything around me felt alive, and I did, too. Part of me wanted to whoop and holler. I was captivated by my own experience in a way that was new to me. Sure, I wanted to know where I was going. But I was the central character in my own drama now—I made this happen, when I chose to jump. In falling, I was carrying responsibility for myself in a way I never had. I felt more complete, more whole, more fully embedded in my own existence than I had ever thought possible. I may have disappeared from the physical world, but in this one, I got found.

I don't know how long I fell. It felt like a long time. But what's time in a tunnel? I can't say. I kind of feel as if I have an understanding of the relativity of time now, how it depends on perspective and circumstance. I know a bunch of it seemed to pass that I can't really account for. I can't imagine that I slept while falling (!), but I can't account for every minute, either. I know I had random thoughts, of Reggie, of my mother, of being a child, rolling down a grassy hill at twilight, with other kids, of hearing the call to come in, and not wanting to.

Then suddenly, when I was at my most relaxed, it was as if a gust of wind pushed me into one of the openings in the wall to my left, and I landed on my behind, rolling over to a stop, against a side wall. I had landed in a three-sided rock room. It took me a minute to realize I'd actually come to a stop—the sense of falling stayed with me internally for a minute, as my organs settled into an upright orientation. I wanted to hold onto 'stop' for a while, to believe in the ulti-mate goal of gravity again, which isn't falling but landing, as Newton's apple did. I felt intensely awake and aware, wondering what would happen next, knowing I had been stopped for a reason.

I looked up just as a young man, out of breath, wearing what looked like a white space suit, without helmet, loomed into view over me. He had a great shock of kinky hair that was reddish in color, skin with the hue and sheen of dark, well-oiled walnut, and eyes that glowed gold. He had small gold hoops in his nose and ears, and they glowed, too. He greeted me enthusiastically, infectiously, reaching down to take my hands and pull me to my feet.

I gave him my hands without thinking, as I stared into his face. It's a beautiful, happy, open face, with a wonderfully wide smile. He knows me—really knows me—and is genu-inely happy to see me. I notice I can see him in the dimness and think it's because he's radiating a gentle light. Then I think maybe there's a light behind me, illuminating us both, and I turn to look before I realize it's *my* light, a light radiat-ing from me. I attributed it to being in his presence, which somehow upped the energy ante, making it possible for me to glow. I associate the light, the glow, with the feeling I'm feeling. I *like* him, really like him. I feel as if I've missed him, a lot, so much it hurts. I find that, without knowing why,

I'm glad to see him, and I'm greeting him enthusiastically, too. Tears are on my face, though I can't even say who he is.

I felt the whole story of me, as I knew it, shifting and changing, and I knew I *needed* this story, this bigger story, to understand the purpose and meaning of my life. Anything else would just be a footnote or, worse, a fiction. And I suddenly realize I love this strange spaceman. I've never felt closer to anyone—not Reggie, not my mother, not Miles, not anyone.

The Void is something more than a pathway to somewhere else. It's a place of meetings, gatherings, like this one. A place you can meet your larger story, through people like this shining man. I'm overcome. Who'd have thought, when looking into the darkness of the Void, you could meet your own light in it?

I ask him, as I continue to hold onto his hands, who he is, where he came from, where we are. I'm so glad to see him. He continues to smile, moves away, crouching down to start a small fire, and says, "Well, you must have sent out the call."

"What call?" I ask, surprised.

He gestures to me to come over and sit down by him; he has the fire going, in a low spot in the rock floor. He smiles at me and laughs. I laugh, too. It just feels good to laugh. He begins to answer my questions, looking sideways at me, as he produces a pan to boil water in and the water to go in it, from a thermos attached to his pocket. He seems to be watching me, to see if anything resonates with me.

"I'm Guy," he says, looking to see if I already knew that, but I didn't, despite how well I know I know him. I'm so happy to be with him that I cling to his every word.

"We've had a team connected to Station 1 for as long as any of us can remember. Not that that's saying much, because time doesn't exist for us *here*. Not the way it does for you *there*. We just know that we come together here in this no-place place whenever any one of us gets a call. The call usually just appears in our knowing, and we direct our attention here, and everything else follows."

He notes my confusion and says, "You'll just have to take my word for that." He smiles again, and I feel lit from inside by his smile. "Sometimes the call goes out to the whole team, sometimes to just one or two of us. But we always come. Unless, of course, we can't." He smiles mischievously at that last part, leaving me wondering.

"This time the call was for all of us. I thought it was to be a 'production,' for one of Lynette's people."

Of course I didn't know but was getting the idea that he and his 'Team' were somehow engaged in looking after those of us currently on Earth. Who or how I didn't know.

"I don't know for sure how big the Team is," he said, answering my question before I even finished thinking it. "It can grow or shrink at any time, based on people's progress, based on individual Team member challenges, based on need, all of which can then be telepathed, one to the other. It feels as if it's been the five of us core members, including you, for a while. We're part of the same cohort— we started existence together—and we've known each other for eons, literally." He knows I'm not quite catching on yet.

"Known is not even an encompassing enough word for what we've been to each other. You tell me a word for it. We've been each other's midwife, mother, father, sister, brother, torturer, betrayer, lover, child, killer, priest, concubine, teacher, and more. We've breathed each other's breaths, died each other's deaths. We've been that close, and closer. Sharing skin and scent. We've been *one*. Remember?"

I just look at him, mesmerized by what he's telling me. He looks back, in no rush. "I remember," he continues, "when I was a person once on Earth, late at night, staring at a clear sky full of a million stars and feeling one with all the world, and every single person in it. I was nothing, and I was something, and all of it felt immense. It's like that for us, here, but multiplied a few thousand times."

He laughs, rubbing his face, stirring loose tea leaves into the now-boiling water. "I know you and you know me, inside and out, in a way that is much more intimate than you know yourself."

It makes me think of Reggie—how she was me and I was her, while still being ourselves—so close we knew each other's thoughts and feelings, yet so respectful we didn't touch that knowing, just accepted it. But that seems a pale shadow of what he's talking about.

"In between being people on Earth, we come here or a place like this—an agreed upon gathering place with a set of coordinates, and we've reviewed lives, laughing and crying, deeply moved by our own and each other's performance, by how hard we tried, how much we messed up, how much we meant well, how painful it all was, even when we thought we were having fun or being successful or were at the top of our game." He shakes his head and laughs again.

I'm trying to keep up and focus on his words, when I suddenly realize he's not speaking—*he's directly communicating inside my head*. He's sharing what he knows and answering questions I'm not aware I'm even asking, so I stop trying to keep up and just let it come.

"We've plotted and planned lives together, and then gone and lived them, together or in opposition to each other. Or we've done this—offering the best, most heart-felt kind of support we can think to offer to those living the life, as forcefully and strategically as we can from the other side in this no-place place. We're reminded, as we watch our people how unutterably, unendingly hard it can be to be a person. And how heartbreakingly hard it is to try to reach them. Most of us think of Earth as the ultimate trial. We know that we ourselves have been broken by it over and over, crushed to nothing before we began to even gain a toe hold on the essentials.

"Having pulled the necessary and legendary 'wool of forgetfulness' over ourselves when we enter Earth, we face the assault of being human alone, in a human body, sure we are ultimately 'born alone and die alone,' or even that it's all 'dust to dust.' We weep, we moan, we fornicate, we lie, we steal, we sell ourselves, we run, we hide, we commit all sorts of sordid, unspeakable acts, all to avoid actually believing the untruth we've created—that we're born alone, die alone. The truth is we're never alone—birth, death, whenever! How's that for irony?" He laughs loud at this, his breath fanning the small fire.

I watch as he stirs the brewing tea. He pours some into the cap of his thermos for me. I take it gratefully.

"Most of this kind of talk makes your fellow Team members here laugh uproariously. It's so ridiculous to us, while we're here, that all of us are capable of veering so far off our carefully laid plans while under the influence of life on Earth. And we do it over and over again, despite our sober, sacred oaths of allegiance to the plan.

"But we're all up against Earth's strong and long-established institutionalized thought when we're there. Established Earth thought stands in direct opposition to all that we know to be true. And people on Earth, mostly, won't stand for what we know, not for a single minute. On Earth, what we *know to be true* is all dismissed as delusional babel, at best. At worst, it's treason, sedition, or even evil—crimes punishable by death. Think about your own American history. People have been *hung* for just talking the way we talk." He grins and continues, before I can think of a reaction to that.

"Anyway, I do digress, a habit across many lifetimes, I'm told. Don't hesitate to call me on it, please. To get back to your questions, I'm the one who refers to this place as 'Station 1,' and I do it on purpose. I do it because it reminds me of watching *Star Trek* on Earth. Watching that and seeing that vision of the future allowed us to see reality ahead of schedule, to know that there was more to come. That was terrifically heartening. And, as we've all learned the hard way—by ignoring them—we come to know everything through these kinds of *connections* to what we like, to what matters to us, even if it is a television show." He laughs again. "Yes, television is a distraction, but like almost anything else, it's not all bad. You all spend so much time with it, we've come to know it better, too, through your references."

I sit, mesmerized by him, my tea forgotten. Our conversation is happening in my head, as if he's inside it. To describe the closeness of that—as close as your own thought—is impossible. It's as much about having a feeling as it is about having a thought or a dialogue.

"As for the *call*, like the one you just made, it usually just appears in our knowing and then we *will* ourselves here, to Station 1. What kind of call, you're asking? It's a call for services. Our services, to be specific, because we're cohorts, having started out at the same time, and because we've discovered why we've survived and we know how to use that hard-won knowledge. If you combine all of our experiences on Earth, we've survived most of whatever you're going through there, along with stuff you couldn't now imagine surviving, most of it more than once, and some of it with you.

"The difference between you and us, in this moment, is that we can access full awareness of our experiences—what to do, what not to do—but you're not usually privy to that awareness where you are. Sometimes, you exist *here*, right where we are now, answering calls about us."

He looks over at me. "You still want to know why we come. We come because the call means there's an opportunity. For service. Let me tell you what I mean by that archaic old word 'service,' because I don't mean what you people on Earth often do. I don't mean that we go into your personal business uninvited or that we try to 'fix' things for you, so you don't have to. We don't try to spare you any of your own experience, or tell you what to do, even if asked. We're only allowed to provide hints, clues, and opportunities, so you're reminded you have *choices*.

"You're not a victim of someone else's choices, you're not caught in pre-determined anything, but at the same time nothing is random (pretty much nothing—hah!). So, we might try to point out the obvious in a situation: 'Hey, remember when you did this before?' Or remind you of a connection: 'Um, this person you consider a perfect stranger has been your child.' Or state the obvious, to us: 'Don't forget that you know the inner workings of most anything, even if you think you've never seen it before.' We do this out of love, for those we love, hoping they get the love.

"Say you're the reason for the call," he smiles, "which you are. This time. But say you're someone who is experiencing a trauma or a vacation or a significant anniversary or birthday or loss—some kind of trigger. Something big. That's our opening to get in there and engage with you on a connecting level. You're shook up, whether you're consciously acknowledging it or not—due to turning 40 or 60, or realizing you've stayed in a relationship too long and don't know how to get out, or you just don't know what to do with yourself without all your usual distractions. Shook up in a good way or a bad way, doesn't matter. You're off balance, not tied down as tightly as usual, and that attracts us. However *you* see it—as disaster or confusion or euphoria—*we* see it as *opportunity*. It's provided our window of opportunity to serve. And we know we have to act fast. Your attention span while you're there is usually short when it comes to things like this! You can be pretty quick in creating a distraction for yourself. After all, you're living in a world of distractions!"

He laughs again and gives my shoulder a push. I push him back, delighted to be playing with him in this way. He acts as if I've given him a powerful push and rolls over to his side and then back up. We laugh again.

I can't argue with him. I remember all the times I decided to have a cigarette, or go for a run, or watch an old movie—anything to shut out uncomfortable feelings. How does service help, I wonder.

"Why service?" he asks. "Without service, no progress is possible, for anybody. If we don't offer help to each other, no one gets 'past' anything, or achieves understanding of it so they don't have to do it again and can stop suffering. We're *all* each other's burdens!" he said with a laugh.

"No matter how stoic or how much of a John Wayne anyone is, their progress is not made without our help. Even 'accidental' help, a movie or a book or a phone call out of the blue, originates with us and our service.

"Once you recognize the importance of service, you're no longer in opposition to anyone else. You understand that when we become aligned with each other in this way— one for all and all for one—there can be no more war, no more violence toward each other or any other living thing, no more human-caused suffering in the world."

"Service brings about necessary change in the world and in us. From service we learn understanding and for-giveness. So, we come to your call—see, that wasn't really an endless digression—because we have an abiding love for you that permeates our being. This is what we all do for each other. It can be no other way."

He looks at me and then says, "And, yes, we do come for ourselves. Because there is no separation. It's a bond stronger than life."

CHAPTER SEVEN

The Group

DUNCAN ROBERT SUGGESTS A little break, and I nod at
him gratefully, shaking out my stiff writing hand, which has
been clenching my pencil tighter than usual. Miles stands
up and stretches and moves to the sideboard for more tea
and something to eat.

"How are you two holding up?" Duncan Robert asks.

"It's a lot to take in. I'll be grateful for the notes." Miles
looks at me.

"I have no idea what I've got," I say honestly to Miles.
"I think I've kept my head down most of the time, so maybe
I got most of it." I look up at Duncan Robert. "I just keep
trying to imagine what it must have been like for you! And I
can hear the questions my editor will have."

"It was wonderful for me!" Duncan Robert says, grin-
ning ear to ear. Of course it was, I think. How could he
question it, when it was happening to him?

He turns to Miles. "What's that thing you say to your
beginning writing classes? About the old Greek definition
of a gift? When you're telling them what their writing can
be for them?"

"Something you wanted, something you needed, something you never thought you'd get?" Miles asks.

"That's it!" says Duncan Robert. "That's exactly what
I got!"

Miles and I look at him and then at each other. I've rarely seen anyone as happy as Duncan Robert is sharing this story. Maybe it's a real relief to him to finally get to share it.

"Okay," says Miles, as we settle back into our places, he and I on either end of the couch, Duncan Robert in his wing-back chair. I've taken off my shoes, un-tucked my shirt, and pulled my hair back in a pony tail, making myself right at home. Miles has taken off his shoes, too, so that he can put his sock-clad feet on the coffee table. Duncan Robert reaches over the coffee table to pick up one of my tablets and a pencil. He hands them to Miles.

"In case you have any questions. I know it's hard to interrupt me once I get going. I don't want you to leave without your questions answered. And let's order lunch at the next break. Remind me, because I'll forget."

Impossible to imagine interrupting him, I think. Look what we're hearing. I pick up my pencil and notebook again.

Duncan Robert starts again.

A group of three what look like regular people dressed in white walks through the opening in the back of the cave, the opening that must lead to another tunnel. They're looking at each other happily, and they let loose a gusty exhale of commonly held breath. Then they turn to look at me.

I stand up, trying to take them in, and they surround me jubilantly, greeting me, putting their arms around me, cheering me.

"I didn't know he'd actually be here!" "God, it's good to see you!"

"Look at you! A guy!" They laugh.

"A young guy, too!" They laugh some more.

I have the oddest feeling, stepping inside their ring of intimacy as a member, into an utter explosion of love. And it all feels real, absolutely authentic. And I've never felt more loved. I can feel their energy even now—their positive regard, their open state of mind, their clear intentions.

We all sit together around the fire, laughing and talking.

"You jumped! You actually jumped!"

"No one does this! You're a hero here, you know. Word spread like wildfire."

"The fairies want you for speaking engagements," one of the men laughs. "Autographs! Photo opps!"

"The Bird People think you must be one of them!"

"You made us proud that you're one of us," Guy says. "But you've surpassed us. We're here to learn from you!"

"Wait!" I say, laughing, too. "I'm still trying to remember who you are!"

"Earth time will do that to you," Guy says, "but it will come back to you."

"Well, let's help him," the woman says.

Then, they make a simultaneous decision that they'll introduce themselves by telling how they're each connected to me. They'll do this in the form of a story about a significant lifetime or piece of a lifetime that we shared, person-to-person or guide-to-person. In my mind they are 'guides,' but they refer to each other as 'cohort,' a more democratic term. They tell me it's natural for me to have trouble thinking of us all as equals while I'm still on Earth.

"We're gods to you!" Guy laughs.

"Or ghosts!" one of the men adds.

I look to the person sitting on my left, a woman, and she says, with a slight Australian accent, "I guess that means I'm first!" She laughs. "You can call me Lynette. That's the last name you knew me by."

She's a short redhead, wearing a kind of gossamer white robe, as are the rest, except for Guy, who looks like he just hopped off a spaceship. She notices me looking at her robe, and she laughs again. "So that's what it looks like to you! Crikey! There's no seeing through it, though!" She laughs once more, realizing what I was unconsciously doing before I do. I blush.

"It just looks very pretty and sort of timeless to me. I forget I'm wearing it. Anyway, we've known each other through many life times, so it's hard to choose just one.

Wait, I know! I can tell you of one that we *all* shared—we began that lifetime together and we ended it together. It was a good one that maybe you'll remember."

The others nod.

"We were monks together, in England, in the thirteenth century. In fact, you can still see the remains of the monastery today, in north Yorkshire. It was perfect for us. We were together, doing work we cared about, in a beautiful place. We lived in community, a self-sustaining community, so we had duties indoors and out, we saw sunrises and sunsets regularly, we ate well, we laughed a lot."

I have questions, and I know she knows it. She continues, working her answers into her telling.

"We were scribes and we created illuminated manuscripts. In other words, we worked on every phase of producing copies of existing books, from stretching and scraping the parchment from animal hides for the pages, to cutting to the proper size, to planning our layout of the text, to determining which letters and passages would be illuminated. Then we scored the parchment with our design and added the text. Illumination came last, followed by binding, with leather and wood. I had a passion for it, and so did you.

"We worked from an exemplar, an original manuscript approved by the church, but we took it to a new level, burnishing it with gold and silver, to exalt the text. We saw our illuminations as works of art praising God, giving thanks, so our days were spent in creating art that honored and gave gratitude for the creativity of others, in service to God. What could be better?

"And we got to be creative, too. It took much skill, and it could be exhausting work but we were proud of it. We worked closely together, often at high desks set on the edges of the monastery's courtyard, enjoying and being inspired by the sights and sounds of nature. We had all been classically educated, and spent our days praying, talking, reading, writing. We slept well at night.

"Usually, we copied the Bible and books of common prayer or religious commentary, for the monastery's own library, to sell to other monasteries, and for teaching. The illuminations made all of these books incredibly valuable. As it happened, the monastery had an extensive library of early secular works, too, some of the world's greatest works of philosophy, politics, history, and literature. We usually weren't allowed to spend our time in copying these books, but occasionally a wealthy patron, who often couldn't read, commissioned copies of one or another for his private collection, to impress his friends.

"We read and re-read those, as we believed they required a different kind of illumination than the religious books, and we wanted to do them justice. We were much taken with these works, recognizing the expansiveness of their thought and expression and their honoring of the capacities of man, and we even read aloud, trading parts, as we planned and executed their illumination.

"We knew that the church had moved closer and closer to censoring such books, to keep them from influencing public thought. We knew these works needed to do exactly that—have a public life and a chance to gain influence, for the betterment of mankind. So, in reaction, we regularly made plain, private copies of them, in case the originals were allowed to deteriorate or were even destroyed.

"This kind of independently determined activity is considered insurrection in a monastery—an attempt to replace the church's authority with ours—and is punishable by death. By the time the prior and the abbot found us out—and some were happy to report us—we had made too many copies to have a reasonable defense for this crime against the church. They had no choice but to turn it over to the district bishop, and the bishop had no choice but to invoke the highest punishment. All twelve of us—scribes and illuminators alike— were hanged. They hung us together, from the south wall of the monastery on an early spring morning, when the ground was finally soft enough to receive a shovel." She paused, and then looked at me, reassuringly. "I see what you're thinking, but dying with others, in support of a common cause is a wonderfully exhilarating experience *you yourself* have had more than once. This one was particularly sweet. We had accomplished what we had set out to do."

Even now, I feel this life on a heart level, more than I know it on a mental level. When she describes working at high desks and the sense of community, sights and sounds and smells come to me. It's as if it has always resided in the storehouse of my memory. She is studying me, to see if I have more questions. I ask why we did it, why we chose that life.

"For fun!" she says playfully, but seriously, too. "For the potential to enjoy all that life offers—food and nature and creativity and each other and work we loved. But, as importantly, for the chance to advance, by addressing a wrong and attempting to right it. Sometimes truth is not relative or situational or optional—not yours or mine, but ours. Sometimes you have to stand up for it. And we *did* that, through our actions. It was great to see what we could do together. It takes a lot of coordinating to have that happen. We didn't betray each other. We hung together. Literally," she adds with a smile.

A tall man looks at me and then explains further. "It's about the forging of the self through common experience." For what purpose, I wonder to myself, and his answer follows immediately. "All of this serves to develop and strengthen our authenticity—the ability to not just know but to act on one's own directive, thereby taking a risk. Taking the risk ensures the forging of the self. What else could we be here for except to construct ourselves in this way? Earth provides the challenges, which in turn provide the opportunities, to do this. That's all that's asked of us—to meet the challenges by taking the risk of being and expressing ourselves. Why? Because that's what makes us happy. And 'happy' is our prime indicator that we're doing what's right and good for all of us. This is why she told this story—it illustrates exactly this life-giving point."

Lynette looks at me and says, "He's good at explaining, isn't he? He's still my teacher."

"And you mine," he says back to her warmly.

"It's because we come from good," she says in answer to another of my questions. "It's what we know, how we feel aligned. Think what the world would look like if everyone was feeling truly happy."

Guy says, reading my mind again, "You're wondering how all of this got started. Maybe the story of the origin of our cohort can be for another time, after you've met everyone."

I look around and feel such an affinity to this group around the fire. I'm drawn to their sense of it all as fun, as well as work they give their lives for. I'm moved by their honesty with me and each other. I feel as if we are picking up where we left off. I'm exploding with questions but I'm not anxious or mistrustful, as I usually would be. This amazes me.

The tall man is sitting next to Lynette, and as I look to him, he smiles. It's such a warm, inviting smile that I break into a broad smile back. His features are more rugged, darker. He looks Middle Eastern, with piercing, direct eyes, hair combed back from his high forehead. His body is lean and taut, like a runner's.

"My name is Kahil. I'm going to tell a story of how we helped each other, across a long span of time. It was a place that brought us together. And we were both women!" He laughs, enlivening his stern good looks.

"It was post-Civil War, in America. You had journeyed to a teaching post in northern Maryland, near the Pennsylvania border, not twenty miles from Gettysburg. You were a tall, strong-minded woman, and you were proud of yourself for having journeyed alone, all the way from Albany, to take up a position that would make you self-sufficient.

"Your family remained a constant reminder that you were a failure as a woman and an embarrassment to them for not having married. You'd had only one real offer, from a much older man who'd been widowed with five small children, who'd insulted you when you'd refused him. You had passed thirty and found being alone much more appealing, and even satisfying, than marriage seemed. You loved teaching, as you always have, and felt it was important work. You looked forward to being on your own and making your own home. You'd arrived in Pennsylvania to find that your quarters were under repair for the next few weeks because a large leak in the roof had become apparent during the spring rains. The school board had decided that you could stay at the farm of one of the area's largest landowners, who was away on a cattle buying trip with his wife. It would serve him to have his kitchen remain functional and his house kept occupied and tidy while he was gone.

"After getting over your initial disappointment following your long trip, you discovered it was a large house, with rooms upstairs and down, and a spacious porch in the back. He had much acreage and a large pond. The grounds were being looked after by a neighboring farmer's son, so your duties were minimal.

"You were told to stay in a small bedroom on the first floor, but something about the room made you uncomfortable, and you kept smelling something burning in it, though it was much too warm for a fire. So you slept instead on a sofa in the side sitting room, just off the main sitting room. You settled in to the comfortable and well-appointed home, enjoying the cool mornings and the quiet nights, the smell of fresh cut hay, and the sounds of nature all around.

"Now, here's where I come in. One night, a few days later, you were sitting on a sofa in the main sitting room, facing the large staircase that gracefully curved down from the upstairs, its bannisters gleaming in the firelight that you read by. You were engrossed in the teacher's manuals you'd been reading, but suddenly you felt the hair stand up on the back of your neck, and you looked up the staircase. You saw a woman coming down the stairs, looking at you.

"That was me," he said with a proud smile. "I didn't mean to frighten you, but I did mean to get your attention.

You were the first person I felt drawn to in a long time. Most people I avoided. You froze, sensed the woman must be a ghost, even though she looked so real you could see the tiny tucks going down the front of her black dress, the narrow band of lace at each cuff, and the small crystal earbobs showing beneath the dark hair drawn over her ears into a low bun in the back.

"I was well-appointed, too," he laughed, "and my name was Lucy. I came downstairs and sat in the chair opposite you, and told you my story. And you listened, despite your initial fear. You anchored me with your listening. You can't imagine now how important that was. I had been aimlessly floating in a field of misery, unable to find my way home. Continued trauma will do that to you.

"You were afraid, but you felt drawn to me, too, so you stayed with me rather than fleeing out the door, as so many would have. I told you how my family lived in the next farm over and had arranged my marriage, at age fifteen, to the man who used to own the house you were staying in. My sisters and I expected arranged marriages but always wished for at least a livable match, if not one with romantic potential. We were young, after all, and still felt at home with hope. But this was a man without feeling who valued his hunting dogs more than he did his wife, and I begged my family to take me back, even running away a time or two. But they wouldn't do it because they were afraid of him, too, and they made me go back each time. 'We made a deal,' my father said. He'd gained a parcel of land and some cattle and horses, and didn't want to give them back, so he gave me back instead.

"I lived with the man a while, gritting my teeth and bearing it, giving him three children he completely disregarded, growing vegetables to feed us all, and working as a field hand for him whenever he required it. This worked, with me as slave labor, until he became abusive of the children. Then I stood against him, and we battled fiercely, until he decided I was more trouble than I was worth, and he was going to kill me.

"He never doubted he had the right to do so. I was his property, purchased just as his other farm animals had been, and most of *their* lives ended in slaughter. He determined to drag me down to the pond, to drown me. He hadn't so many options open to him—rifles were single shot then, a knife would have been tricky and terribly messy—you get the point.

"I saw what he had in mind, and I fought him. He battered me badly and with his greater strength, finally succeeded in drowning me. I hardly remember the details of it, I was so frantically concerned for the children.

"He rested a moment, after I was dead and he'd pulled my body up on the bank, catching his breath, and contemplated what to do with me. He knew the pond wouldn't keep his secret, and he knew enough to want to keep it secret, if only because mistrust or disdain from his neighbors might affect his standing in the community and hence, his income.

"He decided he'd do what he did with the animals—quarter and piecemeal me, and then he would feed me to the fire. Think of the man it would take to accomplish such a task—to the mother of his children! He couldn't do this outside, because it didn't afford good hiding, so he used the fireplace in the small sitting room, taking his time, being thorough about it, distributing the ashes in the garden.

"It took most of the day and night, but his rage had made the children scatter, and I'm glad they weren't there to witness any of it. When it was over, it left me lost. I was lost in it all—his rage, my helplessness, the loss of my children, my shame and demoralization at believing I was the cause of it all, feeling as in pieces as my body was. I didn't know where to turn, how to get back to anywhere, wherever anywhere was. Time passed, and I just hovered at the house, reliving it all, blinded by it, coming to believe this was my deserved fate.

"Then one day many years later *you* came, and I felt our bond. I was amazed at how much better I felt having you there. You changed the feeling in the house, introducing air and light, and your presence focused me, brought me to my senses. I knew myself again, and I began to see my side in the story, to believe I had a side to anchor in. But to really believe it, I desperately needed someone who could see it, too. I needed a witness. Someone who could know that I hadn't meant to abandon my children, that I hadn't caused my husband to kill me, and that he was seriously deranged.

"That night I determined to come down the stairs. There was such a peace and quiet in the house as I hadn't ever felt there. I was drawn to that peace as surely as a moth to a flame. It was the only way I could see to get home to myself. It felt safe enough to try. I couldn't have imagined the power of your listening. I would have been afraid to hope for that. My words, as I spoke them, showed me that it had all been real; your listening showed me that the telling could be borne, and that by telling them, the events could be understood, through compassion, and forgiven.

"You didn't judge, you had compassion—I could feel it. Not pity, but woman-to-woman compassion. You knew that you yourself had come close to feeling forced to enter an unwanted marriage, but you'd been able to choose for yourself, to say no. Your family had seen to your education, so you had a way to be, on your own in the world. You recognized the ways we were alike, and I was made whole by that. By your being *you*, you showed me how to be *me*—calm and compassionate with myself, forgiving, understanding.

"We do it because we love each other, now and always. I thank you. I thank you for honoring our bond, and making progress possible for both of us."

Kahil looks at me. I have tears in my eyes, and he does, too. "Did you see me the next morning in the mirror upstairs, when I came to say good bye?" he asks.

"I think I did," I say, surprised at the surging memory of another lifetime. "I remember seeing a face, surrounded by stars, with such a feeling of joy emanating from it that I was overcome."

"That was me!" he laughs. "You reintroduced me to my joy. I thought it was lost to me forever."

Miles stops us as this point, overcome by the last story. He pauses to pull out his handkerchief and noisily blow his nose.

"Of course, I've heard about stories like that from that time—arranged marriages, cruel or indifferent husbands, the feelings of women disregarded—but never from someone who was there. Wow."

It feels very real to me, too. I have to get up and move around. I go to the window and open it, in search of fresh air to blow away the lingering effects of that story. I'm beginning to get a clue about the bond Duncan Robert shares with his cohort, though it's unlike anything I've ever heard of.

I look at Duncan Robert and think about how he has all the indicators needed for a psychiatric explanation of what he's experienced—the missing father, the sometimes tense family life as a result, all begetting a childhood quest to be seen, heard, valued. As an only child, he'd probably have a strong imagination and be good at dissociation. I knew from my own research that his experiences would be labeled 'anomalous,' the equivalent of 'crazy' for us laypeople. His stories would be cataloged with alien abductions, extraterrestrial visitations, ghosts, spirits, and all the other trivialized other-worldly stories. Why was I finding value in it? Maybe I just saw it as a legitimate part of reporting, especially since these kinds of stories were increasing, across the world. In the past no legitimate newspaper would have even considered them. I liked to think I bowed to a higher god than sensationalism, but this is pretty sensational. How far could we go with this and still believe?

"Let's order some lunch," Duncan Robert says into our silence, calling us back to ourselves. "I've got some menus here. Take a look. I think I'm actually hungry." He laughs.

I realize I'm starving. Miles decides he's going to have a club sandwich, with fries, so I know he's hungry, too. I feel like breakfast, so I order scrambled eggs and toast, with a side of fruit. Duncan Robert orders a large bowl of vegetable soup and a side salad, which seems like a lot for him, too. While we wait for the food, we settle back into our places, except for Miles, who lies on the floor, to stretch his spine, he says. I stretch out on the couch.

I ask Duncan Robert what it was like, to hear his life told to him in that larger way.

"I don't know if I can explain it. First, I could feel myself expand," he says. "I began to see myself as so much larger than I'd ever thought, spreading out across the Universe, touching time in various places, interacting with it in a way that fed my spirit. Then, I could see how the members of my cohort were spreading with me, and we were like a river through time and space. The fact that we weren't separate made us much more helpful to each other and to all those we came in contact with—even if they were killing us!" He laughs.

"It isn't easy to play all the parts we do. Think about it. Earth is a pretty violent place, and we don't seem to get the lessons very quickly!" He pauses to think a minute. "To answer your question, those stories are life-changing information, and my life has been changed by them."

I feel pretty sure Miles's life and my life have been changed, too, and we've only heard the stories second hand. That's how much power they have.

There's a knock at the door, and lunch is served. I don't think we spend more than twenty minutes consuming it, without much talk. We put the trays outside the door, so we won't be disturbed, and get ourselves our hot tea. We settle back into our places, and I take a minute to sharpen a few pencils and turn to a fresh page in my notebook. Miles makes a couple of brief notes in his notebook, and puts it back on the coffee table. Duncan Robert, who has been sitting quietly, begins again:

The group on the ledge agreed to a small break after Kahil's story, and Guy and I talked while he fixed me another cup of tea and made some toast over the fire. I get the sense the others don't need to eat, but I'm grateful for the warmth and sustenance of it.

I'm still spinning after that deeply moving story and feel I have to get back in balance. I ask Guy about this place where we are. He tells me that the tunnel system runs underneath most of the world, connecting its major places. It has been there tens of thousands of years, and much commerce and trade has gone on within it. People have lived in the tunnels, too, when the ash from erupting volcanoes made agriculture impossible and dropped outside temperatures uncomfortably low. People have stayed there to avoid robbers, bandits, and warring tribes. They've birthed their children there, bred their animals, ground their crops there. People have created quiet places of study, contemplation and ceremony. As much has gone on in the tunnels as above them, he assures me, if not more.

I find this incredible, but I decide to believe him.

He notes my momentary struggle with disbelief, says, "Even UFO activity!" and laughs. "After all, we all come from the stars anyway. By my reckoning, I think we're now somewhere under the Carpathian Arch." I look at him questioningly, and he says, "I think it's Romania nowadays. Borders have been moved a lot, what with all the wars and political dealings, but don't get me started on the uselessness of borders—or wars!" He laughs again, shaking his head.

"This one," he gestures to what I now think of as my tunnel, "connects Romania to Egypt and on to Tibet. Afghanistan is connected to it, too, and Russia. You have no idea. There's so much more that you don't know than you do, while you're on Earth. Oh, there are those who do know, but they still believe that power resides in secrets, so they're keeping them.

"Funny, when we're on Earth we don't fear these secret keepers—we trust them with our money, we elect them to high office, we allow them dominion over our children—but we do fear the extraterrestrials, even though many of them have given us nothing but help. True, some don't have such altruistic motives, but I think we're usually capable of telling the difference."

He sees my question and says, "Oh yes, extraterrestrials showed us how to make homes underground and above, how to grow things and manage resources, such as water and minerals and energy and our own health." He hands me my thermos cup of tea and puts the toast in my other hand.

"They've offered us service, and were often our first examples of that."

I'm drinking my tea, eating my toast and feeling better for it, mentally zoning out for the moment, as I do when I'm overwhelmed by incoming information. I look up to ask Guy another question and notice, seemingly out of nowhere, a great horned owl sitting opposite me, near Lynette. It startles me, and I start to scoot back, away from the fire. Lynette laughs and says, "He's here for you, you know."

"What do you mean?" I ask, thinking of all the old Native American stories connecting owls with death.

"A little too Harry-Potterish for you?" she asks playfully. "He's got a bond with you, too. He's your totem. He's why you have an owl calendar in your kitchen and why Reggie gave you that little owl fetish you still carry. He comes to help you in that way animals do, showing you your connection to the natural forces as your guides. He keeps you close to the outdoors, where you find renewal. He's part of why you haven't given up. His name is Anai, but he can tell you that himself."

I'm not surprised there are animals down here. I just didn't know any of them might be for me. I give a little bow to the owl, who gives a friendly bow of his head back. His eyes, with their nictitating membrane moving up and down, seem to have a life of their own, so I can't be sure where he's looking, and he swivels his head around in a way that seems impossible. But he's incredibly beautiful, feathers gleaming in the firelight, eyes an intense highlighter yellow, completely self-possessed as he fluffs his feathers and settles into his spot. He makes contented little chirps. He's come to listen, too.

"This is a good time for me to tell my story," says the other man, who is medium height and build, his features suggesting Southeast Asia. He looks at me across the fire, his beautiful black eyes and hair gleaming in its light, as I sip my tea. "My name is Uche," he says with a kind smile, "and you and I have been together in many lives, too—husband and wife, mother and child, and so forth." He smiles again as he feels my question about our apparent outward differences.

"Sometimes this color, sometimes another—colors have their own lessons but are ultimately meaningless," he answers. "We all have 'a bond stronger than life,' as we like to say. My story involves you and me and a few others, who aren't with us tonight, it's one of my favorites.

"We were together on Atlantis. We lived in one of its larger cities and were considered fairly prosperous. We were friends and co-workers, and raised our children together. We were engaged in what we liked to call the 'health and hygiene' of the government-regulated work force who made up the industrial and technical workers of Atlantis. We were responsible for those who provided essential maintenance of the giant crystals that provided our energy, as well as the workers assigned to the production of food and necessary other goods. We determined and managed their births, their work, their family planning, their disputes, their deaths. Nothing happened to them that we didn't know about, and many of their children shared our birthdays and carried our names. We knew they were not as us and never would be, because we had controlled their genetic development. No more than one-sixth of our genetic materials had been introduced into their own original animal materials, to create useful intelligence without enabling a move to dominance. This was part of a huge intergalactic experiment to create a super slave race that would ensure the protection of necessary resources for the continuation of the intergalactic races. We believed the project was a success and we had created the most productive, efficient, cooperative slaves possible.

"This is why Atlantis accomplished much in the areas of transportation, energy transference, transmutation of metals, and so forth. At its peak, it had millions of citizens, and we needed a trained and focused population of workers we could depend on to keep it all going and progressing. We did our jobs and did them well, and expected these workers to do the same.

"Yes, you might call them 'slaves,' but we didn't. We thought of them as a vital working population in partnership with us for shared progress. We treated them well— they didn't want for food or shelter or medical attention; they weren't over-worked, in fact they even got holidays. We took care of them. We thought of ourselves as good people, by the standards of our time. We did not think of ourselves as 'bad' people. But of course we were. By any proper definition that included depriving someone else of their right to freedom and the pursuit of happiness, we were 'bad' indeed.

"Oh, our job had some concern with 'health and hygiene,' but it was mainly involved with suppressing and sterilizing the workers, so we could control and limit their activities and reproduction for our own purposes. Their existence made ours possible.

"We couldn't have them producing either too many or not enough children, or getting too many other ideas of their own. Sterilization and genetic work allowed us to control and maintain sex, size, and docility, along with their reproductive capacity. We were trying to clean up some genetic damage, too, from earlier extraterrestrial races that had engaged in experimentation to create the slaves on Earth to begin with. Of course we had to engage in some experimentation as well, in the beginning, though we felt we handled that pretty responsibly, disposing of the less successful results discreetly.

One night—you may remember this—we had gone together to a closed session called by our highest government officials for those of us who oversee the slaves. This was unusual and quite hush-hush. We knew something serious must have happened and we were curious. We went to the Auditorium of the Crystals and watched as the ruling council filed in from a side door onto the stage. All twelve members of our ruling council were present and sat at a raised table in front of us. They took turns speaking, beginning with the most senior member.

What we heard stunned us. Not only did our leaders think the experiment had not been a success, they believed it should be terminated, the current generation of slaves liquidated, including their children. Measures were already being taken to ensure future generations were without the fatal flaw that doomed the current slaves.

They said our earlier efforts were to be commended but now our cooperation was needed—it would require the best efforts of all of us—to begin to remove the slave populations from each of the major cities. Step one would be their emigration to the uninhabited territory in the east, avoiding any resistance or insurrection.

"What has happened?" one of our co-workers asked in alarm. "We're stunned by this news!"

"In our zeal to make sure they were educable, for the more complex technical tasks, we unknowingly encouraged chemical reactions within the endocrine system that led to a greater freedom of thought than we had intended." They paused, looking at each other as if deciding how much to say. "They've discovered joy."

An audible gasp went through the audience. The worst case scenario.

"We asked ourselves, what should be the solution to this terrible problem? There will be no containing it. They are intoxicated by it and want to experience it every day.

They will want it for their children and grandchildren. We must put an end to it or it will put an end to us. It will inspire them to want to manage their own joy and we will be in their way.

"We are not monsters. We know many of you have come to depend on your slaves, have even grown fond of them, as of your own children. But we ask that you don't waste your sympathy on them. Save it for our own blood. That will keep us strong. Don't ever waste it on anyone else in the world."

"What will happen to them?" someone called out.

"Do you imagine there can be settlement villages for them? Where they could plan and make trouble for us? There is nothing we can do with them. Maybe the strongest can live on in the east, helping to cultivate the swamps, if we keep them isolated from each other. The majority must be eliminated."

"Eliminated?" a man called out. "Do you mean killed?"

Another gasp.

"Women and children, too?" There is a general unrest in the audience, a rumbling.

"We are letting you know our thinking! It is not an easy solution, but we can retain our decency as we toughen our resolve. We have the moral right, the duty to future generations, to eliminate those who would eliminate us."

"But they've done nothing!" another woman cries out.

"Might the discovery of joy not be a problem?" shouts a man.

"The scientific evidence is clear. There is no doubt where this leads. We have seen it develop on other planets, leading to revolutions and coups. We must be proactive so we are not doomed to reaction, which is much bloodier and much harder to recover from. We will look back on this as a page of glory in our history of genetic progression. It is to be celebrated that we discovered this flaw that could have been fatal."

"But why women and children? They could be sterilized!"

The leaders look at each other, and I thought this would not bode well for the woman who keeps asking this question.

"First, we have to wipe out all trace of the defective genes. Second, our first loyalty must be to our own blood. That is what interests us. We cannot allow any possibility of plotting, rebellion, or sabotage, which they are knowledgeable enough to commit. The slaves interest us only in so far as we can use them. That is what they are for. Otherwise, they are of no interest. There is no place for sentiment. This is a natural necessity, of the highest order."

Those of us in the audience began talking to each other, mentioning specific slaves who have become essential to us, who should be exceptions. Some people are crying. Their slaves have become surrogate families and children to them. We know that some have had children with slaves, though it's against the law. We feel we do not have a concept of decency to encompass what is being asked of us. We are not machines. Just as I was wondering if the leaders had an insurrection on their hands with us that night, one of them spoke quite severely to us.

"We are the ruling class! We cannot be weak on this. Our responsibility follows us through history into the future. We would be judged weaklings and criminals to our children if we allowed their children to grow up. There is no retreat from this. It is important we resolve it in our time. Future generations might not have the courage."

We are quiet for a moment, having interpreted correctly that more resistance should not be expressed there, that night, or we would be seen as siding with the slaves and perhaps suffer their fate.

The most senior leader speaks again. "Humane methods of elimination are under discussion. We will convene another session to finalize these with you. The solution will occur in stages and will require your complete cooperation. Know that this solution is the final solution. There will be no further questions on it. There will be no further discussion on it, either here or amongst yourselves."

They leave the stage, our cue to leave the auditorium as well. We file out quietly, not looking at each other. We believe we have no option but to do as they say.

We complied with their directives, right down to being part of the extermination teams in the east. You and I both heard of other's resistance, of people who hid their favored slaves until they could move them out to the far wilderness areas, of people who attempted to marry or adopt them, of people who set up underground settlements. Many of these people were caught and disappeared. We dared not ask about them.

We left that life knowing two things, even before death. You cannot live without speaking out, even upon pain of death. You cannot live following someone else's directives for your life, even upon pain of death. Our lives lost meaning and purpose, and we lived without interest or joy. Those lessons are of utmost importance for all. Perhaps you can see why?"

He looks at me, one eyebrow raised. I look back at him as something slowly climbs out of the murky depths of memory and a chill creeps like a snake up my body.

"Hitler."

"You hear his language in the council's words. Many of those words appeared verbatim in Hitler's and Himmler's speeches, though they thought they were their own. Those words were the heritage of Atlantis, caught forever in the collective unconscious. Hitler attracted them like a magnet because he had the same intent—to remove an entire people by murder.

"Atlantis' leadership council had as heritage the warmongering of their parent planet Mars, and their laws reflect that. The concept of slaves began with the garnering of many captives as the spoils of war. Atlantis profited from the large number of captives by engaging in medical experimentation to make them less trouble and more useful—a master slave race—enabling the Atlantean ruling class to create industries of slave labor. Then, when the slaves betrayed their masters by growing and developing abilities of their own, they were annihilated. Atlantis provided the universal model for successive tribes to initiate the same kind of genocide or ethnic cleansing. As even Hitler noted, it's a monumental task to eradicate a whole people. It takes the complicit cooperation of everyone to succeed. Support has to be handed over. And we handed it over.

"We didn't question anything, and we didn't step up in aid of anything. We let it all happen. And that was our lesson. We didn't do there what we all had done as monks. It led to the downfall of Atlantis, and we were there when Atlantis sank. Many people died, much was lost, and all unnecessarily. I've never forgotten it. Maybe you haven't either.

"Maybe we couldn't have done much on our own to change the situation. But anything we had done would have changed *us*, for the better. And that's our first responsibility, while on Earth. Stepping up is where inspiration begins, for all. We, and others, paid the price for not having done so." He looks at me for a moment, and I look back, grateful for his telling of this story. I've always felt I had a connection to Atlantis.

Everyone pauses a moment, staring into the fire. "But you called it one of your favorite lives," I say.

"Yes, I did," Uche says, "and I meant it. I learned more about myself in that life than in several other lives combined. What I'll do to belong, to be liked, to succeed according to others' standards, to feel I have power and control; what I'll put first to achieve those things and what I'll put last. We were created from good. We go against our good nature at a great cost, to ourselves and others. We create ourselves and our lives down there through interwoven lifelines—by what we do and don't do, say and don't say. If we're not there for each other, other baser influences can take hold of us, determining our course. Atlanteans achieved what the wildest dreams of science could not have predicted, but they could not keep themselves, their communities, or their future safe and whole."

He laughs ruefully and says, "There were lessons enough for everyone there!" "Lessons?" I ask. "Is that what it's all about?"

"Yes. It's what we want a life to do—teach us. This is about advancing—it's everyone's goal. There's no growth in maintaining the status quo, just a kind of slow death for all." He looks at me, and I look back, intently.

"I thank you for the story," I tell him. "The story of Atlantis has always haunted me."

"I hope to provide you peace," he says, smiling.

I bow to him and he bows back to me from across the fire. I mull over what he said about the cost of maintaining the status quo, thinking of my life now.

We've come full circle to Guy, on my right. I look at him, and he dips his head at me in acknowledgment.

"Are you wearing a spacesuit for any reason?" I ask him, looking at the white multi-zippered, baggy but belted jumpsuit.

"I am," he grins. "I just stepped out of a life for a moment, as you've done with your life. I'll step back in at the moment I left it, as you will. In that life, I'm part of a group traveling from Sirius to Camelius X, an Earth-like planet in a different galaxy. We'll face some of the same challenges the extraterrestrial groups who settled Earth did. Can we partner with the beings there rather than dominate? We've been so eager with our planetary experiments that we don't like waiting for a more democratic process with beings seemingly less advanced than we are."

"Why that life?"

"Because I've killed people who got in my way. Oh, not in a while, but I wanted to be sure. Camelius X will be a test."

I look at the strength rippling in his hands as he stirs the fire. He seems formidable, and I'm a little afraid of him now. "And if you fail?"

"I'll start again." He looks at me and laughs, his teeth flashing brightly. "Do you wonder if I will kill you?" He laughs again. "Already did."

The others laugh, too.

"Me, too!" Lynette calls.

"You murdered me!" Khahil says.

"I don't have a particular story. I've been in most of your lives, in major and minor roles. Monk, yes. I was Lucy's dad in the Lucy story, not wanting to return the land I got in your marriage deal. Yeah, sorry. Good lessons there for me, too, in having a strong daughter. Helped me begin to appreciate the value of women, after a string of male lives. Let's see. We were guards in a Russian prisoner camp. Gay, too. I think that life wasn't too bad. No, we didn't torture anyone in that life, though we did in others—we were baby killers, even."

He looks directly at me for a moment, seeing how I'm taking it, judging if he's gone too far. "You can't be a war-mongering planet, as Earth is, without having lived lives in which war ran it's natural course, going from bad to worse. Many lives are spent balancing that.

"We sailed ship together more than once. Drowned together, too, though we didn't know it at the time. We started together and have always counted on each other—a bond stronger than life.

"But you've guessed we don't share many of the 'down-ers' with you, the lives in which we achieved less than success, and of course there were some. Those are for another time. These stories were for 'getting to know you,' as the song says, and to re-acquaint you with us. I always loved Rogers and Hammerstein," he says in an aside, as he hums the tune. "Getting to like you, getting to hope you like me," he sings, glancing at me.

"Songs have their purpose, too," he remarks. "But back to business. I mean, you're the one who called us together, after all."

This startles me. "Yeah, but I didn't know. Had no idea," I say as I look around our little circle, seeing the owl grooming himself.

"Well, yes and no," he says. "The veil *is* thinning. I mean, you jumped because you knew, or believed, in something like this. Right? You felt it enough to be able to jump. Right? At least fifty-fifty?" He goes on, not waiting for my response. "We've done some of our best work with you to help you put it all together!" He laughs. "And had fun doing it! I mean, dreams, nudges, coincidences, ah-ha moments, arranged over and over, these are the tools of our trade. But the tools are limited. For example, you always say you don't remember your dreams, do you not? So, you challenge our creativity.

"You remember you had a friend whose dreams were so amazing you wrote them down and took them to work with you, to share? Like the one where everyone in it had a flaming sword through their heads? You still remember those dreams, and they weren't even *yours*. But we did our best to get to you, through her. You remember that recurring dream you have? The one where you are sitting at a table at the base of beautiful tree-lined hills, watching as groups of people dressed in multi-colored robes walk down from the hills toward you? You seem to be signing people in. That dream always feels profound, and very real to you—the sights, the sounds, the smells—and you remember it. It's the closest we could get to reminding you of our work together.

"And it was you and your mom who shared another dream on the same night, as revolutionaries being chased to your deaths by the military in Central America. Do you still remember that one? That dream felt real, too, as you crouched at the base of some basement stairs, nowhere left to run, waiting for them to come and kill you. You both still remember it. Through dreams, we aim to arrest and engage you, move you, change you—to bring you to yourselves—so that whatever you're doing is informed by these stories from your larger existence.

"Ah-ha moments are our favorites," he laughs. "Nudges are the easiest. Remember the Chinese fortune cookie you got once that said, 'Imagination rules the world'? Nudges can be that simple—a nudge to creativity. In a way, ah-ha moments are easier than coincidences or synchronicities, which require the coming together of people, places, animals, objects. Those can be a challenge to arrange. You know, like a book on a shelf right where you'll see it right when you need to, or even falling from the shelf in front of you?

"Or running into someone in the right moment—think about all the planning that goes into the success of that. When you have one of those, you'll often think back to the steps before that 'chance' meeting, amazed at all it took—bus being late, traffic just so, et cetera, et cetera—all to have your paths cross at just that moment.

"Ah-ha moments, on the other hand, can also require a lot, but they're more singular, with internal shifts and readiness on your part that defy logical analysis. No one can fully explain why that A led to that B for that person. Ah-ha moments need a little miracle. Even we, who help arrange them, can't explain it. Suddenly, a light goes on, and you have a new, enhanced understanding. You're changed, in a personally powerful way."

He looks at me. "You know what I'm talking about. You've had them."

I look at him with a question mark on my face. I know I must've had them, but in that moment I can't recall a single one.

"For you to meet Reggie, for example. Coincidence *and* ah-ha moment. You knew each other, but you formally met on a blind date, something you always said you'd never go on. You went because your boss arranged it, so it was harder to say no. It was on your birthday, too, so there was a reason for a group celebration to be organized. And hers was just a few days after yours. Harder, again, to say no. Reggie was friends with your boss' daughter—a lot went into that set of connections to make them become part of your 'coincidence.' There were a few false starts—then finally it was scheduled.

"This kind of wheels-moving-within-wheels process is almost always behind it when Earth people come together in decision points in your lives. It's not chance. The ah-ha moment was when you two met. You both knew when you met, before either of you had said a word to the other."

"Knew what?" I ask, struggling to remember the details of that moment. "That something significant had happened?"

Then I remembered it. I couldn't disagree. Reggie and I had just looked at each other and known that we would be together, were meant to be together. It *had* felt magical. I sit back, humbled by all the time and effort that had gone into making that moment.

"Thank you," I said, never meaning it more. I thought for a moment, then had to ask, "These ah-ha moments sound like they involve a lot of work and worry. Why are they your favorites?"

"Because we meet there. You and us," he gestures, tapping my chest, then tapping his. "It's tangible—you feel it, we feel it. We're charged by it. These are moments of such alignment, with self, other, and All That Is. That's happiness. We've been able to do something. So these moments are a kind of success for all involved, no matter where the relationship goes. And we never judge it by Earthly standards; it has its own meaning and purpose. And that part is up to you, not us. We just try to create the opportunities, the moments. I will say there's some cheering that goes on here, when we're successful." He smiles broadly. "It's a great job we have, honestly. None better."

I have to laugh now, shaking my head. Who'd have thought we had all these beings, these partners focused on us and the state of our spirit? There *they* are, working so hard to provide the proof we're always seeking. There *we* are looking for it while overlooking it, confused about what we should we looking for, wanting miracles, not expecting the miracles we're getting. He's saying what to watch for, and I think it will take some practice to see it as mattering among all the other glamor and noise going on around us.

"That's where you were—caught in the middle," Guy says, reading my mind. "So you jumped. Every such deviation from the path creates the scars, the bruises, the cuts, the breaks, the bumps that signify a life lived—not denied, endured or handed over to others for the living. Your jumping really did set you free. What will you do now?"

I stare at him, speechless yet again. He's asked me the very question I've wanted to ask him, that I desperately hoped he would answer for me. It sends me reeling, this reversal. Shouldn't he have the answer, in this all-knowing place? What will I do now?

He's enjoying himself. "All that to say, it's not often someone comes to us, especially in the way you have. If people are just existing, looking for their next distraction, they're not trying to reach us and we can't reach them. They certainly wouldn't come here, gathering their Team for a mind-altering performance, such as we're giving now. They might have one to two guides for the rare, maybe even once in a lifetime opportunity to be reachable (surgery, death of a loved one, war).

"None of us could remember another time someone did this. Why would *you* need an answer from *us?* "

I stop and think about this for a moment. I mean, it had seemed like a big deal to me—to make the jump. But if it's a big deal even to them, that's something to wrap my head around.

"Well, more people are approaching us in other ways nowadays, what with the shift and all," Lynette comments. She had been sitting quietly, listening. "You know, like in what they call lucid dreaming, or in meditation. They come seeking us now, rather than sitting passively, waiting for something to happen."

"Yes, but not the Void," Uche says.

"No, not the Void," Kahil says, looking at me with respect.

"By jumping, you've asked for your larger story. Like the Aborigines say, it's always stalking you. But now you're stalking it. You want to be part of your larger story. So, we've reminded you of some of the things you had to forget in order to be able to live a life. We've kept you spiritually anchored here while you're there, on Earth. And we've done our best to keep you spiritually guided, directed, protected. Loved."

The veil is being lifted, the boundaries thinned, and I see what they've been doing. So much falls into place. Now it becomes my job, using my own discernment and creative powers, to see if I can do here what they've been doing over there. *Help. Serve.* Whoa. Of course.

Guy continues to talk, but its as though the words are silent, or in an unknown language. I can't make them out.

He sees my face and stops. Everyone does.

His voice is clear in my head, almost a whisper. "It's a *point of magic* moment! You're at a point, and you have a choice—not just a choice about one thing in your life. You are looking at making a choice about everything. The *purpose of your life*. It's all coming together and we never know what's going to happen next—this can go beyond even our wildest imaginings, lead to the most unexpected outcomes. Here we go. . . magic! "

CHAPTER EIGHT

Did You Hear Me?

"Let's take a break," Duncan Robert says. It's late afternoon, and Miles and I have been stunned into silence for a long while now. It feels unnatural to recover our voices, our sense of being, even. I feel as if we've been outside of time, as we listened, some place of suspended animation. We have to step back into ourselves again. Even though I've been taking notes the whole time—I make sure of this by looking down at my note book, and I've covered pages with my writing—I don't remember it. My right hand could testify, however. It aches from the workout.

Duncan Robert asks us what we're feeling and thinking. "You know, it's the first time I've said it all aloud," he says, smiling. "It is quite a story. I don't know what it sounds like to you."

I talk first, not knowing I'm going to, as I stare out the open hotel window, the breeze cool on my face. Miles is fixing us all glasses of ice water.

"It reminds me of being hugged by Amma," I turn around to look at them. Seeing their blank looks, I say, "You know, Amma, the 'hugging saint,' from India. I was covering it for my editor, when she came to Boston. Her website says she has hugged more than 30 million worldwide, even the Queen of England. And practically every celebrity you can think of. I had no idea what I was in for. She's quite an organization, with quite a traveling entourage.

"Thousands of people come, you're given a number and a group. When your group is called, you join a double line of people, in chairs, gradually moving forward, like musical chairs. Up ahead, she's dressed all in white, sitting on a sort of low throne, hugging people, one after another—families with babies, the old and the infirm, young people, people speaking different languages. Her attendants move you to your knees a few feet from her, asking you what language you speak. You're sort of dropped into a tight group of frontline attendants, dressed in yellow robes, who are plunging people into Amma's lap and then dragging them out, giving everyone some rose petals and, strangely, a Hershey's Kiss.

"I didn't know whether to laugh or run, feeling sort of claustrophobic in the crowd. Suddenly, it's my turn, and I'm thrust into her arms, with mine moved by the attendants to the arms of her chair, so that I'm not the one doing the hugging, I'm the one being hugged. It's not a joint venture. I'm enveloped by something so much bigger and deeper and more profound than I am. Someone with a much larger story.

"And then I'm hearing her say, 'My daughter, my daughter, my daughter,' over and over in my ear, as I'm being hugged by the most loving presence I've ever been around. I remember the permeating scent of roses, which were everywhere. And then falling out of the hug, as her attendants pulled me back to put the next person in. It's quick, but not; intense, but not; profound, but not.

"And now you're a person who's been hugged by Amma. You're not the same you as before. You know you're better for it—you feel that. But exactly how, you couldn't say. Just better. I was charged by that for days after. I'd gotten a picture of her—there's a whole bazaar of merchants at the back of the hall, selling all the memorabilia you can imagine—and even looking at the picture, I could feel the energy of her, the power of her. And it was just good. It was just love. It made me smile. That's what your experience of the Void made me return to."

Duncan Robert nods appreciatively.

Miles, sitting on the couch, sipping his water, says to Duncan Robert, "Your fall, that sense of falling, is what I returned to. From so many dreams that I startled out of, afraid to hit bottom. So many times I imagined what it must have been like for you—my stomach dropping, knees weak, breath gone. It was like having a fear of heights while standing on the ground. It's falling, but it's flying, too. Exhilarating, but nothing to orient you, to hold on to. Without that, who and what are you? Something, or some-one, else.

"Your conversation with your team is like that for me, too. Like a fall—it moves so fast, and there's such depth. I wanted to say, 'Wait a minute, wait a minute,' like Babe says to me all the time. Let's go back to birth, or some beginning place, let's explain it from there. Show me how all these connections developed, how they grew. Let me see how meaning and purpose emerged, so I can understand what it's all about, what it's all for. It was a lot to take in, if that's what I've managed to do." He pauses, looking up at Duncan Robert. "What's it like for you now, in the telling?"

"Like it happened yesterday. And I'm remembering more details, rather than losing them, as I thought I would. It's fresher than if it happened yesterday. And I feel so close to them all," he says, smiling and looking as fresh as he did this morning when he opened the door to us.

"Are you in regular touch with them?" Miles asks.

"I feel their presence constantly. I wake up with them, I fall asleep with them. It's not like they're right there, in my business. It's more like I feel the force of their love and support, as real as my head on the pillow or my foot on the floor. Or like your Amma presence, it sounds like."

"But do they talk to you? Do you have conversations with them?" I ask.

"Yes, I do," Duncan Robert smiles. "Do you with Amma?"

"Well," I fumble, caught by his question, wondering now why I haven't tried. "No. I guess I didn't think to."

He laughs. "It's okay. It's a different kind of experience. Just wondered."

"Did you hear *me* talking to you?" Miles asks, looking at him, clearly thinking about all those dark nights after Duncan Robert jumped.

Duncan Robert looks back. "Yes, I did. I heard your questions and your cries and even your accusations. Did you hear me answering?"

"No. I didn't," Miles says. "Maybe I wasn't really listening."

"Well," Duncan Robert smiles, "sometimes I think you were answering yourself, for me. Other times, it wasn't really me you were talking to. Sometimes it was you talking to you, finding out if you could really go on, if you wanted to. I realize how hard it must have been, after I jumped. I felt it, too. I don't think either of us realized how hard it would be, we were so caught up in the idea of the jump. I was so eager to find something, anything, that made me feel real.

"When Babe came, though, I felt there was a way you could hear me, through her. She was new to it all and open to learning everything, so she was receptive to hearing my voice, too, incorporating it into everything else she was learning. She didn't reject intuitive flashes that came to her or sudden ideas I nudged her towards. After all, she wasn't carrying the burden of my jump the way you were. So, she was often the bridge for me to you. And sometimes, she was the bridge from you to me. Sometimes, when you talked to her about me and the jump, I could feel as if I was getting the gift of your understanding. And maybe even your forgiveness."

Miles looks at his hands and takes a minute to clear his throat of the emotion lodged there. "I was angry at you. Irrationally, I know. I just missed you so damn much. And it almost came as a surprise to me. I thought I was so cool—in my acceptance and support of your decision. I thought that's where I really was. So, what a surprise, when I cried like a baby, and not just once, either. I might as well have been where Silvia or Reggie were, trying to talk you out of it, asking you not to do it. But, honestly, you don't need my forgiveness. I should be asking for yours. I did work my way through it, though, in my own weird way."

Duncan Robert smiles again. "I loved it. It's like you got it. You really got it. That's why I call it a gift. And your work with your students! The stuff about the importance of a jump, no matter your age or circumstances—who could have said it better? We could learn so much from what kids hang on to, and you were giving them stuff to hang onto. And you add to that the stuff about the Void—it is an invitation to the jump. For what other reason would it exist? As a repository for our fears? The Universe doesn't work that way. Nothing is a static repository. Nothing. You put it all together in a way that's really useful. I think you should do a course on the Void."

Miles laughs. "I do have a lot of material. But I barely had that thought myself! I don't know that they'd let me." He laughs again.

"Well, they live with a Void," Duncan Robert says, "only a few miles from their door."

"Yeah, but that's just it. They don't want to stir things up, you know. God forbid they should disturb the status quo."

"I wondered how you knew what had happened at the Void," I say, before I think, not meaning to interrupt them, thinking they had forgotten I was there. "You knew when I got to town to do my story, that I was talking with Miles, and my experience at the Void. Didn't you?"

"Yeah, I did know—in a general sense. I had my thoughts and my awareness on Miles a lot, and I got where I could sense what was going on with him. I'm sure it was with my cohort's help. Then you became part of what was happening with him. But pretty soon I realized I had an awareness of you, separate from him, some of it in dreams. I dreamed you standing at the edge of the Void.

"That was a powerful moment. I think we all met each other there, on some level. I knew what was happening. But I didn't know how it was going to turn out any more than you two did," Duncan Robert says. "That was quite an achievement, Babe," he looks at me with admiration in his eyes. "You actually went to the Void and took a real look inside. That's fearless! The Void took you to your deepest fear and showed it to you in a new way, so you could confront it. You're a powerful person, Babe, and I'm glad to know you."

"Whew!" I say, remembering that day. "Thanks, Duncan Robert. That means a lot, coming from you." I am a little choked up.

"Really, I'm no different than you. Just a little more connected."

"But you've jumped!" Miles and I both say, sharing the same thought, almost shouting.

Duncan Robert laughs. "Okay! I'll grant you that."

"It's your experience we're talking about now. What was it for you? What did it answer? What do you make of it?"

Duncan Robert looks at Miles with seriousness. "Here's what it makes me think of—Einstein's observers of lightning—one on the train, inside, one on the bank, at the side of the tracks, outside. What did they see, when did they see it? You're on the train—you understand the explanations of the people on the train. I've gotten off. I have a different explanation of that lightning. I can't put it all into words for someone still on the train. No, it doesn't mean you have to jump. It just means I might not be able to explain it to you, to your satisfaction. It's specific to me— you know, your jump is your jump."

"Well, it makes me think of Higgs Boson," Miles says into the pause. And they both laugh.

Clearly, that's an inside joke, so I ask, "What?!"

"Who understands that?" Duncan Robert asks, chuckling.

"Well, maybe it's childish, but I thought you might be able to explain things like particle physics," Miles says, with a little laugh. We were both thinking his fall had somehow made him smarter, more all-seeing and all-knowing— therefore, able to explain even particle physics to us. We couldn't imagine such a profound experience as he'd had in the Void hadn't given him some sort of advantage over everyone else on Earth. That would be part of how he'd been changed by his jump.

"What I think," Duncan Robert says, "is that the fall accelerated my energetic force or speed to match that of my cohorts in the cave, so it was like we were all standing still. Does that make sense? In reality (whatever that is), they're operating at a much higher speed or vibration than we are, but because I jumped, I caught up to them and could have a conversation, a meeting, for a while. The Void is a place, like a vacuum, where things become equal, so it's easier to see things, be with things, as if all are real. The length of the fall gave me time to catch up. Now, that's Einstein-ian, I think. And maybe the veil is thinnest, possibilities greatest, when you're with the energy of your cohort—a bond stronger than life. "

"I created something, a situation, that allowed me to find myself. It was an act of creativity," he says again, "not desperation, as I thought. It was the most creative thing I could do. It certainly wasn't a small act. It gave me plenty of room!"

Miles and I looked at each other as we both think of the Void, the grass around it as green as the greenest things of spring.

In a way, Duncan Robert has de-mystified it. In a way, he has made it more mysterious than ever. Any jumper could still never know what he or she might encounter down there.

Now that we have his answers, such as they are, all that's left is our answers—what we put together now. Do we have any? Our buffer is gone—the person who stood between us and the Void, who protected us from the Void, in a sense. He's told us what he could of it. Now, what will we do with that? We didn't realize there would be that kind of shift—to us. What are we going to do with that? It's like when your parents have died and you know you're next— there's nothing between you and death now. It feels that open.

I am suddenly struck by how far we've gotten from any discussion of death! At the start, both Miles and I (let alone everyone in town) thought that jumping and falling must be about that, at least partly. How else could a jump and fall end? I think of the people in the village who felt sure it was an act of suicide. I blurt out, "We've haven't talked about death at all! It's all been about life."

"And the best kind of life! Happy, with meaning and purpose," Duncan Robert says. This gave us all pause.

"Wow. Find your instructions for living in the Void," Miles shakes his head and laughs. "We could bill it as an adventure trip—like an Alaska cruise."

"You'd have to be careful," Duncan Robert says. "You'd have people suing you for failure to deliver. It wouldn't work for everyone." They chuckle.

"You boys do egg each other on, don't you," I observe.

"Yeah, we're quite a team," Miles says.

Duncan Robert looks at him and says, "You know we are. I couldn't have jumped without you."

"What do you mean?" Miles asks, looking sideways at him.

"Our conversations took me, inch by inch, closer to the Void. We rehearsed it all, together, in those conversations."

Miles is stopped by this. But he doesn't argue. "I'm bothered by that," he says, with a frown. "I think the same thing was happening in my conversations with Babe, which took her to the brink."

"Wait a minute," I say to Miles. "I've been called to the Void since I was a child. I had to go. You didn't push me there. All your talk just helped clarify that call. Going there helped me see I'd always had a choice."

He doesn't look convinced. He's still frowning.

"Look how important we are to each other," Duncan Robert says. "Look how we need each other."

"I'm not so sure," Miles says. "Is it the right thing we do for each other?"

Duncan Robert looks at him. "Those conversations were acts of creativity—they went where they went. We let them. I think it was us at our best. We didn't let fear stop us, not-knowing stop us. We just went there. Did our homework, asked questions, thought, worked things out for ourselves."

"But it feels like we assumed a responsibility there maybe we didn't realize we were assuming."

"For my life?" Duncan Robert asks. "*We* never had that. *I* always had that. And I was aware of that."

Miles frowns. "It's just scary to think about. I guess most of us are used to thinking of death as something out-side of our control, not knowing when it will come or how, rather than stepping up to a moment and then finding our-selves moving beyond it."

"You guys love each other and you know it," I say. "There's your protection, right?"

Miles looks at me with tears in his eyes for the ump-teenth time that day, saying not a word.

Duncan Robert suggests gently, "Let's get back to the story. There's not a lot more to tell. I was right at a moment of choice, Guy's 'point of magic.' He moves back to the couch and picks up his glass of water.

Break is over. I pick up my notebook and shake out my fingers before picking up my pen. Miles lies back on the floor, to stare at the ceiling as he listens.

CHAPTER NINE

The Conclusion

THE FOUR OF THEM, plus Anai in owl form, are looking at me in the soft glow of the fire. I'm looking back at them, feeling such a part of everything here that I swear I can feel the walls breathe with me. And I am more present than I've ever been, inhabiting every part of myself down to the smallest of my cells. I think, startled, "This is what joy is."

But I knew the time to go was coming. I could feel it.

"Yes, we could use your help." Guy looks at me.

I realize I've been asked a question, and I think I know what it is. It feels like the heart of my 'point of magic'—it feels that big.

I feel all the old boundaries between me and everything else melt away—at that moment the world was without boundaries, as it was meant to be. I look at the Team. I can feel them—their feelings, state of mind, intentions, love. The joining of my and their energies has breached the barriers. I see their example of how to live without boundaries. Their pure feelings for each other give them their high energy—a kind of enthusiasm for themselves, each other, and their own experience.

So I'm having all these realizations, and they sound in my head the way they must be coming across to you, too— half-crazy, jumbled up over each other, overwhelming— but feeling so right, so true. They were asking me to do what they do. I was their opportunity to serve. And you're mine—you two. There's not a doubt in my mind what to do. That's why I'm back and talking.

"As soon as they knew I wanted to do it—to serve as they serve—I knew it was time for me to go. They had things to do, and I had a life to figure out. We hugged, we laughed, the owl Anai and I touched foreheads. They teased me about working harder to remember my dreams now, knowing they've gone to a lot of trouble; reminded me to put myself outside as much as I put the cat out, because Nature is important for both of us; told me to capture and hold close those moments of unexpected joy, to fuel my spirit when times get tough.

"Your own joy is your best resource, don't forget," Lynette said.

Guy added, "We're closer than ever now, all of us. Call on us. We'll hear you. We'll come."

"Yes," Kahil agreed, "no one was ever meant to do this Earth stuff alone. No one ever could."

Uche nodded, as he held both my hands in his, saying, "A bond stronger than life." That still gives me chills.

There's not much more to tell. I didn't want to go. It was only the strength of my commitment to my purpose that made me able to go. Leaving seemed so unnatural, so wrong. It didn't bother them in the same way, of course— they are so used to parting and coming together, and keep in constant contact telepathically. They are always in each other's presence. I was still working on trusting that.

They said they were going to help me teleport back to where I came in, explaining that they know how to transport matter instantaneously from one spot to another, and could lend their energy to mine to make it possible for me. I asked what this would be like for me, and they said it would be a little like coming out from under anesthesia, but they were going to make sure I remembered everything.

Guy said, "And I don't think you'll have any nausea," and laughed uproariously, which I found less funny though

I was relieved to hear it. I stood in the center of their silent group and closed my eyes. I could feel their hands on me, at the center of their energetic attention, and I surrendered to the wonderful feeling sweeping over me. I felt myself floating off.

The next thing I knew, I was lying in the damp grass near the edge of the Void. It was still morning; the sun was still low on the horizon, its light slanting through the trees. It took me a while to collect myself, to fully realize where I was, to sit up and try to regain a sense of reality here, while the cave still felt more real. I was glad to have come back to such a peaceful place.

I don't know how long it was before I got up, knowing I was going home to say goodbye to my mother. I didn't question it. It just felt right. Before going, I walked over and stood at the edge of the Void and looked down. I could still see where my shoes had flattened the grass before I jumped. I stood there and spread my arms and closed my eyes and gave thanks. That was all I knew to do. It was a place I had trusted more than I had trusted the world, and it had proved trustworthy. I felt as if the Void received my thanks because I imagined I felt it tingling a bit at my feet. I don't know if I'll ever jump again, but I felt as if I could. I have no fear of it anymore.

I go to see Silvia, who is, of course, over-joyed to see me. The first thing she wanted to do was feed me, so I stayed for one of her great breakfasts—vegetarian omelet, just like I like it, homemade biscuits, fresh-squeezed juice—you know what I'm talking about, Miles.

Then I put a few things in a pack, getting away with telling her only the high points of what happened in the Void. She says she can tell I'm different, but she's happy with what she sees because I seem happier. So she's okay with my going, knowing I'll still be in the world and she'll be able to have contact with me. I tell her goodbye and I assure her I'll be in touch. I leave while it's still early, on foot. I like that. Ever since reading the Transcendentalists in English class, I imagined I would do this at some point in my life.

I wandered the back roads for a while, walking, camping, "living rough," being away from everything, yet more a part of everything that's really important as I see it now. I had realizations out there it could take your whole life to achieve—and that's if you were lucky. What had happened to me was all consuming. I needed to be alone, because I couldn't use words as a means of experiencing or understanding everything. I just felt I needed to be alone and outside. Nature would support and ground my understanding.

The first step, it seemed to me, was to trust that I could find my own way with this. I had taken the pain, the disappointment, the boredom, and my lack of a life into the Void with me, and I came out without those things. The jumping—the falling—healed me. It brought me an internal peace I couldn't deny. I needed to look at what I had now in place of all those things cleansed away by the Void. But really, I began to integrate my experience in the Void because it feels like the most true thing that's ever happened to me. I trust it, and I want to build on it, live it. I know that life, like a story, has a beginning, middle and end. My experience with the Void has changed the middle; it's loaded the end with possibilities it never had before—it's no longer predictable.

Much of my time was spent alone, in contemplation. I can give snippets, like the afternoon I met an elderly woman on her back step, who fed me and read my future in egg whites, from eggs she cultivated for just this purpose. She looked up at me with an open, wondering face and told me I must be a mystic, because the future she saw for me was beyond this planet. She said her mother, who had taught her the skill, had seen a future like that once in a man, and the man was named Edgar Cayce. He had come to town with his photography equipment one summer. She didn't remember meeting him, but her mother never forgot.

I met another woman who is the keeper of an ancient crystal skull, one of the original thirteen skulls, to be brought together at the end of the Mayan calendar, she said. It speaks to her and will speak to anyone else willing to listen. I listened to it, and it carries messages of immense change for the world. I thought that was pretty far out, but in a way I expected it—I knew I was different now, so the people I was meeting would be different. These people are out there, if you're looking for them, and meeting them showed me where I fit now.

I met an old man who is a beekeeper working to save the environment with his hives. He told me that they had found honey in Tutankhamen's tomb, and it was still edible, after 2,000 years. Aristotle kept bees, he said. Bees argue and then reach consensus through dance. He loved that. And they die to protect their mother. Darwin said their death, when they sting us, serves evolution because they've died so that their mother, the queen, can live and keep the hive going. The old man also said 3.5 grams of bee pollen a day contains all the nutrients needed to sustain life.

I didn't want to hold onto the past any more, to have more past than room for present in my awareness. Lingering in the past inhibits creativity, and life and progress depend on our creativity.

My life now is devoted to maintaining the truth I have gained. I know I can't act outside of this with immunity now; it would cost me in ways I might never know the full extent of. I'm part of a Team, a cohort, and I won't forget that. It makes me think of the words to that old Walter Hyatt song, "When I remember your life, I remember mine."

I'm no longer checking to see what anybody else is doing. I'm no longer wondering or caring what they think of what I'm doing.

Right now, I have a dog and I need to get back to check on him, feed him. I'm still doing odd jobs and some healing work, in partnership with some like-minded people. And I'll be in touch. That's important for all of us now, because

I've taken you two on, as part of my Team here. None of us know what that means at this point, but I'm not worried. I know we'll figure it out. We figured out today, didn't we?"

Duncan Robert gets up to leave, looking around as if he might have left something, though he brought nothing in with him. He tells us to stay as long as we'd like. The room is paid for, for the night. We hug. We all have tears in our eyes. "A bond stronger than life," he says, with a smile, and then he's gone. We watch from the window as he walks out of the hotel, around the corner, and out of our sight. It's hard to let him go. Everything in me says not to. I turn to Miles and wrap my arms around his waist, burying my head in his chest. And then I just cry. He holds on tight, too, and I feel him cry with me.

CHAPTER TEN

And Then They Know

We order from room service again, as the sun is beginning to set. We've been here since the morning, and we're exhausted from it all. You'd think we'd been doing heavy lifting. We're too tired and confused to talk, but we can't help but talk.

All of a sudden, we hear some loud thumping coming from outside, and we go to the window. A fireworks display has begun, down by the river, and I remember that it's Labor Day. A celebration must be going on, and it seems very appropriate. I have to smile. So does Miles. We watch for a while, as the colorful light blossoms explode into the twilight sky above the trees on the square, disappearing almost immediately, leaving little puffs of smoke behind.

I look over at Miles and think of how comfortable I have become with him. We've been through some really unsettling, and even deeply disturbing, stuff together, but we've never lost our ease of interacting, our respectful way of waiting for each other and helping each other to whatever understanding seems possible. I'm grateful for that. I can't imagine going through this alone, which makes me think of what Uche said to Duncan Robert. None of us is supposed to go through any of this alone.

We go back to the couch and settle in again.

As he leans his head back on the couch, I ask Miles if I can look at the notes he's made in his notebook, because I did see him writing from time to time, as Duncan Robert talked, and I'm thinking he may have caught some things I didn't. He doesn't open his eyes, but he hesitates and then says, "Sure, but they're my notes, based on the questions I came in with and the answers I think I got. They're not based on what he said, but what I heard, if that makes any sense."

"It makes sense," I say.

He opens one eye to look over at me, raising one eyebrow, too. Then he closes it again.

I sit on the couch, my legs tucked under me, reading his list of questions and answers aloud, as I sip my still-warm cup of tea. I realize the questions went unasked—we just listened. The answers are his, too, which is kind of eerie. He writes them in first person, as if it is his own jump he's writing about. They're kind of based in Duncan Robert's words and kind of not.

"Questions," he's written at the top of the page. A list follows, not numbered. There are answers, indented, after each question, just a few lines each.

Tell us why you jumped.

In good part because it was there. And nothing else really was.

Tell us where you've been.

Right here.

Tell us about the jump.

Exhilarating. First it was dark and I was afraid—afraid I'd made the wrong choice, like they all said. Then my heart lifted like a sail. All feeling left all other areas of my body and gathered in my heart. My heart swelled, and at the same time it felt light. Then I felt my heart burst. It's an incredible feeling, being turned inside out, made vulnerable to the world.

I felt more aligned with the Void than I ever had with life. With life, I always felt out of sync—behind, out of step, anxious, frantic sometimes, not feeling enough of anything—smart, quick, tall, aggressive, handsome, good. With the Void, I felt perfect.

Were you scared?

Paralyzed. Unable to breathe. Not sure I could respond. But when I realized it was happening, I let go. I laughed, I cried, I was moved by my own actions. I couldn't believe what I had done. It was the most authentic act of my life—done by me, for me, and for no other reason.

Did you feel alone?

Honestly? I never felt alone. I felt completely surrounded by presences. They laughed with me, screamed with me, held onto me.

Are you glad you did it?

More than I can say. And I'm grateful to the Void, for its constancy, its inspiration, and its enlightenment. It has never left us. It is always there, waiting for the next one to jump.

I closed his notebook in my lap. Miles has been watching me read, and as I look over at him, his eyes meet mine. We look at each other for a moment. We have to pack up and go back to our lives, to our jobs, to our friends and families. I'll be sitting at a computer screen, trying to fit this story into a manageable, publishable form, probably forced to squeeze half the life out of it to satisfy Henry. Miles will be preparing for school to start, to teach some inhumane number of classes to an uninterested flock of freshmen. He would describe them more charitably, I know, because he really does love his students. We'll both be trying to hold onto and sort out all that we've just heard. And waiting for more contact with Duncan Robert, the leader of our Team down here.

We continue to look at each other, knowing the biggest question without saying it, feeling it filling the air between us.

Are we the next ones to jump?

CHAPTER ELEVEN

Carrie Jean

THE MORNING SUN SLANTS through the trees and disappears into the dark hole that is the Void. A group of raucous crows gathers around the edge, squawking to each other the way they do, pecking at invisible things in the grass and in the air. The sun picks up the iridescence of their feathers, edging the black with purple and green. I wind my long hair into a loose bun, securing it with a stick, and think about how my Granny Noreha would call them a storytelling of crows, rather than a flock or a muster. In her tradition, they are the keepers of spiritual law through the telling of stories. I love their sounds and consider their presence a good omen. I stand at the edge of the woods that stop short of the Void. There is a little meadow in between, carpeted in dense, knee-high grass that grows right up to the Void, almost hiding it. Even from this distance, I can see the path of two sets of footprints crossing the damp grass, up to the edge of the Void. Crossing, but not returning.

I saw them jump, both of them. They didn't see me, but I saw them. They stood a few feet back from the edge. Holding hands, they looked at each other, calm as ice. Then they ran the few steps to the edge and jumped, clearing the sides of the Void and disappearing. I held my breath, as if expecting them to reappear, peeking over the edge, telling me it was all a joke. I had been pretty sure they were going to do it, because I'd been called here, but still, seeing it left me breathless. I thought my heart had stopped with my breath. It was just so final. They existed in my world one moment and then they *didn't*. No sound, no panic, no hesitation, no leader and no follower.

Should I have tried to stop them? Not that I could have. They walked into the clearing with purpose, and they hurtled themselves forward into the Void with the same purposefulness. It felt natural, easy. As it happened, I was mesmerized by it, as if into a trance. To be honest, intervening hadn't even occurred to me.

I wondered what would happen to them now. I stood quietly for a while, not ready to abandon them yet. I'd known someone else who had jumped, and I hadn't been there to witness it. It helped to be here for this jump. So I stood and watched for a while, as the sun began to warm the clearing, and the crows continued holding court.

I was so engrossed in my secret watching, I could not have noticed that someone else watched me.

CHAPTER TWELVE

Miles

I CLIMB OUT OF the little Cessna 172, tie the ropes to the lift struts and tail, slide the rudder lock in place, securely tethering her to her spot near the frozen dirt runway, between the runway and the hangar. I chock her tires and begin wiping off all the signs of flight on her—the bug juice, the dirt, the oil—as I was taught fifteen years ago by my first trainer. I automatically check for any signs of wear and tear as I do so. I feel the late afternoon cold in my hands as I work, and the multi-colors of the fall leaves are so bright they argue for my attention.

This isn't my plane—I rent it occasionally, for $35 an hour—but I've been taught to treat every plane I fly as if it was, leaving it in good shape for the next guy. I have to pay for fuel, too, and any runway costs, but I still consider it a good deal, for what you get. I was bitten by the flying bug years ago, when I first read a battered copy of *Jonathan Livingston Seagull*, by Richard Bach, that someone had left on the Greyhound I was taking to see a girl, the name of whom I can't now remember. I'd been young and 'high on life,' as they used to say, excited about collecting experiences of all kinds, ensuring I'd have all kinds of stuff to write about, because writing was what I thought I wanted to do. It was a romantic notion, and flying was part of it, as were outdoor adventures, travel, and girls. I dabbled in all four, while getting my education, working odd jobs to support myself, and writing on the side, as I found time.

The one real reason for flying, Bach said, "is the finding of life itself, and the living of it in the present." Just as you get a broader view of the world from up there, you get a broader view of your own situation. I agree with that, and since life itself has provided much to stir me lately, I've taken to the sky again to settle my thoughts. After coming back from seeing Duncan Robert with Babe, I'd been overwhelmed, emotionally and intellectually. The aloneness and the silence in the plane had stitched my thoughts and feelings back together again, just as Bach said they would—leaving me feeling like singing, as I did on my best days up in that cockpit, knowing no one could hear. I was glad to be singing again, having wondered if I would.

As I walked away from the plane towards my old pickup, I knew, first, I needed to talk with Silvia. I had just spent more time with her son than she had in over a year. Second, I needed to begin to get my affairs in order, so I could make the jump with as little on my mind as possible. I knew Babe was doing the same, and it wouldn't take either of us much, since both of us live fairly simply. We plan to jump in May, over spring break. It is mid-October now, which allows us both plenty of time to do what we need to do. We won't have the holidays with our families, since we don't usually spend them with family. Babe doesn't, because of work, and Silvia hasn't made much of any of the holidays since Duncan Robert left last year. Besides, her work as church secretary keeps her pretty busy during most holidays, so I'm usually on my own.

Our parents have been gone for years now. We are only a year and a half apart in age, and we were always close growing up. We hung out together, sharing friends, all through school, and people often asked if we were twins. I thought that was more because we were always together than because we look a lot alike, which we do, though I see it as the usual sibling resemblance.

I went off to college first, attending the university near Portsmouth, not far from the village, and she came up often, meeting whomever I met, learning all the places I knew, hanging out with me and my best friend Tom. I had been attending the university for a year, majoring in English, when Silvia came up to begin her studies in nursing. She wanted to be a midwife.

Tom and I met attending many of the anti-war and human rights protests on campus, eager to voice our opinions on the over-involvement of our government in too many places in the world, from the Middle East, to Africa, to the South Pacific. We discovered we were both English majors, interested in becoming writers, and we decided to share a loft apartment. Silvia lived in the dorm and hadn't made many friends there, as I remember. So, the three of us were together most of the time, reading the same things and discussing them, seeing the same movies, going to the same protests.

I often think the protests, more than anything, forged the relationship among the three of us, enlivening and uniting us in an enduring way. They were some of my fondest memories. Usually held around lunch time, they brought together students who had some free time, provided us with free pizza, and kept great debates going on the finer points of whatever U.S. engagement we were protesting. Silvia and I were impassioned protesters, and began to help to organize the marches and find funding for their operation. Tom was more along for the ride, enjoying the camaraderie of the gatherings and finding all kinds of things to write about. Protest was all I wanted to write about, though, from early on. I sought out all the forgotten vets I could find in order to collect their war stories, which I then could weave into an argument against war.

As for Tom and Silvia, they're an example of why I've always considered good conversation the best aphrodisiac for a relationship. I could see how one conversational topic led to another and another for them, deepening their relationship incrementally. I can't say when I felt the energy change, but I soon came to fully understand the concept of "third wheel." I was close to Tom and I could see they were both happy, so it was easy to be genuinely happy for them.

Silvia and Tom's wedding came that following summer, and Silvia quit her studies because she was pregnant by then, with Duncan Robert. Tom quit, too, and they moved back to the village, where Tom tried to find work to support them. I never understood their move back. Tom was a writer at heart, and a good one. He needed to have time and place to do it in order to thrive. I lost the everyday contact I'd had with them because of that move, and threw myself into completing my master's degree in the writing program, funded by a teaching fellowship.

I soon discovered that my real interest, and my strength, was in teaching. I liked doing it, and I liked myself when I did it. I knew that my writing, while serviceable, would never be as good as Tom's, and that knowledge didn't break my heart the way I thought it would. More and more, I wanted to tell other people's stories, particularly war stories, which I found deeply moving, and I knew they could provide background for my teaching.

I talked with returning vets, coming home after tours of duty in Iraq, though there weren't many returning at that time unless they'd been terribly wounded. I discovered that several of the older faculty on campus had fought in Vietnam, and their stories had had time to merge with the details of who they were then and are now in a way that made them powerful tools for teaching. I continued to enjoy teaching; it made me think and laugh and feel really alive. It wasn't as all-consuming and solitary as writing was. I found I had room to be, which suited me, and I happily settled into the routines of teaching, reading and writing that continue to define my life. Life was good, and I assumed it was for my sister, too.

What I didn't know, however, was that Tom and Silvia were heading for divorce, a decision they would make when

Duncan Robert was three. Later, after talking at length with Silvia over late-night coffees, I wondered if Tom's trying to be something he wasn't had just worn them all out. There wasn't a job left in the village he hadn't tried and failed at, and not tending to his writing regularly seemed to rob him of something essential for his well-being. The part of him that knew joy diminished almost to the point of non-existence. So, he took what was left of himself out of the marriage, said good bye to his son, and promised to still provide for them in whatever ways he could. Tom told me he thought it was too late for him to try to be a student anymore, so he set out to write, supporting himself any way he could, which was easier when he was alone. He had some success with his writing, too, and sent money to Silvia regularly.

I know Silvia and Duncan Robert haven't seen Tom since, his work and life taking him in and out of the country. Silvia has kept him as the dad in Duncan Robert's life, not letting his absence obscure the fact, hoping they'll connect at some point. She stayed on in the village, liking that she could at least give Duncan Robert constancy in that way. She has worked almost twenty years now as secretary at the one Catholic church in town. Though she neither practices the faith nor believes in it, she feels herself lucky to be an essential part of the community. Duncan Robert grew up well supported, on all sides. I'm struck by the sad irony that he was named for two fathers—Silvia's and my father (Duncan) and Tom's father (Robert), but he never knew either of them. And of course he's never really known his own.

The divorce, however, gave *me* the unexpected gift of knowing Duncan Robert. I had some vague romantic notion of being the popular uncle, the one who only got to visit occasionally, and was all the more loved and longed for because of it. That was hogwash of course, and I instead found myself working hard to woo this active, discerning kid who regularly looked at me sideways, measuring the sum total of me in that look. I had no way of knowing what that look found in me, or didn't find. But without a shadow of a doubt, it began to matter to me more and more.

I finally admitted to myself that I was captivated by this boy—how he thought, what he might say, what he might do next—I had begun to love him. Duncan Robert was teaching me things that I couldn't learn anywhere else. So when I completed the master's program, contrary to what I thought I would do, I took a job teaching at the community college not far from the village so that I could be near Silvia and Duncan Robert. This arrangement also suited me better than I could have imagined. Duncan Robert and I grew to be very close, camping and hiking together, sharing books and music, and all the things that mattered most—including, eventually, his jump.

So, I'm here at Silvia's, to tell her about Babe's and my conversation with him. I pull into her driveway behind her old Subaru Forester, the back of the car still plastered with anti-war stickers. I pause a moment to see if she has any new ones. I savor the old ones—*Republicans for Voldemort* and *How many lives per gallon?* I spot one I haven't seen: *How far can you go without destroying from within what you are trying to defend from without?—Dwight D. Eisenhower.* Good one, unexpected source. I'll have to ask her about it.

I follow the side brick walk, some signs of early frost in the shade of its borders, to the back door of her little cape cod, which is complete with black shutters at the narrow windows and fanlight above the front door. The back door opens directly into the kitchen, where I know she'll be. She has lived in the same house for all the time she and Duncan Robert have been in the village. I love her house. It feels like home to me. I open the door to see her, as expected, at the kitchen sink, washing lettuce.

"You're going to jump, aren't you?" She doesn't turn around to greet me.

I turn from shutting the door. "What makes you say that?" I have come to talk about Duncan Robert, not me, and she is going to fix dinner for us. My hard-won calm is threatening to desert me.

"You might just as well tell me, Miles. I know you. This has been coming for a long time." She continues to wash her lettuce.

"Don't you want to hear about the interview first?"

"Oh, all right. I know the answer anyway." She dries her hands and turns to hug me, and I hug her back, still glad to be here.

And she does want to hear about the interview. We sit at her kitchen table to eat the good stew and salad she has prepared, sharing some wine, too. So I tell her everything I can remember and say that Babe has an article coming out in the local paper in the next week or so, and she can talk to Babe, too.

Silvia has been in regular contact with Duncan Robert since the day he came out of the Void, which was the exact day he jumped in, so she already knew he was all right and where he was living and so on. She hadn't known the peace and understanding he'd discovered through his experience, though she'd guessed at it. I am able to provide that.

She listens quietly. When I finish, she says, "I thought I had failed him."

"Why?" I ask, surprised. "How could you have thought that?"

"Because he couldn't find his way. That's why I supported his jump. I thought I'd let him down. That he had expected things from me as a mother I wasn't capable of. From the very beginning, my feelings for him had taken me beyond any place I'd ever been before. I didn't know how to do it. He had to be the teacher. You know our parents were the kind who never showed emotion. Everyone went to their rooms when they were angry. And it was an unspoken truth that going beyond our assigned roles was not appropriate or acceptable. I don't think this was true for you, but it left me feeling like an outcast most of the time. Nothing I thought or did seemed right."

I sit amazed to hear this. She's never said any of this to me before.

"And that's what I think Duncan Robert felt, too. I hadn't been able to save him from it. But he didn't stick at that spot, as I had done. Look what he did instead! I so admire it—finding his own way, creating his own beliefs to live by. He jumped! My god, the courage that took. It still blows me away. I don't think I could do it." She ruminates for a minute. "But if he hadn't come out, I probably would have gone in!" She laughs.

"The Void probably wouldn't have let you," I say. I don't know if I could have handled both of them jumping.

"I know, I know." She looks at me as if she's the older sibling. "It's just funny. His jump has made me feel like a better mother." She smiles and hugs me, and I hug her back.

CHAPTER THIRTEEN

Miles and His Students

A FEW WEEKS LATER, I'm in one of my small night classes on basic composition at the community college. The college is just one town over, about seven miles from the village, so I know the students have heard about Babe's interview. Her article is out now. I don't expect them to talk about it, though. It's a topic no one really talks about in town—things are whispered, there's some random gossip hinted at more than stated, but that's all. It's kept behind closed doors, and I plan to honor that. Between now and next spring, the Void doesn't need any more attention cast on it.

There are five students there that night, three males, two females; one male student is absent. Most are non-traditional students, as they say, meaning not eighteen and fresh out of high school. More like twenty-five and up, and a product of the school of hard knocks, living on the fringe of purpose and ambition but driven to attend college to find some kind of future.

I'm doing a traditional writing exercise, without really thinking about it. I'm passing around the old cardboard box with a mismatched collection of odds and ends in it for them to choose from. Once they've chosen, they're given ten or twenty minutes in class to write on their object—manufacture a story about it and share it with the class. The box holds an old tube of fire-engine red lipstick, almost completely used up; some keys on a flimsy key chain; a frayed shoelace that could be from a child's shoe; a small battered blue flashlight; a pack of breath-saving gum with a couple of pieces left in it; an old Ray Bradbury paperback; a funeral home hand fan, inscribed with the name of the funeral home and a heavenly host of angels. Fodder for fiction, as one student called it.

As the box is being passed around, a male student named Lonnie in the back calls out, "Can we write about the Void?"

The room gets quiet. They all look up at me, standing by my desk, pen in hand, poised over the grade book open on my desk. I mark Nathan, the missing student, absent. Attendance is 20 percent of their grade. I know why they're asking, but I'm not going to discuss the interview with them.

"Sure."

"But we haven't experienced it," Lonnie says "and you always say it has to be our truth. Can we write about something that hasn't happened to us?"

I stop what I'm doing, put my grade book down, and sit back in my chair. I look at them, realizing it's an important point for me to make.

"I had a professor tell me once that my forte is war stories." I pause and breathe a moment. "Have I ever been to war? No. In fact, I do the opposite. I protest wars, any and all wars. But can I tell a war story? You be the judge. Let me tell you part of one that I heard from one of my older friends who did go to war, in Vietnam." I pull some typed pages out of the back of my grade book. They've served this duty before.

I'm not really trying to distract them from the Void, I tell myself, and I don't think I could. I'm trying to answer their question about telling others' stories, while making sure I'm being a good example for how it's done. And if I can get them to join hands aboard the love train and forsake war forever, as the old anti-war song says, so much the better. I start to read to them.

"O'Reilly was a young eighteen when he went to war, fresh out of high school and fresh out of ideas of what to do with himself. Every male in his family before him had enlisted. They weren't good at getting educated and didn't have the means for it anyway. There was no family business to go into. Enlisting offered their first chance at picking out a living wherever they could.

"So, scared to the point of throwing up outside the recruitment office but figuring he was due to be drafted anyway, O'Reilly went in and enlisted. He threw up the moment he came out. Vietnam was on, and he knew that's where he'd be going.

"After three months of training at Fort Lewis, Washington, and Fort Polk, Louisiana, and a thirty-day pass home, he was on a twenty-hour flight into Cam Rahn Bay. Once there, his company was assigned to the Central Highlands, the border between North and South Vietnam.

"Around 350 American soldiers were dying every week in Vietnam. And an estimated thousand North and South Vietnamese men, women, and children were dying every week during the worst of it. But O'Reilly didn't know those figures. His days were organized around patrols into the rice paddies and the jungle, to keep the army's hold on the territory secure. The only thing worse than the daytime marches, he learned quickly, was the nighttime ones. It was on these night patrols that most of the original men in his company—men he was there to replace—had been killed or badly injured.

"Their patrols were single file, each soldier keeping a space of ten feet between him and the soldiers in front of and behind him, because of land mines. Soldiers learned all about land mines and what they did to a human body, because they saw it firsthand. It wasn't long before his best friend, Bob Bywater, was killed by a mine. The two had connected during their first days at boot camp when they were assigned as battle buddies, meant to always travel as a pair, having each other's back. Under the circumstances, they'd grown as close as brothers.

"One sweltering hot morning they were out on patrol, crossing the rice paddies on the dikes that ran between the flooded areas of the fields. O'Reilly followed Bywater, matching his steps without thinking, when Bywater stepped on a mine.

"The explosion knocked O'Reilly from his feet, ears ringing. He saw that Bywater's legs had been shredded badly by the blast, and he was losing blood quickly. It flowed into the watery field. Bywater was yelling for help, but his fall had set off the gas canister at his waist, releasing a particularly lethal form of tear gas. Everyone who tried to rush into the narrow space on the dike was forced back by the gas. They watched helplessly as Bywater, within the cloud of the poisonous gas, bled to death. O'Reilly never moved from the ground where he dropped. It was as if his own legs were useless, and he sat watching and listening to Bywater call, 'Help me, O'Reilly. Help me,' more and more softly, until he called no more."

I put the pages back into my grade book and then look up at them. They're quiet.

"O'Reilly told me that story forty-three years after it happened, and he still had tears streaming down his cheeks when he told it." They're quiet.

"So, does that answer your question about telling someone else's story? The idea is that your truth is in the telling, too, not just theirs. Could you hear mine?" I ask.

One of the two girls, Carrie Jean, says, "Yes."

"What did you hear?"

"That you hate war."

"How did you hear that?"

"In your description of the stupidity of it, of sending men marching in broad daylight out into an open field, unprotected. Of wearing so much equipment it can turn on them, as if they were the enemy. Of someone needing help, and no one can. It makes me hate war, too. Isn't that how we know it is truth? We feel it as our own?"

I gaze at this tall Native American girl and wonder at her. I like her answer. Her mind works like a writer's mind, clear and straight to the heart of the matter. Obviously, she has a base of experience and wisdom beyond her years. I know that she's part of the Tribe, the loosely affiliated group of Native Americans that live just north of town, between town and the Void, but closer to the Void. That's all I know about her. I've had members of the Tribe in my classes before, but they're not usually talkative.

"Is she right?" I ask the others. "Do you agree with how she describes truth?"

"Yes," says Donal, from the back row. "You know it when you hear it. It has its own fit." He nods at Carrie Jean.

"And my truth is different from O'Reilly's truth. He believes his time in the army made a man of him, though he's still confused by his experience and says he wouldn't recommend it to his sons," I tell them.

Lonnie, the boy who originally asked the question, says, "Yeah, I can see how you can tell someone else's story, but I don't know if I can do it that good." They all laugh.

"Well, you can't," Kevin, the third boy in the class, says from the back of the room, and they all laugh again, including Lonnie. Kevin can almost always make us laugh.

"Okay. I'm setting the timer."

They shuffle their things for writing and get quiet. They look at me expectantly.

I set the timer for twenty minutes. As it starts ticking, their heads go down. Twenty minutes is enough for them to write three or four pages and still allows enough class time for each of them to read their words aloud.

Every single one of them writes about the Void.

I know this before they're even through. I feel as if the Void has taken a seat in the back row with the other malcontents and is ready to speak its piece. Then the time is up.

The first story is read by Donal, who almost always chooses to be first. He is a member of the school's tiny football team and takes the stature this gives him on campus seriously. He goes first as though it is his duty to volunteer. His story is about the continuing nightmares his little six-year-old brother, Brogan, has about the Void. The family is a large, close knit one without a lot of resources, so Donal and his brother share a room.

"I read to Brogan every night, trying to replace the bad stories with good ones so he can fall asleep. Kids at school talk, and Brogan has heard things he doesn't know what to do with. Things that make it sound like the Void could come and get him from his bed, and he'd be gone forever, never to see his family again. They laugh at him when he cries."

I wonder to myself if Donal is affected by these stories, too. Maybe he's reading them both to sleep.

Kevin, a welding apprentice, steps up to the front of the class next. He reads to us of feeling the call of the Void, like in *The Call of the Wild* he just read for his English 101 class.

"I feel the call," he tells us. "I'm drawn to jump, and it scares me. I think the Void is like the *wild* in the book, something bigger than all of us that we all have to eventually surrender to, because it's in our nature to do so." He looks sincere and worried as he reads.

"For Buck, the dog who is the lead character in *The Call of the Wild*, surrendering to the wild is ultimately a good thing—he lives happily ever after, a legend in his own time." He stops and goes back to his seat.

"Kevin isn't quite sure how to reconcile that successful surrendering that Buck did with his view of the Void as a scary place. How do you surrender to that? So he stays uneasy about it, and we hear that in his writing, don't we? He writes on a descriptive rather than an interpretive level. Do you know what that means?" I ask them.

Monica, the other girl in the class, says tentatively, "I think so. He's doing what you always call coloring within the lines. You want us to color outside of them."

"Exactly," I say, and Kevin nods. "We want his truth." He knows he's struggling with this, but it's a worthwhile struggle.

The boys are sticking together, it seems, and Lonnie, a full-time student living at home, reads next. He writes of knowing Duncan Robert, of them working on cars together, how much fun that was, and now he's gone, and there's no one else like him to work with, to learn from.

"Why did this have to happen? Where did he really go?" His tone is belligerent. "My girlfriend says there's a lesson in everything. Just what was I supposed to have learned from this?"

He looks challengingly at me, sure I'm willfully withholding the answer, as I sit in the front of the room over my grade book.

"I've got no answers," I tell him. "I'm just hoping to cure you of run-on sentences before the term is over." They laugh.

"But I'm still moved by what he has read," I tell all of them. "I can hear the honest expression of the anger at this unexpected loss behind his words—no chance to ask why, or say good bye, or are you coming back. He's captured real loss."

They look at Lonnie with respect. He blushes, confused. Usually his anger gets him in trouble, especially in a classroom.

Monica is the first girl to step up to the front of the room. She tugs at her short skirt on the way up, making sure it covers what it needs to. She tells the story of her friend, who went out with Duncan Robert in high school once or twice, who still has a crush on him.

"They drifted apart, and my friend never understood why. She always felt it was some shortcoming on her part." She looks up at us for a moment, pain in her eyes. "Now she's left wondering if she had any part in his jumping, because we don't really know why he jumped." She closes her notebook, gives one last tug to her skirt and goes back to her seat.

"This is the stuff of good stories, isn't it?" I ask them. "The friend has made an emotional investment in someone and it hasn't paid off. What other stories does it make you think of?"

"*Romeo and Juliet*," Carrie Jean says, "or *West Side Story*. They all loved each other, but it still didn't pay off."

"*Great Gatsby*," Kevin, our resident reader, calls out.

"*Carrie*," says Lonnie, and they all laugh, but I can't disagree. The literature classes here all talk about the stories of Stephen King, since he's a fixture in these parts.

I notice that their stories are confessional, as if they were compelled to write about the Void, but they feel guilty doing so, as if they've betrayed a common code. I don't know what to do with that. I can't absolve them. I don't have even the imaginary power to do so. But I know they think I do.

So I ask them, "What do you want, by writing and sharing these stories of the Void?"

"I think we need to know," Lonnie says.

"Know what?"

"What we're talking about," Monica says honestly.

"What do you mean?"

And then Donal, their self-appointed leader, says, "We need a trip to the Void."

They all look at me in agreement, in defiance, expecting me to say the things adults in authority say to them— parents, law enforcement, pastors—who say it directly and indirectly. *Stay away from it. You'd have to be crazy or have a death wish to do otherwise. We forbid you.* No one ever takes into account just normal, natural curiosity—or the fact that forbidding it, trying to make if off limits, just energizes curiosity into action. This is where they are now—energized by all the communal forbidding. Ready to take action.

I suggest we talk about it, hoping to defuse some of the energy. They're disturbed by it all—the existence of the Void, Duncan Robert's jump, his return. They know that Duncan Robert is alive, and yet that somehow makes the

Void more disturbing to them, the return having generated an on-going story that lives rather than one that ended and could be forgotten.

I find myself talking to them about Voids in general, the things I know, because I do know a lot now. I do it because I hope it will help. It helped me some, after Duncan Robert jumped, as I thought back on our talks before the jump. Then, it had helped me to think generally about the Void, when everything in me had said to follow Duncan Robert, to help him, or save him somehow. How could I possibly let him jump alone? What kind of uncle was I?

But my feelings about it had remained mixed, like theirs now, and Duncan Robert had known it. I hadn't been sure. I worried if it was the right time. I felt the tug of responsibility here, in this world. Clearly, I didn't feel the call. We both knew that meant there could be no jumping for me.

Jumping is for clear feelings, clear purpose only. It's like unconditional love. You had to have that kind of clarity, that kind of certainty, to jump. And I didn't have it. Duncan Robert told me I had to respect my own humanness, my own instinct on this, and not feel guilt. Funny, I thought at the time, that's just what I would have told him, had the situation been reversed.

So, I worked at that. I could tell them what I'd learned. It didn't mean anyone had to do any jumping. I look at them a moment, not entirely sure I should proceed. It's one thing for them to write about it, another for their authority figure to talk about it, without seeming to encourage it.

"The Void is always there," I tell them. "We seem to continually create the idea of it, tell the stories of it, include it in our philosophy and religion. We need it. It's the collection place—the dump—for everything we don't want. We create it, and we fill it— tossing our deepest fears together in one place, under one name, and then treating it like a real place. It's been around too long to just be imaginary. We know that better than anyone, because we've got one right here in our woods.

"And jumping? I see jumping as an act of life—jumping rope, jumping into water, jumping into someone's arms, jumping for joy, even jumping out of a plane. Jumping is natural to us. We like it because it brings us into an immediate and intense awareness of ourselves at a moment in which we're at our best—a moment of choice, of courage or joy or just plain fun. It can be empowering. We forget that, by the way, as we get older." I'm into it now, excited to be telling it. It definitely feels like coloring outside of the lines.

"But a jump into the Void is a different story. We don't do it for fun, or on a dare, or because of a random urge. That's what bungee jumping or sky diving are for. It's not a place for suicide, either. The Void calls for a jump *into* life, not out of it. You've seen that, with Duncan Robert's return."

"Like *Dante's Inferno*?" Kevin asks, and while taken aback by his question, I'm reminded again that I always know where they are in their survey of literature classes by their associations.

"Well maybe. 'Abandon all hope, ye who enter here,' I say wryly, remembering the poem. "Sure, or Captain Ahab being dragged to the bottom of the ocean," I continue.

But I get blank stares on that one and remember they won't get to *Moby Dick* until next semester. "The Void provides an opportunity for a transformative journey."

"Why would we need Voids?" Donal asks.

"Why would you think?" I need to answer that question with a question.

"Are we supposed to jump to find out?" Kevin asks apprehensively.

"Are *you* going to jump?" Monica asks accusingly.

"What you're feeling, in part, is the lure of the Void, which talking about it can trigger. It doesn't mean anybody will be doing anything." I look at their upturned, unconvinced faces. "It's like talking about food." I try turning to something more familiar, less scary. "Pretty soon everybody's hungry."

"Or sex," Kevin says, and we all laugh. Almost nothing works as well as laughing to break the hold of the lure.

Towards the end of class it's clear that they want to take a field trip to the Void and have class there. They remain unwavering in this. I know they will go, with or without me, and I now feel responsible for having led them in conversation on this. So I opt to go with them, and they spend the last of their class time planning the trip.

It doesn't fully sink in until after class, when I have time to process what has happened. I am aghast. This is the *last* thing Babe and I want—to bring more people to the Void, to generate more attention. They'll tell friends and family! Word will get out, even though they've all sworn secrecy about the trip. I know there's no such thing as secrecy in a small community. I'll be called by irate family, the police, my own school's administration. True, people have their classes meet all kinds of places—the library, the museum, outside on nice spring days, even coffee shops or private homes. It's not a big deal. But still, I might be in some serious trouble here, doing something that engages liability issues and that suggests—or confirms—a serious lack of judgment on my part.

I decide to confess it all to Babe, steeling myself for her response. She needs to know. Besides, I want her input.

But, wonder of wonders, when I tell her, she doesn't agree at all. I sit quietly at her kitchen table in her tiny apartment above the bank as she explains. She is glad to see me, having been working alone at her computer all day. She fixes us her favorite chai tea with some cinnamon-raisin scones she made that morning, and I drink and eat gratefully, exhausted by the drama I've created in my head around this incident. It's tiring to play all the imaginary parts, I think with a laugh.

"Now think about this a minute," she says. "The Void has existed longer than this community. What are we doing? Still trying to pretend it doesn't exist? Or that we can keep people from it, like in a police state, by ordering them not to go near it? We think we can rule it off limits, without ever saying why? Treat people like children? What would Duncan Robert say?"

I think her question is probably rhetorical, but feeling better now in her warm kitchen I say, "Is that like what would Jesus say?" I smile, but she's on a tear now.

"We forget that people can and will do what they want, right or wrong. They're supposed to! We cannot, and have no right to, try to control them, to prevent them the exercise of their own will, as long as it doesn't harm anyone else. We seem to have an endless supply of rules, whether or not rules have ever really worked. Oh, it's true, they can work for lots of things, like traffic or education or work, but . . . wait a minute. Wait a minute. I sound like him, don't I?" She looks at me with wide eyes.

"I am ready to jump, aren't I," she whispers.

I look at her with a question on my face.

"I think we live our lives waiting for, looking for the rules, to tell us what to do. And Duncan Robert was trying to say look how we've become our own jailers!" She looks at me again, really alive now. It's quite a turn on.

"There are no rules for any of this Void stuff, Miles. Your students are making their own as they go. And I think it's good." She brushes off the scone crumbs that have fallen, in her excitement, on the front of her flannel shirt.

I look at her with the unadulterated admiration that I'm feeling. The sun has come out in my world. There are no places for secrets to hide any more. In her presence, I feel good again.

And that makes me remember Carrie Jean's story. I tell Babe about Carrie Jean, and I dig her paper out of my bag to read it to her:

I have lots of Void stories. I live with the Tribe, north of town, and they watch over the Void. I don't know if I belong to the Tribe or not. I do know I belong to my Granny, and anything I know about the Void comes from her. She visits it almost every day, and I go with her to ceremonies, to call on the ancestors and natural forces. I got my medicine bag at the end of my coming of age ceremony there, when I was about twelve.

(I tell Babe that at this point, she reached into her shirt and pulled out a small, worn, beaded buckskin bag on a leather tie to show us.)

That night, I stood at the Void and watched it breathe. We had no fire. We used the stars and waxing quarter moon for light. Me and the other twelve-year old girls stood near the edge of the Void, in our new, women's ceremonial dresses, to receive a blessing. I'd been to these ceremonies before, but never observed the breathing of the Void before.

The ground swelled as the Void drew breath, and I felt myself lifted. It sank when that breath was expelled in a shower of colorful living sparks that shot far up into the night sky, not returning to Earth. I looked at the girls next to me, but they were staring straight ahead, as if they weren't seeing anything. As the breathing continued, I looked out into the crowd of observers. They weren't looking up at the sparks either. But they had been joined by a crowd of colorful, glowing others, who were pointing to the sparks and laughing and dancing. These people were looking at me, too.

They were telling me that I'm part of a larger tribe now, and my job is to carry that tribe's messages to the world. People need to be able to find those messages in the world now. People who are looking for them and don't find them can go badly astray, losing all that's deep in their hearts. Then their hearts become empty shelters for anyone's messages.

Some of them didn't glow but were like ragged dark tears in the dark, without features. They stood at the edge with me. I knew they were people who hadn't found those messages in the world and in their turmoil, had jumped into the Void in search of them. The Void had allowed it, for its own reasons, but not because it has the answers. The Void doesn't have them. Only people do.

I stood at the edge of the Void and watched the dancing and the lights for a long time. My Granny came to me and said, "They're going now." And I knew she had seen them, too. I turned to ask her and saw that everyone else had gone and we were alone at the Void.

"The Void is looking for those things, too. Especially now," she said. "You will help to find them."

CHAPTER FOURTEEN

The Students at the Void

THE STUDENTS AND I go out to the Void late Sunday afternoon, when everybody is off work and it's still light. We thought about going at night, but there are no lights out there and it's a new moon. Auspicious time for new beginnings, Babe had said to me portentously over the phone before I left. Plus I'm thinking that at night it might be more patrolled out there since Duncan Robert's jump and all the talk generated by Babe's article. Soon it might be prohibited. No one can get rid of the Void, but they could fence the area, which is exactly what Police Chief Nguyen is considering.

Half a dozen high-schoolers went out there to party one night about a week ago. This is unheard of. No one knows what all happened for sure. A fight. Some dares. Things got thrown into the Void, like lit cigarettes and beer cans. Maybe some girl's underwear. They were freaked by strange globes of light that came out of the Void, and the air felt strange to them, they said, as if electrically laden. Some heard low sounds coming from the Void. Of course they were drunk, but none of them will go anywhere near the Void now. And they're strangely quiet about it, even though they know it could get them lots of attention and maybe even admiration, which high school kids are usually pretty big on.

My students want to show me they're serious about this trip, not like the high-schoolers, so they make an inordinate amount of preparation, bringing enough gear for a weekend camping trip. I know, from their side talk, that they have spent time talking about what to wear, jackets, lucky caps, what kind of shoes. They come with water and blankets, flashlights, lanterns, snacks, because they know they'll be out there for a while, maybe even 'til it's dark, and they will get hungry. Some have brought a locket, emblem, charm, for luck, a favorite photo. All have brought pens and paper, and some have clipboards to steady their writing. They're quiet, subdued, as they create a cozy little encampment with all of their stuff.

They have surprised me by keeping the trip a secret. I haven't received a single call. This level of secret keeping is unprecedented in all my life, especially by students, who so often feel like cogs in a big machine, under someone else's power. That kind of situation can make a secret really valuable currency on the climb to wherever you might be trying to get to. I'm a little in awe of their seriousness, wondering what purpose it serves for them.

What have they come for? To look into the Void? To feel it? To find out if they can conquer their fear of it? Most have never been this close to it—too scared, even as daredevil kids. There were just too many other places to go for fun or excitement, they told themselves. All this was, of course, before Duncan Robert's jump.

A couple have brought their digital cameras or phones and are checking each other's out, taking test pictures of each other and gathering around each other's little screens to look at them and laugh. They start to relax a little. Nathan has brought his sound equipment. He's the youngest in the class and works as a part-time amateur music producer, occasionally missing class because of his late-night work in the school's recording studio. Though he missed last week, someone informed him about tonight's field trip. He had heard about the sounds the high-schoolers heard, too, and has come prepared to record the sounds of the Void, as an experiment.

He's usually pretty quiet in class, around his older classmates, but he seems in his element here at the Void. Nathan tells us he plans to listen to the recordings he makes later, maybe speeding them up or playing them backwards to see if there's anything to be learned from them.

The picture takers have noticed that small multi-colored orbs have appeared in their pictures, usually just a couple around the people in the pictures.

"That's classic around places with supernatural energy," Monica tells them. "I saw this on some of the shows on cable about the paranormal."

They get me to take a picture of all of them sitting on the edge of the Void, legs dangling in. Monica is certain that having all of them at the Void together will produce lots of globes. They station me on the opposite side of the Void, crouched in the grass, to be at their level.

As I look through the lens, their legs seem to disappear into the Void, and I'm a little spooked. I take several pictures with each of the three cameras, and they all gather to view them. Sure enough, there are globes and other light effects in the pictures, whether attributable to the fading light now augmented by lantern light, or the effects of being this close to the Void, they don't know and neither do I.

Someone throws a lit match in to see what it does, and someone else takes a picture of it before it goes out. They look at the view of the match on the digital camera, and I can see the spectrum of colors around the flame. It's a beautiful picture, the little light in the Void.

Someone makes a joke, comparing the Void to the old cardboard box I use in class as a writing prompt.

"Except it looks more empty," Donal says, laughing.

"Does it?" I'm thinking about the people Duncan Robert ran into down there.

The students are quiet, maybe thinking about the same thing.

Their voices in the semi-darkness remind me of all of the camping trips Duncan Robert and I took, and I'm comforted by their sounds. I let them do all these things with cameras and sound equipment and gear before they settle down to write, knowing they can't write until they feel they've come to know the Void a bit, gotten comfortable with themselves around it.

The light is starting to fade as the sun sinks through the surrounding trees towards the horizon. They seem excited, but excited like at a school dance just before it starts or at the car races or a Halloween party. That kind of energy. Even though they seem to like being near the Void, they still have a healthy respect for it, not getting too close to its edge, not dis-respecting it in any way—no jokes at the Void's expense, no throwing trash in or anything like that.

The Void is a keeper of something ancient—of something we don't know or don't remember or almost remember. I ask them if they feel a sense of history here with the Void.

Kevin says, "I feel the portal-ness of it."

He looks around to see if there are any other sci-fi fans. "It's a *Star Trek* term, having to do with an opening to somewhere bigger, like the place that holds the secrets of the origins of everything."

Nathan gives him the old Vulcan, split-fingered salute. The two of them then knock fists in tribute to each other's knowledge.

Most of them agree that the Void has a knowingness of some kind.

Nathan, who's definitely more talkative tonight, says it has a strong, all-knowing presence, but benign, non-reactive. "It just is. And it wants us to just be, too. Live and let live."

So I say, to begin to move them towards writing, "Think about this. You're doing all the things you'd do when visiting a monument or point of interest on holiday—you're looking at it, photographing it, photographing yourselves, talking about it. Eating and resting beside it. You feel safe enough to do these things. And you're learning something about yourselves, too, in relation to this monument and what we know about what it commemorates." I'm picking words they don't usually use, trying to reframe the scary Void of their childhoods.

"Do you like yourselves around it? And each other?" They look at me, bemused.

"Let me show you what I mean. How many of you have visited the Grand Canyon?" Two people raise their hands—Kevin and Carrie Jean.

"How did you feel about it?" I ask.

"I was blown away," Kevin says. "I've never forgotten it. We spent the night at the bottom, and the stars were so close, they felt inhabited. I've never seen them that way again."

"I was awe-struck, too," Carrie Jean says. "And so was my brother. We felt big and small, and we wanted to live there forever. I think I was eight." She laughs. "But it reminded me of home. Even though the government claims the land, the Native Americans there look after the Canyon. It's their sacred place, like the Void is for the Tribe."

"Now, how many of you have been to Plymouth Rock?" I ask, knowing the answer. It's in every family's photo album around here.

All hands go up, and they all laugh. Despite its historic significance, the rock is small and nondescript. You'd miss it if you weren't looking for it. It tends to underwhelm its many visitors. The park it's in, Pilgrim Memorial State Park, is just off a busy highway in Plymouth, and the rock star's home up the way often receives more attention. But still, it commemorates something, which is why they go.

They hardly think of the rock as a monument anymore, and don't go any more unless they have to. Now they have a counterpoint to write from or at least think from, if they didn't already. They're re-anchored in themselves, their own experience. They're almost ready to write.

They're quiet for a few minutes.

"What makes a place sacred?" Kevin asks out of the quiet.

Nathan, who seemed absorbed in his own thoughts, says, "Maybe just what we were talking about. You'd let your kids play here. You could sleep here. You come here for private moments—for the peace it provides for thinking about the things important to you. You're more yourself here, your best self, than maybe anywhere else. You feel accepted. It's like a good friend." He pauses a moment, looking toward the Void. I'm impressed by where his thoughts have taken him.

"Whatever might have happened here, in the past, the Void didn't do it. Maybe it witnessed it. But it didn't do it," he finishes, a little defiantly. I wonder what Nathan knows about what might have happened in the past. No one else says anything for a moment. Then Carrie Jean speaks.

"We've all heard stories about Tribe people jumping, but no one is sure what did or didn't happen here. And of course the Void didn't do anything. It's a sacred place." She looks troubled. "These stories are old. We may never know the truth."

They've all brought their journals, which are a part of the requirements for the class—another twenty percent of their grade. These journals are writers' journals, not just any old *dear diary*, I've told them. They are a place to capture the workings of their imaginations.

This is why I agreed to come here with them—as a writer's exercise. By being this close and being able to actually look into the Void, they can imagine jumping if they want, or just note their feelings in being so close, what it evokes for them. I've told them I believe that this place has the power to set their imaginations free. And coming here to the Void with the intent to write legitimized their trip, sort of. At least it made my original discomfort manageable. I still don't know what my department would say about it, but I haven't told anyone there, or anywhere, either. No one except Babe knows.

I turn the timer on for twenty minutes, its familiar ticking their signal to begin. They write steadily.

For those moments that they write, I allow myself to feel good—about being here, about doing this. I see the stars twinkling beyond the group's soft lantern light, I feel the night wind move across my face. I feel the peace and renewal of being outside at night, with the night's small sounds and smells released with the day's heat. I find I'm grateful to be here and don't want to be anywhere else at this moment. I have to smile because that's how I usually feel around the Void. So I smile at the Void. I'm thinking of Babe's earlier comment, about knowing she's ready to jump, and I know I feel the same way. I'm at home with the idea, even looking forward to it.

The timer goes off, startling me and them. They've been absorbed in their writing. One by one, they read their stories aloud in the light of the lanterns and flashlights. There is silence between each story, until someone fills it with more reading. I don't choose who's next. They choose themselves, as usual. They've moved closer together, so they can hear each other better. Some wrap the extra blankets around themselves, feeling the chill of the late October night and maybe an internal chill from the stories. They are quieter than usual, without any side conversations, checking of phones, or the general restlessness I'm used to on their weekday night class after most of them have had a long day at work. They don't look at each other, either, staring ahead of them or glancing toward the Void.

Carrie Jean, surprisingly, goes first, something she's never done. The low light shadows the angles of her face and puts gleams in her long dark hair. She looks fiercely Tribal.

"I wrote about my twin brother, Jimmy Lynn, who jumped to his death from a twelve-story building two years ago, after he moved to the city alone to find work. I must have been looking for him here.

"We were both tall, like our mother. Made for horses, our Granny said. She kept our hair like she had our mother's, according to tradition, long and never cut. I was always caught between our tradition and your world. Your world has 'way fewer rules! But I'm not the right color for your world, and I don't carry your culture in my blood. I think my brother felt the same way. Whose rules do we follow?

"We are Tribe people first, me and my brother, raised in the Tribal community. Does that make us Native American? I don't know. It's hard to know our culture nowadays, there's been so much intermarriage. So many comings and goings. Usually, I think of myself as a part-time Indian, like Sherman Alexie says. Do you know him? He's an Indian poet and filmmaker, and he's really funny. He comforts me. I don't know our heritage for sure. I think we're Algonquin and Sioux and Navajo, but I think there's some African slave and French Canadian in there, too, and maybe even some Irish. You tell me what to make of it," she says, looking up at us. "Maybe it's no different for you."

"We were raised by our Grandmother Noreha, our mother's mother, because our parents have been gone a long time. The story is that our mother killed herself, jumping to her death, some say into the Void, but our Granny has never said a word about it, and we never really wanted to ask. It was enough to know our mother was gone, that we didn't have her. People say our father fled right after that, never to be heard from again.

"I never knew either of them," she says, "but that doesn't mean you can't miss them.

"My family was my brother and my grandmother. My brother killed himself. Now it's my grandmother." There are tears on her cheeks.

"I'll tell one story about him, so you can see what he struggled with before he died." She looks towards the Void as she talks, the light breeze moving through her hair.

"One morning, when we were thirteen, we were standing out on the road, waiting for the school bus. It's the same school bus you probably rode, but it picked us up first, so it was always really early, before the sun came up. We were half awake, never feeling we were even on our way to starting our day until we were on the bus, moving. Suddenly

Jimmy Lynn points. I thought he'd seen a quail or wild tur-
key, so I casually look. What I saw was smoke coming out
of the house across the road from the bus stop. Not a lot
of smoke, but as the top edge of the sun cleared the horizon, we could suddenly see the little house was filled with
smoke. That's all you could see at the windows, just thick
white smoke.

"The bus pulled up right then—we hadn't even heard it
come around the bend. Jimmy Lynn yelled to the bus driver
to call the fire in, to the volunteer fire department. The
driver, Meg Shirley, had a radio phone, and she was a volunteer fire fighter herself, so she knew what to do. Before
Meg could stop him, Jimmy Lynn ran across the road and
up onto the porch of the house.

"We knew who lived there—it was Henry Chepi and
his wife Anna. They were at least in their eighties and
pretty frail. I knew he was going to try to get them out. Meg
yelled for him to get away from there and something about
back draft. I ran over to stop him, while Meg did her best to
keep the rest of the kids on the bus as she radioed the call.

"I heard the fire siren go off on top of the tiny general
store at the cross roads a half mile back up the road, and
I knew help would be here quick. Practically every adult
is a volunteer, and no one ignores the siren. It might be
their time of need someday, so they know to be available for
everyone else's fire. Jimmy Lynn had his jacket off when I
got up the porch and he was winding it around his hands.
He said the front door was locked and too hot to touch. He
was going to try to break a window.

"'They're in there!'" he said fiercely to me. I took my
jacket off, too, scared but knowing we had to. We pounded
on the windows, but they just wouldn't break. I've never
seen anything like it. We know how easy old windows are
to break.

"Firefighters started to arrive, pulling on fire jackets as
they ran, grabbing the hose off the truck, running to connect it to the lone fire hydrant at the side of the road. Don

Bannerly, the chief volunteer, yelled at us to get off the porch.

"His brother Sam came over, while pulling on his heavy gloves and fire coat, and said, 'Give it up now. We'll take care of it. This is a fire that's been burning for a long time, Jimmy Lynn, prob'ly all night. The inside of that house is like an oven. You open that door and a whole lot of heat will come out of there, and it will be ignited into fire by the outside air. If you were standing in its path, you'd be one crispy critter right quick.'

"Jimmy Lynn looks up at him, and Sam says, 'Those people are long gone. They've prob'ly been turned to ash by now. That's what happens with such intense heat for so long. But, Jimmy Lynn, they would prob'ly have been asleep while the fire did its slow burn. The smoke would have got them while they slept. Most likely they never would have noticed a thing.'"

"Jimmy Lynn and I moved back off the porch, out of their way, holding onto each other, which we hadn't done in a long time. Something was on his face that I couldn't read. The firemen took their axes to the door handle and then jumped back. The door exploded open, and heat and fire blew out of it, then subsided. Smoke kept billowing out, but the firemen went inside with hose and axes and shovels, testing the floor as they went. They broke out some of the windows, and more smoke came out. After a little while they came out and stood around in the yard talking. They were waiting for the ambulance. It would take what was left of the Chepis to the hospital, where the coroner was waiting.

"We could hear that they had found the couple not too far inside the front door, side by side on the floor. One of the men had touched one of the bodies lightly on the shoulder as it lay on the floor, and the whole body crumpled in on itself. They were just ashes to ashes now.

"We didn't get on the school bus that day. We went back to our Granny's house. At least I did. Jimmy Lynn took off for the woods and stayed out there until dark. When he came in, he didn't talk, and he stayed that way for a few days, not going to school, hiding in the woods. I left him alone, knowing from experience that was all you could do. Towards the end of the week, when I was in the little general store up the road, picking up some flour for my Granny's flat bread, Sam was in there. He saw me and came over and pulled me aside.

'I tried to talk to your Granny,' he said, 'but she didn't get it. The old people always have their own version of things. So, I'll try tellin' you, and maybe you can help your brother. I hear how he's hanging out in the woods all day, not going to school. I think he's suffering from what we call survivor's guilt. He wonders why those nice old people died, and he's still alive. He wonders why he couldn't save them, and if a better boy would have found a way. He's prob'ly thinking the same thing about his parents. They'd be here now, if it wasn't for him.'

"That stops me in my tracks. I look at Sam, not knowing how he knows, not knowing how to say thanks for giving me the key to my brother, for helping me understand myself. He just chucks my chin and says, 'That's okay, Carrie Jean. I been there, too. Just go talk to him.'"

"So I got two things that day that my brother didn't get: a good man who's a role model and an understanding of what is and isn't our fault, couldn't be our fault. I got most of that in one look.

"I did talk to Jimmy Lynn, and I do think he understood about the survivor's guilt and got some comfort there. He started going back to school, but I always saw some kind of permanent lostness hanging over him that I couldn't chase away. It was with him the day he left to go to the city, six years later. He carried too many of his parents' choices and actions with him. I don't know why. Maybe it was that lack of a good male role model. I have Granny, who I still think is the strongest female role model you'll ever find. But whatever he had or didn't have, I loved him.

You can see how the loss of Jimmy Lynn was a hard loss for me. Maybe I should have expected to find him again, here, tonight, at this place of jumping. I thank you."

She stops and closes her journal, looking up at me. I give her a nod, and she nods back. She's already grateful to the Void, I think, whether she knows it or not. And this, I know for sure, is what the Void does. It produces your own truth for you, no matter how well you've hidden it.

I look to see who's next.

Kevin, the reader who quotes Dante's *Inferno*, is next. He smooths his short blonde hair with the hand that holds his journal and uses the other hand to tuck his neat black t-shirt into his creased jeans. His timing is perfect, and he instinctively moves us away from Carrie Jean's deeply personal and heartbreaking piece to something more universal. Kevin writes of the Void as though it contains nine rings of hell captured in the Earth. It's a story straight out of the *Inferno*, but he describes the rings in his own way, with rings for having no friends, the wrong clothes, or not fitting in. He tells about those who've jumped into the rings, like Dante's fortune tellers, out of a desire to belong. They end up having their heads on backwards because, by jumping, they've forfeited the right to have a future, so they can't look forward to anything. It's an ambitious story and I commend him for attempting it.

The relief on his face is evident to all.

Monica speaks up next. As she stands up, she switches her journal from hand to hand, wiping the alternate hand on her jeans. She isn't usually nervous. She takes a deep breath, shrugging her blonde braid off her shoulder, and begins.

"A leap into the Void is free floating into the Universe, in search of meaning," she says, and tells a short story of totally surrendering and being turned inside out by an experience she imagines of jumping. It's over before I have time to get into it, but when she finishes, I see tears gleaming on her cheeks in the lantern light. Some piece of it got into her.

I look around and see that Nathan has stepped up to the edge of the blanket to read next. He is tall and stands straight, and the light polishes his dark skin. His short dreads bob as he talks, both hands gripping his journal.

"I feel as if I know the Void, as if I've already jumped," he begins. I'm arrested by his first words.

"I see the tunnel in the dim light, the walls decorated here and there with graffiti or maybe rock art. The feel of the fall is with me, along with the time to think that falling grants you. I get a sense of other tunnels, other falling bodies."

I'm chilled, hearing Duncan Robert's descriptions come from the mouth of this boy. This kind of detail wasn't in Babe's article, because it had to be kept shorter. How can this be that he describes the fall in almost exactly the same way?

"I land on a ledge," Nathan reads, "on the side of the Void, and an angel comes to visit me, from out of the dark, hovering like a hummingbird. This stereotypical angel, with flowing robes and giant wings, extends his hand to me, urging me to take it, to come with him.

"Most birds either soar, relying on neighboring winds to move them in the air, or flap, creating carrying winds themselves, to get somewhere and then land. But not the hummingbird. It can hover at will, with or without wind, staying exactly where it wants to be, neither being in flight nor having landed. The angel is the same."

I think about what I know of hummingbirds. Their shoulders trace a horizontal figure eight in the air, over and over, a sign of the balance of the up and down lift they achieve. Some birds have to leap to fly, but the humming-bird is able to lift itself straight up. It's not hard to imagine the angel, hovering near the ledge, extending a hand to the boy. I can easily imagine this happening in the Void, and I'm shaken by the vision of it, transported by it. Nathan's voice calls me out of my reverie.

"I'm afraid that if I go with the Angel," he concludes, "I'll never be able to return to the clearing at the Void, to my life. It'll be like dying. I back away, refusing the angel's hand, and I slip off the ledge. I start falling again. I fall and fall, and the next thing I know, I wake up, here at the Void, as if I had been dreaming. But I know I wasn't." A look of wonderment still sits on Nathan's face.

There's a moment before the next reader steps up. Maybe the two students left find Nathan's story a hard act to follow. I would. Lonnie steps up, leaving only Donal.

"I've always been afraid of heights," he says. You'd never guess it by looking at him. He exudes a compact strength. He's dark and muscular, shorter than Nathan and Kevin by a few inches, but more physically powerful. His eyes are almost gold, and they flash in the light.

"I've been plagued by that fear all my life." He flashes a smile. "It's probably good I didn't jump freights like the other kids, but I still didn't want to be known as the kid who couldn't. And I didn't outgrow it, as my parents promised. It only got worse as I got older.

"My senior prom was held at a big hotel in the city. I went with this girl in my class, Colleen, knowing I would score that night." His face turns a little red, but he keeps going. "I had reserved a room at the hotel and everything, like a lot of the kids were doing. I was feeling grown-up, on top of the world. But then it turned out that my room was on the 9th floor. I'd never been in a hotel, so I didn't know that when I got up there my fear would kick in and I wouldn't be able to move away from the wall farthest from the row of floor-to-ceiling windows that looked down on the pool. I was literally paralyzed. Colleen had to shut all the drapes, which helped only a little because I was sure I could feel the building swaying. I guess you could say I was unable to perform that night, and I was eternally grateful that Colleen had gotten too drunk to remember. She was so sure we had done it, she told all her friends." He looks at us and laughs, shaking his head.

"My fear is there all the time, so coming to the edge of the Void was big for me, and I thought I might make a fool of myself somehow. But I felt called to try it. I'm so tired of being afraid—no flying, no high seats in stadiums, no skiing, no hiking, always making lame excuses for it, knowing everyone knows. I came here and much to my surprise, I found it felt friendly! This Void isn't out to hurt me, I knew that immediately. I felt like laughing. I even came to the edge with all of you, for the picture taking, and it was all good."

He's silent for a minute. "As things got quiet, and everyone started to write, I looked over at the Void, feeling peaceful, and I felt it looking back at me. That's when I figured out that my fear isn't of heights but of jumping! People had tried to tell me that before, but I never got it. I hadn't cared what they were calling it, I just didn't want to have it. Now I could see that the fear of jumping was underneath my fear of heights all along. I always equated jumping with death and that was my real fear—which is everybody's real fear! So now, for the first time, I have a handle on what I'm dealing with and it feels more normal to me. I feel more like you." He looks at them all with a grin. "Only better!" They laugh.

I don't know how much of that was written and how much he was just telling, but Lonnie is so pleased, I decide to let it go. This is the best he's done all year.

But he's not finished. "The Void spoke to me."

No one says anything, wondering if he's joking.

"The Void told me that there is no death. Life doesn't end. It just changes. And changes again. And again, more times than you can count. If we can believe that, we'll have no fear of jumping or of anything else. Life was always made for living, not dying," he says.

His eyes are shining as he looks up at me and says, "I may beat this thing yet." Everyone laughs. He looks at them seriously for a moment. "After all, I'm not afraid of the Void anymore." Then he moves back to his place on the blanket.

Everyone waits for Donal now. He centers his journal on his lap and begins to read, without moving up to the front of the group. His thick curly auburn hair shines in the light as he bends his head to the journal in his lap. His large hands rest open on his knees.

"I wish I had brought Brogan with me tonight, so he could jump into the Void."

Someone exclaims, "No!"

"Brogan was always a jumper," Donal says, with certainty, "from the time he was little. I remember when he was two and a half, he had a favorite little bench he kept in the living room, at the end of the couch. He would hold onto the arm of the couch as he climbed up on this bench that was maybe ten inches off the floor. He was about thirty-one inches tall then, so we're talking a third of his height. He would face forward, hold out his arms, airplane style, concentrate for a minute, and then jump. He'd land flat-footed, so pleased with himself he laughed out loud, and then he'd do it again. He'd do this over and over—I counted twenty-six times in a row once—before he'd get tired of it. He wasn't doing it for an audience. Usually there was no one in the room but him. I'd be in another room and hear him laugh, and I'd know what he was doing and come to spy on him. It made me laugh, too. I tried to ask him why he did it, and he'd just laugh and say, 'It fun, Donal!'

Donal looks up at us, love for his brother shining on his clear, honest face. "I loved the way he said my name. He made it sound like a foreign word." He looks back down at his journal, turning the page.

"When he was four, he would jump off the back fence, which was as tall as he was. By five, we couldn't keep him off the shed roof, easily twice as tall as he was. He still said he did it for the fun of it, and you'd hear him laugh as he did it. The sound of his laughing is one of the best sounds in the world; it makes everything seem perfect. Now he's six, and he's not jumping any more. He's not laughing any more, either. Oh, I know you'll all say, don't worry, Donal, he'll probably jump again, when he gets past this fear he has. Yeah, maybe. But I look around at the other six year olds, and they're not jumping either. They're racing each other or fighting or watching videos, like their big brothers. I don't want that for him. I want Brogan back. I want Brogan to jump. If that's gone, I don't know who he is. Maybe that's crazy. But I heard what you said about jumping." He looks at me, accusingly, and then they all do.

I look back, feeling a little hollow inside. Why do they think I have all the answers? Did I ever feel that way about my teachers? Maybe I did.

"So, when I sat here tonight, my first time at the Void, I thought this is where I should bring Brogan. I could take him to the edge of the Void and show him he has nothing to be afraid of here. I could let the Void reintroduce him to the idea of jumping. I mean, Duncan Robert jumped and he survived. And he sounded like Brogan in that story—happy, at home in his own skin, glad for each day. I want that for Brogan. Does that make me a terrible person? I'd be willing to jump with him. I could even hold him when we jump."

He looks at me again, and I feel a little nauseous. I take a minute to breathe, trying to stop the picture in my head of a child jumping, and the feeling of being responsible for it.

"Donal, I bet you were a lot like Brogan when you were his age. Look how you've turned out. Is that so bad? It looks pretty good to me. You've told an incredible story."

Donal slumps in his position on the ground now.

"He's better than me. He's got more good."

I'm at a loss about what to say next, and suddenly I wish Babe was here. She'd know what to say. Somebody needs to say something to this dejected boy.

Then a voice wafts out of the darkness.

"That's how I feel about my brother."

Donal turns to look at Carrie Jean, and she moves to his blanket, putting an arm around him when she gets there, smiling at him. He leans against her, though he's easily twice her size, and cries softly, quietly. She just sits and lets him, without saying another word. Brothers are being comforted, I think. They're all getting and giving things they didn't get and give at other places and times, with other people, living and dead. I'm so moved, I hardly know what to think.

The last writer has read. They pause, and it feels as if the night pauses with them. I look at them, sitting cross-legged on their blankets, some of them holding hands, leaning against each other. They've somehow all moved closer together. We all need a break, so I suggest that before we move on. They look at each other and laugh, stretching arms and legs and voices, chattering. They get up and move to ice chests and picnic baskets, distributing water bottles and thermoses with hot tea and coffee. They pass around bags of cookies and chips, really hungry suddenly, which is not at all unusual after an emotional purge, I know. It's as if we've literally cleared the way for food. I'm hungry and thirsty myself. And they'll soon be tired, too. So, I ask them to settle in with their food and drink, so that we can wrap things up quickly.

I ask them my questions, and they talk. They had to come, they tell me—they were already disturbed by what's been happening at the Void. Coming is better than not coming. Lonnie says it's like hearing footsteps outside your door in the middle of the night—you want to open the door, to settle it one way or another, but you also want to get under your bed or put your head under the covers. Your heart pounds in your chest either way. The difference, you realize, is that part of you wants to be alive, to find out, and part of you wants to be dead, to never have to know. He wants to know.

Monica explains her position. "It's like the time, a couple of years ago, when I witnessed a car wreck on the freeway, right in front of me. I mean, we're all doing at least 65 miles an hour, and a pick-up just nudges the Volkswagen Beetle next to it, as it tries to change lanes, and the next thing I know, the beetle is flipping over in mid-air, and I'm not knowing where it's going to land. All I can do is hit my brakes and try not to have to veer into anybody near me. All of us come to a stop, the Volkswagen is upside down, one lane over, the pick-up has finally fish-tailed to a stop. Cops come almost immediately, and one comes to my window to ask what I saw and who I am. Though nothing has happened to me, I don't have so much as a scratch on me, I'm upset enough that I can't remember my phone number or address. I'm doing good to remember my name. The cop reassures me that this is pretty common and not to worry, they have enough witnesses, and to call if I remember anything more. All I know is, I'm messed up in some way I can't lay hold of but is very real. That's how I feel tonight. The Void hasn't done anything to me, but the possibility of it doing something seems very real. Does that make any sense? I mean, it's not going to grab me, but it's like it has somehow." Others nod. She adds, "That feeling stayed with me for a while after the wreck, and I think the Void feeling will, too."

Carrie Jean says, "At first, I couldn't help but wonder if my brother was in there, right? Like, is that what it's for? Is that where people go to die? Is it like the path to heaven or hell? But as I laid there in the grass, I suddenly knew that my brother had gone on, not down into some hole in the ground, that this Void wasn't like some mass grave that had my brother." She gave a little laugh. "Doesn't that sound like a movie—*The Void That Ate My Brother*? But I just felt my brother's freedom, and it made me feel free, too." She laughed again. "Does *that* make any sense? Probably not."

Much of the sadness has left her face. The smile that's forming there doesn't seem so foreign anymore.

Donal says, "I thought I might feel the urge to jump, like it might be calling to me to jump. I've heard it has that power. But I ended up feeling pretty peaceful here. Like, it didn't want me, and maybe it even wished me well. It made me feel like everything's going to be all right, including my little brother. I know *that* doesn't make any sense!" More laughter. "The little twerp," he says, also smiling. "Maybe I *should* bring him here."

"I thought I did jump!" said Nathan. "I wanted to imagine what falling into it would be like, and I just laid there on my blanket and closed my eyes and imagined it. And it was so real. I just ended up writing what I saw. You know, like you tell us to, with your Dragnet theory—'just the facts, ma'am.'" I had to explain that reference to them, but now they like it.

So, I ask them, "Is this your story of the Void, then? A happy, feel-good kind of place?"

"I don't know. I still wonder why our town has one, and there isn't one anywhere else. I still wonder what it's here for. Maybe that's why no one talks about it—they don't know what it's here for. Why can't geology explain it? Or archaeology?" Kevin asks.

"No money in it," Lonnie says.

"What do you mean, no money in it?"

"No reason to spend money on it, to figure anything out. It can't make anybody any money."

"I think they tried, over the years," Monica says. "They did some tests, like dropping ropes down, to find its bottom, like they did with Bottomless Lakes. And they couldn't find any bottom. I think they've tried to send spelunkers down, but they didn't see much point, since it seemed pretty featureless in there. Maybe they could do more, now, what with all the technology."

"Yeah, if there was money in it," Lonnie adds.

They laugh.

"But why is everyone so afraid of it? Why weren't we allowed near it? Why'd they try to fill it in? Just because people might jump?" Monica asks.

"Because somebody did jump," Lonnie says. "I remember a story, a long time ago, from my cousin, who is part Algonquin and part Lakota. He said he knew there was somebody who jumped, over a lover's triangle or something. He said the older generation knows more than they're telling. They value their traditions more than they value people. And they try to blame everything that goes wrong on white interference, so you never know what really happened. But he said that's what doomed the Void."

Carrie Jean looks at Lonnie. "I've heard that story, too." That troubled look has returned to her face. "Sometimes they even say that's where my mother jumped. But my Granny doesn't say, and I think if it was true, she would have told me."

The group gets quiet, thinking about this and staring towards the Void. It's time to wrap it up for the evening. It's class as usual next week, and they are to write in their journals in the meantime, look at their pictures, and see what more they might have to say about it all. They pack up, which takes several minutes, and move toward their cars, talking quietly as they go. I'm giving a couple of them rides, so I pack up, too. I'm thinking about the Void and its long history and how I'm about to become part of it. I know I can't tell them that, but I wish I could. I wonder if Babe is still up.

CHAPTER FIFTEEN

Babe Remembers

IN THE WEEKS THAT follow our visit with Duncan Robert, I find myself inventing a kind of training for the jump, primarily to quell my anxiety at waiting for it. The jump isn't until May, when Spring Break is scheduled, but still, I try to eat healthier foods and exercise more, though I can't seem to quell my addiction to french fries. They're comfort food. The waitresses at Alpine Alley, my favorite café in town, say, "Well, we can fix you a grilled cheese," when I ask about getting anything vegetarian.

Under pressure from Henry, I finished the article within a week or two of the interview, and he published it as quickly as he could, so that it was out by mid-October. Of course he compressed and cut a good part of the life out of it, but the story line is still there, and the readers know Duncan Robert not only survived his jump into the Void, he survived what he ran into down there, too. I don't know what anyone really thinks of what he ran into because they're strangely afraid to talk to me about it. They say nothing unless pressed, and then they think what I want is a compliment. The best guess I can make is that they want to think I made it all up, like the old newspaper serials. After all, *they* haven't seen Duncan Robert.

My anxiety drives me to walk in the early mornings, before the sun is up, so I can catch the sunrise, feeling as if the sun feeds me, too. Often my walks end at the Void. I can't say I plan it, but there and back is the equivalent of a good 10K, with a few gentle hills thrown in for added benefit. And it is the source of my anxiety. I find I have to keep moving, re-directing my attention away from the jump and back to more emotionally manageable things, or I tend to stop breathing and become catatonic, staring into space for long periods, a cup of cold tea halfway to my mouth or sweat pants half on or standing in the middle of a room holding an empty envelope. Sometimes I walk twice a day, sunset as well as sunrise. I think I'm trying to walk myself all the way into my decision to jump.

Miles's work as an adjunct professor at the community college keeps him busy—the interminable prep for his classes and always the grading of papers—he keeps a stack in his car, on his desk, and beside his bed. They never seem to diminish. He teaches four classes in writing composition, even though three is considered a full load for a tenured person (who would also have grading help). He likes to give lots of assignments, too, to keep the students writing so much that they can put pen to paper with ease and produce a stream of words with a beginning, middle and end. I envy him his preoccupation with work, knowing there is solace in it for him.

I, on the other hand, am in the worst possible place with work—in between things. I don't know when my next pay check is coming, I don't know what to prepare for, and I try not to think about the fact that I don't have any savings. But I am a writer, that is my craft, and this is one of the few ways I know of to try to make a living at it. I'm not cut out for teaching, like Miles. Watching him only confirms that. He has a seemingly endless supply of patience and a huge reserve of calm, with a mind able to hone the argument in a paper down to its core and know if it is good and why it is good. Or if it isn't good. He has a sure and stable confidence that doesn't second guess itself or let you do so either. I often feel like one more student in his presence, but do my level best to keep this hidden from him, usually through shameless posturing.

Miles is a runner, another reason for me to get in shape. He and Duncan Robert often ran together, on the back roads, to stay in shape for backpacking and skiing. Even so, he's not without vices. He does smoke from time to time, still allowing himself a cigarette or two after dinner, only rarely three.

"What makes a three-cigarette day?" I asked him once.

"Student grades have gone out," he said.

I laughed.

"I'm serious," he said. "It can bring out the worst in them."

"Really?" I can't remember ever having argued with a teacher over a grade, figuring they knew what they were doing, generally speaking, and I deserved whatever they gave me.

"Oh, it's really just a handful of them, but it's the same bad arguing tactics over and over."

He didn't elaborate, but I know he isn't an arguer. I imagine him calm and sure in the face of those entitled students.

As a newspaper person, I don't argue, either, having learned the hard way that can shut down an interview quicker than most anything. Maybe that's why neither of us has argued about the jump. In that hotel room, after Duncan Robert told us the story of his jump and left us to go back to his world as he would now create it, we had looked at each other calmly and known that we would jump, no question about it.

So maybe there was nothing to argue about—no pros or cons, no cost-benefit analysis, no logic model. Not that we weren't scared; any normal people would be. But before we even heard from Duncan Robert, Miles had spent months after his jump learning everything he could about jumping and about Voids, trying to piece together the whys and wherefores of it all. And I've been building a background in it practically all my life. We've got a familiarity with the Void most people don't have, and we agree on what we know.

Miles has the added experience of knowing a jumper. Duncan Robert is one of his two remaining family members, close as family can get. So close Duncan Robert could tell Miles he was going to jump, and Miles didn't try to stop him. This means Miles is following in a trusted family member's footsteps.

What am I doing? I'm following a childhood call, a hunch, a feeling. Well, that's what makes a good newspaper person, and I'm being that, too. And who am I kidding? I can't *not* do it, no matter how it unsettles my days and my nights and my sense of who I am. I have the peace of knowing I'm doing it.

Duncan Robert came back to talk about it, and for a few weeks I knew people in town talked about it, and the article brought some out-of-town visitors—the curious, the thrill seeking, the self-appointed overseers of such public happenings. While that brought some extra revenue for the local businesses that catered to the tourist trade, some people couldn't help but believe it was for the wrong reasons. Most town people believed they were being laughed at behind their backs, and they didn't like it.

Meanwhile, Miles and I went on planning our jump. We need to prepare our loved ones, and we want to spare them as much shock and worry as we can. We need to tell them as early as possible, to give them time to ask all their questions and get as used to the idea as they can. It helps that we both have small families. Miles has one sister, and I have two, Marla and Kelly. None of our parents are alive, and we're not close to any extended family. Of course, for Silvia this will be the second jump of a close family member, so I wondered about her reaction. I still have a picture in my mind of her looking for comfort at the Void after Duncan Robert's jump, tossing flowers into the darkness, hoping somehow that he knew. But Miles has been to see her, and she seemed to have known before he did that he was going to do it.

As for my sisters, I don't feel good about this. Miles and I weren't each other's opposing voices, but this is where I think my sisters will come in, loaded for argument. Both will think jumping is an act of willful and senseless insanity. And though it occurred more than twenty years ago, my act of jumping will remind both of them of the unexpected loss of our parents, something we never talk about any more, but something we haven't completely made peace with, either. It doesn't seem we can ever stand in a Zen place of complete acceptance of it. I don't mean to make all of us pick that scab again, but I don't mean for it to stop my jumping, either. I'm a rip-the-band-aid-off kind of person, so I want to get the telling of them done.

CHAPTER SIXTEEN

Babe and Her Sisters

SO, THE FIRST THING I really do to prepare for the jump is to bring my sisters to town, the last of my immediate family, to tell them I am going to jump and to say good bye. I plan the logistics of the visit, but my emotional control feels as thin as paper stretched over sharp objects. For all three of us, our early acquaintance with disappointment in life keeps that feeling at the ready, along with self-righteous anger. I remember one visit with Marla. She felt abandoned by our long absence, but rather than talking about it, we fought fiercely about how she hadn't heard from Kelly in a while. I tried to defend Kelly, and we almost ended the visit screaming at the top of our lungs and slamming doors. But we've held together through a lot worse than that in life, and we have a solid foundation. It's a tie that binds but can still feel tenuous, riddled as we are by our fears about the permanence of any relationship. I know I'll be testing it yet again.

Silvia found us someone's holiday cabin just outside of town to use for our reunion, since I'm still living in the little studio apartment above the bank. I gave them a just a couple weeks' notice, asking them to come a few weeks before Thanksgiving, but my sisters came—Marla, the older one and Kelly, the younger one. I, Babe, am in the middle (in more ways than one, I've always thought).

Being the coward I am, I told them in a later email about the jump, attaching a copy of my article, so they'd know the need for a visit now. They haven't had a chance to voice how appalled they are, so I know they've come full of dire admonitions with the intention of talking me out of jumping. I'm prepared for that. I know how crazy it sounds, and I'm sure I'd be doing the same thing, if roles were reversed.

I find I'm inordinately pleased that they've come. I can't help myself. I smile when I see them and rush forward to hug them. They've flown in together and rented a car to drive to the village. They're a little travel weary, unsure of where they actually are and worried about the loss that may be their reward for coming. Their tight smiles betray the fact they've been talking and their guard is up against something unnamable, something that their own sister is making them shake hands with.

I look at Marla, with her pale hair tucked neatly into a bun at the base of her neck and her travel clothes still fitted crisply to her thin frame, and know that she has brought her matching pajamas and robe and slippers; she has brought her own teabags because she always has only tea and toast for breakfast; and she has brought her own pillow, because you can't be too sure. Marla is an art historian, with a master's degree, working as a curator in a history museum outside of Portland, Oregon.

Marla is really a kind of hero of mine, though I've never told her that. She and her husband Cal (her high school sweetheart) adopted two kids. They started as foster parents, going through the state's long and trying process of screening and licensure, and caring for kids who'd been in the state's care since they were weeks old and had been moved dozens of times. These kids stole, hoarded food, had night terrors, and acted out their anger at an uncaring world in an array of unspeakable ways that must have driven my fastidious sister crazy.

I would go to help when I could, having gotten approval from Henry to do a series of articles on the state of foster care in our state. The problems are pretty much the same nationwide, but I had no idea what I was getting myself into. I was there one weekend when they had temporary care of an infant—just what everyone seems to want most, and in theory more pleasant than sullen or abused teenagers. Well, this was an infant who seemed to be feigning his own death. Lethargic was not a strong enough word for the lifelessness of him.

"Failure to thrive," the caseworker called it. "It's how infants express grief and loss."

It knocked the wind out of me. All of a sudden I knew I couldn't survive the telling of his story. But my sister could and did take in all their stories, without batting an eye. These are the horrors you read about in the newspaper and maybe sometimes wonder what ever became of those kids. Well, if they're lucky, my sister and others like her are what became of those kids. Marla and Cal were a way station for something like sixty-seven kids in a two-year period.

"It isn't hard," she said. "You just treat them as if you love them, before you do."

Always considered the 'wild one,' Kelly is sort of bad-girl pretty, with unruly hair and funky clothes, everything a little unkempt and mismatched. She takes pride in this image of herself, cultivating it by being a partier, a dabbler in drugs, a singer with a heavy metal band in New Mexico, where she lives. Her boyfriends are always a little scary, with obscure histories and tattoos that could be prison art. Her day job is design—bohemian interiors, alternative store windows, ethnic restaurants.

But Kelly is a caregiver, too, in her own way. On the side, she rescues animals and has for years, both with official groups and on her own. She regularly works with hospice part time, too. She is assigned one dying person at a time and spends up to a year with that person and his or her family, helping them sort out the dying in ways that none of them could on their own. She doesn't say much about it.

"This isn't necessarily anything healthy," she said once. "It's just us endlessly offering the help to strangers that we never got ourselves. Maybe some time I'll get over it." Then she laughed.

We had almost never talked about the sexual abuse by our father that had haunted our childhoods, and that I had revisited when I stood at the edge of the Void. Kelly acknowledged she always thought *something* had happened, and had even had a therapist she visited for a while tell her so. Kelly stopped seeing the therapist after that because, she said, she didn't want to know. She knew her limits, and I had to respect her for that.

When I asked Marla about the abuse, she denied that any such thing had ever happened, suggesting without actually saying it that she thought I suffered from some form of mental delusion. Then she started in on her reminiscences about our childhood, always building a tidy and well-ordered picture of it. This smacked more of delusion than anything I could ever dream up, but it was so well-suited to her nature, I knew there would be no arguing her out of it. She would never admit that such an offensive thing could have happened in our family.

It reminds me of how I came to be called Babe. My real name is Elizabeth. I'm called Babe because that's what Marla named me, shortly after I was born. Everyone referred to me as "the baby," and for Marla, it became "da babe." Her name for me stuck, unchallenged.

"Come in! Come in! You guys are a sight for sore eyes! How long has it been?"

We come together, right there on the front porch, for our signature three-way hug, so no one gets left out. And we hold on, wobbling and laughing, as they grapple with purses, coats, and bags.

"Let me help!" I grab for the bag Kelly is thrusting at me.

"You look great! You haven't cut your hair!" Kelly cries.

"I think we saw each other last four years ago this summer, when we celebrated the signing of the final adoption papers on the kids," Marla says over her shoulder as she wrestles her own bag through the front door.

"No!" I say. "That can't be right! Four years! We must not love each other!"

"Clearly we don't!" Kelly laughs. "Or we love our own lives more!"

"That can't be right, either! That might be healthy!"

I drag her bag through the front door, as if it was hugely heavy, which it isn't. She throws her coat over my head. We're laughing like teenagers. Kelly and I always do.

Marla is looking out the living room's bay window, and I drop everything to stand next to her, my arm on her shoulder.

"It's quite a view," she says. She turns to look at me. "Nice place."

"Thanks. Miles's sister Silvia found it for us. His house is not far from here."

"Let us help pay for it."

"We got if for free. The people are thrilled to have someone in it. We'll leave them a bottle of wine or some-thing. Silvia will know."

"Where can we put this stuff?" Kelly calls as she heads down the hall. "Show us our rooms!"

I pick up her bag again and follow her. "There's a bed-room for each of us, bathroom at the end of the hall. Pick whichever room you want."

"Wait a minute," Marla says as she follows us. "I'd like the room that faces east, so I can get the sunrise."

"You can sleep in!" Kelly says.

"I get up early for me, not for anyone else."

"Well, which way is east?"

"East is the front of the house," I say.

"Okay, I'll take the one farthest back, so I can sleep in for sure," Kelly says. I follow with her bag as Marla turns off into the first room on the right. Their rooms have double beds, mine has twins. The rooms are a lot like what we grew up with—average sized, mixed furniture, matching curtains and bedspreads, pale carpet on the floors—nice, but a little early-American for me.

As they settle into their rooms and change into more comfortable clothes, I lay out the prepared pasta, bread, and salad I've brought. I've got red and white wine—I don't know if Marla drinks anything these days.

We eat around the large kitchen table, watching the sun's fading colors on the lake. We catch up on the details of their travel, everyone's latest news—Marla's kids are preparing for the annual spelling bee, and Kelly is an extra in a television series being filmed in Albuquerque—and I answer their questions about the town. We'll tour around and eat out tomorrow.

It's like thousands of old times—who knows how many meals we've had together—in which we reaffirm who we are to each other and remember how deeply our ties go, despite the erosion of time and distance and events. We clean up the kitchen together, loading the dishwasher and then take our coffee and plate of chocolates into the living room.

Then we begin to talk about the jump.

"So, you're going to do this thing," Marla states.

"Yeah, I am." I wish I still smoked.

"Can we see it—the Void?" Kelly asks.

"Well, sure. Miles held class out there the other night. It's not closed or anything."

"Held class out there! The school allows that?"

"It's not elementary school. They hold classes wherever they want."

"That's not how I remember school."

"Not all the time." I pause a minute. "Come on, Marla. You're not my mother." I'm fighting against feeling like a bad child. How can she still have this effect on me?

"I feel like you need one." She pauses, too. "What does Silvia say about all this?"

"You can meet her and ask her yourself if you want. Miles says she's not surprised. She knew he'd jump."

"But she has the advantage of having had someone come out," Kelly says. "That's the thing we don't know about you." She reaches her hand across the table between us to take my hand, and we grip hands a minute.

"I do take that seriously," I tell her, "and we can talk about it."

"Well, I'm horrified!" Marla blurts, getting up to pace. "And so disappointed in you! Why would you do such an incredibly selfish thing? I feel as if I'm talking to one of my children! All I can think is that you've climbed on the bandwagon, because jumping is popular now! Your job probably expects it! It will sell papers! And you must be in need of attention yourself! Are you that easily influenced, enough to risk your own life? Did you even give us a thought?"

"Wait a minute," I try to interrupt her flow, probably not a good idea. "Didn't you read the article? You don't see any value in jumping at all?" I'm annoyed that's the only thing I can come up with, but her assault leaves me scattered. She always takes the offensive, firing the first salvo, leaving me the defensive, a position that's scrambling from the get-go.

"Value?" she laughs scornfully, an adult laugh she's good at. "In being a copycat? That makes no sense! I blame Miles for this!"

"You've never even met him!"

"Clearly, your boundaries aren't well set. It's all about working for the media, which is all about garnering attention, and boundaries go by the wayside. Clearly, Miles has romanticized jumping, to salvage the image of his nephew. He wants to make him a hero! For jumping into a hole!"

Out of the corner of my eye, I see Kelly stifling a laugh. I feel my own emotions slide that direction, too, always the path of least resistance. It means Marla wins by default. Kelly and I have been there many times, but I'm not going there this time, even though I did almost laugh at the "hole" comment, too.

"So, I have no mind of my own. That's what you think." Things are still deteriorating too quickly and too thoroughly to see how to salvage them.

"No, it's because you DO have a mind that I can ask these questions!"

"Alright, let's not do this all night. Do you have any real questions we can talk about? I see this as the adventure of a life time." Oops. That doesn't help.

"That sounds like a cheap advertising slogan!"

"For condoms," Kelly adds, and the two of us break into laughter, irritating Marla further. As the big sister, she'd still thinks she should have the definitive word on the subject, and she sees she's not going to get it. I understand that what I'm doing scares her, triggering every mothering urge she has. But I won't take the role that leaves me.

Kelly, on the other hand, is like me, drawn to the excitement of the risk and though it scares her, too, she looks for ways to vicariously share in trying it on.

"Hey, I'm writing a song about it!" We both start to laugh. Marla gets up to make more coffee and stares out the window while it brews.

"What should we call it?" She turns pages in her journal, which she's pulled from her bag, to a clean page. "And you should let me do your horoscope. We should make sure the timing is right."

Something about the jump resonates with her, like she's got a void calling her, too, and she's just been too afraid to heed it. Now I've made it harder to ignore. Her sudden restlessness creates an unease in the room that causes her sense of humor to flee. I immediately miss it, realizing how much we've always relied on it to manage any tension. Now we have to confront the issue head on, which is pretty much never fun.

Marla gets her fresh coffee and comes back to the living room to sit next to me. They want to know why. Duncan Robert did it to find his life, to quell the restlessness that let him know he wasn't in alignment with anything.

"You like your life, your job, your friends. Why would you need to jump?" Marla asks.

Because every life needs a jump, I think, but don't say.

"Doing it scares the crap out of me, but not doing it is worse. I can't imagine wanting to live my life past this point if I don't do it. That's the truth and the best I can tell you."

And it doesn't satisfy them. It's selfish, they say.

"We don't want to lose a sister, and you're too young to die. It's horribly unfair to put us through this." Marla says most of this as she paces the room, but Kelly chimes in regularly. "What's wrong with a normal future—marriage and kids—you'd make a great mom. Don't you want that?"

Most of these questions aren't really answerable, or the answers are obvious—I've learned from Miles that they're just arguments, rhetorical in nature, used to further the user's position.

I'm used to it, though, having grown up with it. Most of us aren't good arguers. After a while they get tired of my answers, and of their own anger at me for choosing to do something that disturbs the order of things. Seeing honest feelings on their faces moves me. I see the consequences for others of this thing I'm doing for me. It reminds me how much I love them and they love me. I know them inside and out, and I still love them. What we have is each other.

Finally, Kelly can't believe there's nothing romantic driving my jump with Miles. "I mean, you're doing the jump together. Hello. Very Romeo and Juliet of you," she drawls. She thinks he's probably attractive and that's what men are for, some kind of romantic engagement, when you're young—and apparently she thinks of me as 'still youngish.' What else could it be, in her mind? When I assure her over and over that our relationship "isn't like that, never has been, we're just the best of friends," she raises her eyebrows and looks at me pointedly, to remind me she wasn't born yesterday. I'm left to assume she's never been "the best of friends" with any male, ever. Her loss.

Arguments exhausted for now, we head to bed. Marla's the early riser, and this trip will be no exception. Kelly's sleep paraphernalia—her lavender-scented, 100 percent light-blocking sleep mask; her hot pink, soft foam ear plugs; her sleep supplements, just in case—will ensure she doesn't get up early. She's brought her chillable, flax-seed-filled eye pillow, too, in case of headaches. Or hangovers, I think, chiding myself to be more charitable. I take to my usual routine—once in my room, I turn the lights out and stand at an open window to say goodnight to the night. It's hard for me to sleep without an open window, no matter what the weather. As I stand in the cool air now, I think of the Void, always in a state of night and always open. I know what some of the village people mean when they say they feel it out there, as if it is a living, breathing thing, waiting. As I tuck myself in, I feel sure that it will find me in my dreams. I wonder what Miles is doing.

CHAPTER SEVENTEEN

Babe and Her Sisters at the Void

THE NEXT MORNING, MARLA has gone to the grocery store early to find some suitably green things for lunch and dinner. Her cheerful mood seems unaffected by our talk the previous night and all the things wrong with my decision. Kelly is up, though not enthusiastic about it, and takes her eye pillow out of the freezer as she talks, placing the cold pillow over her tilted-back face. She tells me that she made the classic move last night, intending to go to Miles' place with a bottle of wine to get to the bottom of the *real* story of the jump. She explains that she was wide awake, unable to sleep after all our discussion of voids and jumps. She started the rental car without turning the lights on, so as not to wake us, and headed back down the road, sure she could find Miles's house, which I had pointed out on our way to the cabin.

I swallow every angry, ugly word that comes immediately to mind, having used them all before with her. This would not be the first boyfriend of mine to receive a late-night visit from Kelly—I'd lost a few to her, and we'd had knock-down, drag-out fights in which we had to be pulled apart by Marla. Once, years later, as I was bemoaning the loss of a boyfriend I had particularly liked, a therapist said to me, "She didn't lose you if she stole him, right?" I understood that fear of being left, but having some kind of logic for it helped only a little. However, when I step back, I find I'm not as upset this morning. I realize I'm not worried about Miles succumbing to her wiles, and I know I would have heard from him if she'd been there.

"I couldn't do it, though."

"What could have stopped you? Surely not the fact I have a professional, working relationship with him that you could have destroyed."

"No. It felt too pathetic to me, too old Betty Davis, you know, in the movie where she plays twins, one good one, one evil one," she says. "You and I are the twins," she clarifies. She didn't have to tell me which role she thought she should play. "Maybe you're too old to play the good twin anymore."

I have to laugh. "Maybe you care about me too much to do it!"

She laughs and says, "No, that can't be it. Maybe I wasn't drunk enough."

"That's hardly possible." We laugh again.

"But I was still too wound up to sleep, so me and my bottle of wine decided to go to the Void instead. I knew it was just up the road the other direction." She lifts the eye pillow from one eye and looks at me a little defensively, a little proud.

So the Void was calling her. I'm not surprised.

"My usual schedule would have me up half the night anyway, and I wanted to see what the attraction is." She takes the eye pillow off her eyes and gets up to pour herself some coffee, avoiding further eye contact with me.

"I'm not exactly sure what all happened after that," she says, "because that bottle of wine did get drunk, but," she turns to me with a genuinely perplexed look on her face, "I think I lay at the edge of the Void and had a long conversation with it."

She shakes her head and continues to the 'fridge, getting her cream and returning to her chair.

"I may have tried to jump in," she says quietly, looking at me. "But I have the distinct impression it wouldn't let me." She stirs the cream into her coffee. "But maybe I dreamed it. I thought there was an old Native American woman there, too. She reminded me of Mom. She knew who I was and showed me lights coming out of the Void." She sips her coffee absent mindedly. "I liked her. I don't even remember getting myself home."

I'm upset by all this, of course. For one thing, there's already been too much attention on the Void lately, and any of it could interfere with our jump. I look at her.

"Are you mad? Did I ruin anything?"

"No. Truth be told, you did exactly what I would have done. " I look at her and smile. I'm not going to be Marla's child and I'm not going to be Kelly's parent, but it's hard. I think a minute, thankful Marla hasn't returned from the store. "Let me make some calls."

I make a couple of well-placed phone calls, beginning with Miles.

"Your relationship with your sister is so mature!" I whisper-shout to him.

"No, it's just been repressed. It got better after Duncan Robert. Kelly sounds like one of my students."

"She's thirty-three!"

"Still, no harm done. And it sounds like she had a bit of an experience out there."

Dammit! He's so kind, I feel like the mean twin.

I talk to my Native American contact at the sheriff's office and find no one seems to know anything about Kelly's outing. I come back to the kitchen table and sit opposite Kelly again. "I think everything is okay. No harm done."

"That's good news." She sighs with relief. "I'm sorry, Babe." She's always sorry after, but she seems a bit more genuinely contrite this morning. She searches my face a minute. "There's really something to this Void thing, isn't there?"

I nod.

"I'm not going to argue against it anymore." She gets up to go take a shower and then turns to me with a grin. "Besides, I thought Miles wasn't your boyfriend!"

Before I can answer, we hear Marla drive up outside. Without saying a word, we know that neither of us will mention any of this to her. This is an old pattern of ours—there are things you can say to Marla and things you can't. She has her patterns, too, as self-proclaimed surrogate mother, that warrant our precautions.

Marla comes in with bags of groceries, exuding order, focus, and good planning. "You two aren't dressed yet!" she exclaims, though it's barely 8:30. "I've got plans for us," she says, as she begins to unpack the groceries, putting them away as she pulls them out of the bags, not letting them rest on the counter for even a moment.

"What plans?" Kelly asks petulantly, putting her cold pillow back over her eyes. "I've got plans, too. To do nothing! I'm on vacation."

"I think you'll like this," Marla says to her and then turns to me. "I thought we'd take a picnic up to the Void."

I look at her, surprised.

"We can see your Void and have time together," she says, "and if I'm not wrong, we can also get some exercise in!"

"How?" I ask, stalling for time as I try to determine if I want to do this or not.

"Aren't there hiking trails up there? I thought I saw some on the map," she says.

"Well, yes, there are." I remember I'd heard that. I've just never gone up there with the intent of hiking. "We could do that."

"Okay, then." She looks at Kelly. "Are you in?"

Kelly raises the pillow from one eye to look back at her. "Okay, but I get a shower first. And another cup of coffee."

"No problem," Marla says, Miss Congeniality this morning. "I've got to make lunch anyway."

Kelly heads for the shower.

"I thought I'd do wraps," she says, starting her preparation. "You get a salad in them, along with your protein." She looks at me speculatively. "So where'd she go last night?"

"What?"

"I heard the car leave. I'm a mom. You always hear."

"The Void. She went to the Void."

Marla pauses. "Wow. At night. By herself."

I hear the admiration in her voice and, surprised, say, "You wouldn't be afraid to do that."

"Well of course I would. I've got no experience with anything like that. I'm like anybody else. It scares me." She looks at me. "Didn't you think I could be scared?"

"Not really. I don't think I've ever seen you scared."

She laughs. "Well, I don't think I've ever seen you scared, either!"

I laugh, too. "I'm scared all the time!"

"You'd never know it. Look at what you're doing! Look at your life!"

"What about my life?"

"Babe," she says intently, "you *never* stayed within the *known*. That's why I didn't keep arguing this Void thing with you. You've constructed a whole life for yourself outside anything that's known to be reliable, safe, or certain. The opposite of what I've done. I live in a community of people doing the exact same thing I'm doing!"

"I thought you disapproved of everything I did."

"Not at all! I worry, like any mother would." She laughs again. "You'd think I could let go of that—of thinking I'm the mother of you two—but I don't know if I ever can. It's like a curse!" She shakes her head. "But I know it has helped me be a better mom to my own kids."

"Really."

"Well, yes. I'm able to let them be."

At that moment, Kelly comes into the kitchen, dressed, wet hair in a towel.

"Great shower," she says, pouring herself yet another cup of coffee. "I'm going to dry my hair outside." She heads out the back door to the sunny porch. "Beautiful day!" she throws back over her shoulder, and I hear her singing something under her breath.

"After all, you two didn't turn out too badly," Marla says with a smile.

"I get up to give her a hug. She gets up, too, and we hold onto each other for a minute.

Within half an hour lunch is made, and we're packed up and on our way. From the cabin, it only takes about ten minutes to get to the Void. It's not even ten yet, and the food is tucked safely into the cooler, so we've got plenty of time for a hike. We walk through the grass to the edge of the Void. Marla stops just short of it.

"Close enough for me! I've got a little fear of heights out in the open like this, without a railing or anything."

Kelly goes to the edge and crouches, looking into it. It's how I must have looked to Miles. "Wow," she breathes. "You can feel it." She looks up at me, and I see her awe. "I feel it."

Marla points out the trail head, just east of the Void. I'd never noticed the little wooden sign marking it before. The trail leads up a gentle hill through a tunnel of trees; it's wide enough for us to walk side-by-side most of the time. The little sign has told us there is a viewpoint about a mile and a half up.

We don't talk much on the walk. It's very peaceful, the light made dim by the leaves, the forest quiet, seeming to have settled into its own morning meditation. At one point, Marla says, "Is this the first time the three of us have ever hiked together? I think it is."

"I think it is, too," I say. "Kelly and I do hikes sometimes when I visit her in New Mexico."

"But you're a walker," Kelly says, "every day, right?"

"I try. It works better than meditation for me."

"I'm the mother of two," Marla says and laughs. "I'm well-exercised." We laugh, too.

Soon we've arrived at the viewpoint, an opening in the trees that lets us look out over the meadow where the Void lives. We can see our car in the distance, parked on the edge of the dirt road. There's an iron bench near the hill's edge, with a plaque on it, in memory of someone long gone. All three of us sit on it to observe the sea of trees that surround the meadow and the road, stretching out to cover the hills that surround us. A breeze moves through the trees around us and down to the grass in the meadow. We watch it move through the grass, approaching the Void as if it is going to jump. It passes over the Void and travels through the grass beyond.

Marla turns to look at me. "What if you don't come out? Cal and I had to plan for our own deaths. You have to when you have children. Have you planned for yours? Have either of you?"

"Hey, wait a minute," Kelly protests. "I'm not going anywhere."

"We all are," Marla says to her. Kelly has no response to that.

"What did you do?" I ask.

"The usual. Saw a lawyer. Made a will. In our case, everything goes to the kids. Decided who the kids would go to."

Kelly and I look at each other. Nothing has ever been said to either of us, so we realize we must not be where the kids are going.

Marla sees our exchange of looks. "Oh come on! This is not about you! We were thinking of the kids. How not to disrupt their lives any more than necessary. I told you. We live in a community of people like us, who deal with fostered and adopted kids daily, in their own homes. Our kids know them. They all go to the same schools, have the same doctors and therapists. That felt right to us. But let me know if you disagree." She looks pointedly at us, then looks away. "These are high-needs kids, you know."

"No, no," I say, "I don't disagree. I just didn't know what I felt. Maybe I felt responsible, as if I should offer. A good sister would offer."

"Me, too," says Kelly. "I mean I knew it would never work, but part of me wished it could. Those are some great kids. And I'd like to have kids someday."

"Me, too," I say. "I'm almost thirty-five! Tick-tick-tick."

"I'm not far behind you! I hear that clock, too."

Marla laughs. "Well, now that we're out of the hypothetical, let's get back to you, Babe. Have you thought about it? About not coming out?"

"It's a good question, because it has two answers. First, I have no doubt I'm coming out. None at all. And yet, it's such an odd thing to be doing—to engage in an act that seems to be courting death—that I can't help but think about it. That's why Miles and I have each created a last will and testament. Mine is in a safety deposit box at the bank I live above. I'll give Marla the key, since she's already a signer on my accounts." Kelly and I both have Marla as co-signer on our bank accounts, something we did from the first time we ever had a bank account.

"What do you think happens when you die?" Kelly asks, leaning back on the bench. "I think there's no real death, just a transition. How about you?" She's looking at me.

"I don't believe in death, either. That's what I've always believed at some level, but Duncan Robert's jump clarified it for me. He came back from the dead, in a sense, and I believe in what happened to him in the Void, too. Everything that happened to him reiterated that life is not about anybody ending, ever."

"I don't know," Kelly says. "I still might scream if the plane went down."

"Do you believe in God?" Marla asks, as she watches the trees.

"I believe in the idea of God," I say, "and I believe we're that idea."

She's quiet for a moment. "I can believe that about my children."

Then I ask a question. "Do you worry how you two would get along without me as your buffer?" I'm only half-joking, because I know this fear lurks beneath much of what they've talked about.

"Yes," Kelly says, and I hear the tears in her voice.

"Yes," echoes Marla somberly.

"But you both know you can and you will?"

"Of course," says Marla. Kelly says nothing.

"You'll have to turn to each other."

They look at each other, and Marla reaches out to Kelly. They take each other's hand, across me, in the middle.

"We do have each other," she says. And Kelly nods.

"And I'm not going anywhere!" I remind them and laugh. They laugh, too.

I look down at the Void, seeing its dark edge. At ground level, it's masked by the knee-high grass that surrounds it. From here, its edge reveals the breadth and depth of it. It seems more its real self from this angle—a dark place that waits. A place deep in me waits, too.

Marla and Kelly are set to leave the next day. They have lives they have to get back to. Before they go, we decide to get matching tattoos—the wildest thing we've ever done together. Kelly and I already have some, but it will be Marla's first. She must really believe I might not come back from this jump and is taken in by the sentimentality. As long as she can put it in some really inconspicuous place—and keep it small—she's willing. Kelly decides we'll get a small black snake, with red and turquoise and white designs. She makes the drawing herself. It looks New Mexican to me, but she says it represents the ancient Kundalini energy in each of us, coiled at the base of our spines, ready to be called to rise up and set us free to be ourselves.

I remember seeing a snake come down from the porch roof of a cabin I was staying in with friends. As we watched, it extended half of its length down through space as if the space had substance to support it, leaving its other half anchored on the porch roof. It lowered that front half right into a fir tree leaning against the porch, into the nest of a small mourning dove, a nest clearly visible to our group on the porch, a nest with two small eggs in it. The dove had left the nest, probably because we had scared her off by coming out onto the porch, and the snake had seen its chance. It moved into the nest, with half its body still on the porch roof, and swallowed both eggs, so quickly, so effortlessly, I could almost believe it hadn't happened. I didn't want to believe it had. Then it withdrew itself back up onto the roof, again as if suspended by invisible wires, and disappeared from sight. We stood there, silenced by the finality of its act. Why were we meant to witness that?

Later, I found a snakeskin tucked into the fold of the bottom step of the back porch. It was beautiful, elegant, like a woman's elbow length opera glove, dropped unheedingly, while she was on her way to somewhere else. The power of that snake, moving in its own world, taking care of business, meaning no harm, just following its instinct to survive, stayed with me, and I liked the idea of having it, symbolically, on my body, especially as I contemplated my jump. I'm doing what the snake did—my jump causing me to shed one skin because, unbeknownst to me, I've been growing another, the one that allows me to jump, taking care of business because I'm driven, like the snake, to do it, to jump, following my instinct to survive. The snake didn't have to articulate why, and neither do I. Feeling the truth of it is enough.

I made provisions with Marla and Kelly that if I don't come back after six months, or they haven't heard from me, they're to come and collect my stuff, such as it is, and do what they want with it. They're the only people in the world it might mean anything to. I just don't want it left for my landlord to deal with. Kelly can have my music and books and anything else she wants. With that taken care of, my affairs are settled.

As I watch them drive off in their rental car, I feel a little melancholy. I wonder if that's what makes me also feel apprehensive, as if the good luck the Void has brought into my life, which I think it has, has to be followed by bad luck. Why do we want the gods not to notice our good fortune? Why do we think the other shoe has to fall? What about the Law of Attraction? Good calls good. Can I get that through my head? We're more afraid of good luck than bad luck. We're unaccustomed to good—it makes us feel prickly in our own skin. We're used to bad. I shake my head.

But, even though I worry, I just can't feel bad about the Void. I think my apprehension is really because I so seldom choose, really choose, to act on my own behalf. It can't possibly feel comfortable to me. And when I'm choosing to do something so far outside the usual range of choices, well, I'm probably feeling in better shape than I have a right to!

I'm glad Marla and Kelly came. It has been great—like a ceremony of preparation for my trip to the Void. I can't deny that I'm hoping the Void will connect me to something more—as it did Duncan Robert—and it feels right to have gotten to embrace these earthly connections before I go.

I go in to call Miles. I pause a minute at the door. That doesn't mean he's my boyfriend.

CHAPTER EIGHTEEN

Babe —Tandem Jumping

WE ARE JUMPING IN the early morning, like Duncan Robert did. It's May, and the temperatures are New England moderate. We're taking nothing with us. I've got a pocket notebook and pen, but I always have those with me. We've kept who we told to a small circle of family, to avoid creating a sensation with the people we work with or with any of our friends. We didn't want to be delayed or stopped, and we didn't want to generate unnecessary worry. All preparations have been made—and after all, we believe we'll only be gone one day in Earth time.

I've been visiting the Void in the daytime, when no one is likely to be there. It was a kind of rehearsal—I wanted to feel easier around it, not just show up the day we jump. I wanted it to feel more everyday than that. Sometimes I took my lunch or a book and stretched out there in the sunlight next to the Void, listening to the forest noises, of which there are many once you get quiet. Chirpings, rustlings, scratchings, whistlings, cawing, wind in the trees, something dropping from a tree. I saw the occasional small animal—meditating rabbits, once a black fox that was startled to see me and ran right up a tree, little curious chipmunks who venture close, once a couple of hesitant deer. None of them seemed afraid of the Void in the slightest. They hardly seemed to notice it. They were more afraid of me, even as still as I tried to be. The Void was part of the whole scene, not something separate and malevolent at all. I couldn't help but take comfort in the natural instincts of animals.

When I told Miles, he laughed. He said, "Maybe that's part of the Void's lure. It can seem normal, like the big bad wolf in Granny's clothing."

"That's not what Duncan Robert would say," I scolded him, shaking a finger at him. "He knows better, and so do you. Stop trying to scare me."

He grabbed my finger and held it. "I hardly think of you as someone who can be scared so easily."

I wondered how I had given him that impression, but I wasn't going to disavow him of it. "Why'd you try, then?"

"I guess I still miss Duncan Robert, my old sparring partner," he said. "We helped each other keep our fears at bay."

"Let's just both admit we're afraid. Is there something so wrong in that? When we're about to jump into a Void?"

"Only if you plan on not coming back."

Whatever his fears, he is going to do this. He's known that longer than I have. He says he feels as if he's been preparing for it since long before Duncan Robert's jump even. Part of him still feels he should have jumped first. Duncan Robert's jump was so hard on him, much harder than he had expected. He hurt—ached—for a long time after. I think he lived outside of himself for a while, until he could manage the compressed pain of living inside. He knew he loved the boy, but he hadn't known how deep that love ran. He had taken it all for granted. And then the jump measured the depth and breadth of it for him.

I know he's glad to know me. He thinks I'm interesting and I make him laugh. Not that he tells me that, but I know it in the ways he seeks me out, asks my opinion, and watches my face as I speak. I know he values our friendship, as I do, and wouldn't want to lose it. What we're doing feels bigger than both of us, and we can use a friend more than a lover to get us through it, even if my heart is occasionally unruly in his presence. We're both glad to not be jumping alone.

So the time is here, and soon we'll be walking through that clearing. The horizon is light and I can hear a few solitary bird chirps. We spent the night at his place—in separate rooms—and neither of us slept much. I got up to make a cup of chamomile tea around two and saw the light under his door. We were up before our alarms went off and are having more tea, sitting out on his porch, watching the shift from dark to impending light. Our stomachs are empty, to be on the safe side. I watch him in the opposite corner of the swing, cradling his mug, staring into the trees. I feel as close to him as I have to just about anybody. Sharing this life-changing purpose has made our relationship into something I can't define, only feel.

We've said our good byes, our final preparations are long done, and I think we've arrived at yet another new point of readiness. We exchange hardly a word. We've achieved a kind of self-aware peace, coupled with only a little apprehension for the jump, not for anything else. We think only of the jump. Silvia pulls up out front in her old Subaru Forester, and we take our mugs inside and rinse them at the sink. I follow him out the front door, waiting as he locks it. We walk down the porch steps, and I almost laugh out loud. Everything feels so significant, on the way to this significant act!

"Morning," Silvia says quietly. She doesn't look directly at us, but I think she has tears in her eyes. I'm in the back seat, and I reach to touch her shoulder.

"Tough duty," Miles says to her.

"It is," she says honestly, looking at him, and a tear slides down her cheek. "But it beats sitting at home thinking about it, like last time." She wipes her cheek and turns the car back into the street. "And, damn it, it's exciting!" She laughs. "Watch me end up jumping next time!"

We're the only car on the road, and the Void is only a few minutes away. At the edge of the clearing, Silvia pulls to the side of the road and turns off the engine.

"I'm so proud of you two!" she says. "But I still don't think I can stay to watch. I don't have that much courage. I'm going to go pick up a paper and some coffee and then come back here to wait for you." She smiles. "We'll see if I can manage that."

She doesn't get out to hug us. We get out and start to cross the clearing. I stop to turn and blow her a kiss. Miles and I smile at each other, and he takes my hand. I look at him and feel as if I've known him forever.

We stand at the edge of the Void a moment before we turn and take some steps back, to give ourselves a little running start, as we've rehearsed. We turn to each other, wordless, and then just do it. It's the most peaceful thing. We run a few steps through the damp grass and then make a little jump. I feel more excitement than actual fear. We're synchronized, and it feels like one jump, not two. Having seen into his eyes the moment before the jump sustains me. Holding his hand helps, too.

We have no moments of panic, as Duncan Robert had at the beginning of his fall, maybe because we're together, maybe because Duncan Robert prepared us for those first disorienting, stomach-swallowing moments. After the first catch of our breath, we just let ourselves fall, without resisting. We expect to be falling for a while, as he did.

Then we begin to separate. The force of the fall pulls us apart, pulls our hands apart. He falls first, ahead of me. I feel panic. *Wait! This shouldn't be happening!* We should fall and land at the same rate, according to the laws of gravity. I researched it! There must be something different at work here. How different?

I see him moving away from me, down. I'm feeling as if I'm being pulled out of myself, down, with him—it's as if I'm looking into his eyes, but from outside my own body. I wrench my eyes away, knowing I have to keep hold of myself, or I might really panic, in addition to losing him. I know he is below me, but I can no longer see him. He is leading the way, I tell myself, and that's a small comfort.

The sensations of the fall are taking my attention, anyway. Now it becomes my fall. *Your fall is your fall*, just as Duncan Robert said.

CHAPTER NINETEEN

Babe's Jump

I WANT TO SAVOR IT, compartmentalize it, treasure all the details. I'm a writer at heart, so I have to capture it to sort for understanding later. I can't help watching myself have this experience. But part of me wants to just let go and fall. How else does the truth happen? How can it happen if I'm always on guard against it?

For some of the time, despite my vigilance, I do lose track of myself and time, just closing my eyes and going mindless. I feel myself lose size and shape and substance and morph into a nameless, faceless falling. I'm falling with the air around me, one with it. I have no more being than that. Yet my own presence, my own awareness, never leaves me, remaining undiminished, strong, purposeful. This is beyond understanding, because I feel miniscule at the same time, tinier than tiny. I laugh. Then I laugh at my laughing. How can I be laughing? I'm still falling. I'm giddy. I haven't even stopped to notice my surroundings. I'm not much of an Alice in Wonderland.

This situation calls for my awareness to be at the forefront. I'm falling pretty fast, but I can see there are some sort of hieroglyphics on the walls. Pictographs, sort of, some maybe of people. I try to study them but can only hold onto glimpses. I might be able to reproduce some of them later on paper. I close my eyes and can't be sure I don't doze or even dream.

I feel a bump and instantly open my eyes. I have landed, right side up, almost sitting. I feel all in one piece, not bruised or broken. Quite the opposite—I couldn't be more excited. I know from Duncan Robert that this is how his adventure in the Void began. I stand up and look around. I see that I have landed on a flat rocky surface, a few feet back from the reach of the Void, and I can't help going to the edge to look over. To see the Void from this angle is mind blowing. I'm in it! Finally. I hold on to the rocky wall to my right as I look up and then down. It's dark, and a little windy. There is a dim glow, as if light emanates from the rocks themselves. When I look up again, I don't see even a pinprick of light to mark the opening where Miles and I jumped. I wonder how many miles I have fallen. I look down again, glad to have something to hold on to, and feel the bottomlessness, a vast openness that goes on and on. I don't want to stand here too long because, crazily, I can feel the urge to jump rising in me. It's stronger down here than at the edge of the meadow. I'm not ready for another jump! I have to see where I've landed first. I look around my rocky room. I've been buffeted into a side cave that's bigger than my whole studio apartment. Higher ceilings, too.

After a few minutes of wandering around, I can see that it has a back opening. I go into it, figuring that if anyone was going to come out and meet me, they already would have. I'm a little disappointed. I find myself in a winding tunnel with a faint light at the end, which gets brighter and brighter as I walk. All of a sudden, as I round a curve in the tunnel it opens out onto a large, beautiful beach, on a stunning day. The beach extends into the distance in front of me to the edge of the water, which is clear turquoise-blue and gently rippled with small waves. The beach is strewn with gigantic rocks, some grouped, some separate. They're as big as buildings, and they have all kinds of interesting crevices and formations where the wind and the water have been at them in artful ways. Gulls wheel in the sky, calling, and some are scattered on the beach in the far distance.

It's a moment before I realize those are people in the distance, not gulls! People! I start to run. "Who are they?" I'm wondering. "And why am I running?" But I can't stop myself. I'm so happy to be running to these strangers on the beach! I feel as if my heart is pulling me and will leave me behind if I resist. I'm glad I've been exercising, because I don't think I've ever run this fast. I can't seem to run fast enough!

The people ahead of me haven't noticed me coming, so I have a chance to try to look at them as I get closer. But as I approach the group I realize it's only one person I'm really looking at and running towards—a tall, thin man in long, flowing white robes.

"It's Philip!" I think, wondering who Philip is. I run through the small gatherings of other people, not even looking at them, until I'm only a short distance away. Suddenly, I'm so overwhelmed at seeing him that I drop to my knees, unable to go further, and I sob with the abandon of a broken-hearted child. I can't seem to understand or control my own behavior. I've never felt so vulnerable and without defense. I know how Duncan Robert felt about the people he met in the Void and how hard it had been to leave them, but what I'm feeling seems beyond that. This man is my heart. The feelings I'm having for him transcend any I've ever felt for anyone on Earth. They transcend any notion of love or soul mate I've ever had, making any other connection seem paltry, stingy, limited, fearful. I couldn't hold this back if I tried.

I sit there collapsed on the beach and cry without will, without desire, feeling as if I've always cried, that crying is my natural state, like breathing. I can't imagine stopping. Yet I've never been happier. His presence surrounds me and the essence of me moves in and out of it. I don't know how else to express it. He is not man, I am not woman, we are filaments of the same strand of soul. I feel him move closer, and I look up. He bends down and takes my hands in his, and I stand, feeling weak as a kitten. We embrace, and I can hardly breathe. Every question I have ever had has been answered, every need tended to, every prayer acknowledged. I'm complete. I'm home.

He laughs. He knows what I'm thinking and feeling. He tells me that this is how we all feel about each other, all of the time, when we're not Earth bound. And we always forget that when we leave here.

"A great thing to return to, yes?" he says, with a slight British accent. I'm still incapable of stringing two coherent words together. I want to ask where I am, why I am, but it's hard to care in his presence. It doesn't matter.

I feel so vulnerable, but I know, at the same time, we're meant to be living vulnerable—that's our natural state. How else can we change and grow and progress? It's the only attitude that makes real learning possible. You have to be open. A plant doesn't grow clenched, protected; it hurtles itself into growing. It may seem slow to us, but it has the plant's utmost commitment and attention. "It has no fear," he says to me, hearing my careening thoughts. This stops me in my tracks. It so resonates with the feelings I had on jumping with Miles into the Void. I just hadn't known what having no fear felt like.

Now, in this moment, in this place, I know it's the most natural thing in the world for me to love Miles. And I do. I'm filled with an absolute certainty and an absolute happiness. At the same time, I can't help but realize we love so much bigger than that, so much bigger than the love of one person. Here with Philip, I can understand how we do it—how it's possible for us to hold so much love.

Philip shares my thoughts as I have them. He tells me this is the meaning and purpose of life for everyone, all of the time—to be open in love. When I feel drawn to another, like Miles, it is to build structure with him—routines, habits, patterns—to ensure time and place for our spirits to co-exist, to learn from and work with each other, as well as sustain each other. I know we are together due to a pre-contract or agreement to do this, in this place and time. In between lives, we agreed to help each other, and we've probably done it before, in different roles in other lives. We do it until we don't have to do it anymore.

As I look up into his face, I know Phillip's energy lifts mine to a level beyond what I can ever achieve on my own, on Earth. You can't be in a bad mood here, I realize. You can't not like yourself or anyone else.

He takes my hand and says, "Let's meet the others, shall we? They've been waiting."

I look around. The others are focused on us, though it hadn't looked like that initially.

"Who are they?" I ask, though I instantly know what he's going to say.

"They're your cohort, along with members of a few other cohorts who have shared lives with you. They want to celebrate your being here. It's a huge step, you understand. They've not seen anyone else do it."

"What exactly have I done?"

Philip looks at me with seriousness. "You have bet your life, my dear. By jumping, you have bet your life that you can make change for yourself. It's why you jumped. It takes such courage because everything in your lives is so programmed to prevent change, to maintain the status quo at all costs." He smiles now.

"You're their hero," he says.

I have to laugh.

"Well, I've never been accused of that before!" He laughs, too, and I wonder if I have.

I turn to meet my cohort—the parts of my original entity who are all living lives on Earth now, too, when not between lives. Some of them are on the beach, and I meet them face to face, maybe a dozen of them. Young, old, men, women—not like Duncan Robert's group, who seemed all to be around his age. I can tell from their faces they have had different kinds of experiences and have different kinds of knowing. Or maybe that's just part of the telepathy that seems always in operation here.

One of them is a woman I saw once, in Tasmania. I'm surprised to see a woman with whom I have had only one encounter, and we never even spoke. I remember being in Launceston, the second largest city in Tasmania, for a conference where I was invited to speak. I believe everyone else they asked had turned them down—it was so far, so expensive, and no one was exactly sure where Tasmania even was. Africa, they thought? Even I had to look it up, not realizing it was an island off the southeast coast of Australia, one of Australia's five provinces, just adjacent to New Zealand. I loved it, and will always remember the magic of seeing wallabies spar with each other, like miniature boxers, in the twilight on the grounds of the Cataract Gorge Reserve, a wild place just minutes from the heart of the city.

I look at the woman, who looks strikingly like me, and remember seeing her in the crowd of evening strollers along the pier one night, on the Tamar River. People were checking out the restaurants and each other, wandering into the shops, thinking about taking rides on the water taxi. I felt so strangely drawn to follow this woman, knowing there was some sort of connection, and hoping the woman knew it, too. She was older, and walked with a younger couple, who looked like a daughter and son-in-law. She had put herself under their protection and seemed fragile somehow.

I tell Philip, "I think she was afraid of me—she noticed me, but only peripherally, and wouldn't look at me head-on. I was a little freaked out—I kept thinking, knowing, she was *me* somehow, some other version of me. I wanted to see her and have her see me, as validation of something. At the same time, I felt as if something irrevocable would change, and I didn't know if I was ready for that. I think she felt the same way."

He says nothing because the woman approaches.

"Babe, this is Hardin," Philip says, just as I'm thinking the name in my head.

"I know."

Hardin and I hug. And Hardin, laughing, says, with a distinct Australian accent, "Of course, I did see you. I'm an aspect of you and you of me. It was my first time to ever see such a thing. I wasn't well at the time, and I thought seeing you meant immanent death!" She laughs again, "I know now that's not the case. And I'm sorry to have missed the opportunity, but I was a frightened little thing in that life. Not like you!"

"Oh, I was scared, too!" I assure her. "It feels so good to meet you now!"

We hug again, and I turn with Philip, Hardin following, to meet some of the others on the beach.

Another older woman comes up to me and takes my hands in hers. She is shorter than I am, with long dark hair flowing in the wind. Her face is deeply lined and darkly tanned. She has on what I think of as gypsy jewelry, large hoop earrings, lots of bangles, and long strands of small gold beads around her neck. She's a strong and handsome woman. Her deeply set dark eyes exude confidence and good will. Her white teeth flash in her tanned face as she smiles broadly at me, waiting for me to know her.

I look down at her, into her eyes, and gasp. "I do know you!"

In half a second, both of us are crying. I look at the woman, keeping hold of her hands. "What I know is that we killed each other. We've died together, too, when someone else killed us. We've had intense relationships. I know, too, that only people who really love each other would do these things for and with each other. It takes planning and synchronization of everything from our births, to a shared geography, to a million other things, and a deep understanding of what it means for each of us, and for everyone else these acts touch, in terms of advancement." I'm out of breath.

Laughing and nodding, the woman pulls me to sit with her on the sand, and I do.

"We burned at the stake together, our stakes near each other. Part of the Inquisition? We committed heresy?" I look at her for confirmation. The woman nods her head. "We were completely present to each other through the burning," I continue, "joined in supporting each other. We rose together from that life, with the smoke of the fire."

I look at the woman again, who nods and bows her head. I look up at Philip. "She beheaded me in another life. She was the axe man, or headman, as they were called, much hated and feared by everyone, near and far. The King's administration did their best to keep the axe men unknown, but people knew, and the men were ostracized, as if the evil they did was somehow contagious, so even casual association with them would pull you into a dark brotherhood. I had committed some sort of usury—making loans with high interest rates that pretty much no one could have paid. The King had made charging interest on lent money legal, within certain limits, despite the church's opposition. But this was what all the money lenders did, or they couldn't have made a living, what with the King's heavy taxation of all of them. I had been caught, though, in part because I was a Jew and Jews were generally hated, and in part because one family I was over-charging had some connections in high places.

"When I knelt to the axe man, I knew we had a bond stronger than life! It was just as Duncan Robert said—we'd played all sorts of roles with each other—mother, father, friend, now executioner." I look at the woman again. "Until we know we're one."

"I am Nika. But you've known me by so many other names, we hardly need names anymore. I use Nika because that was one of my favorite lives with you. It was in Russia. Do you remember? We lived in the city of Kiev, in the Ukraine, before it declared its independence. We were sisters, living with our parents, who ran a small tobacco shop, with our lodgings above it.

"One day our parents went off to a big buyers' market in St. Petersburg, something they'd never done before, about a two-day train trip each way. They never returned.

We never learned what happened to them. We were about fourteen and fifteen, you were still in school. We just kept going—we ordered tobacco, forging our father's signature, we managed the books, we closed the shop for holidays and took ourselves on trips out into the countryside. We'd latch onto whatever group of adults seemed handy and were never questioned.

"Finally we were found out, by an unscrupulous man who wanted to buy the shop out, to curtail the competition. Once he found out, he wanted us to do whatever unsavory thing he said, or he'd report us to the authorities and we'd be put in prison for all that we'd done. We believed him about the prison, and saw it as a prison either way.

"One night shortly after we were found out, we slipped out of the house and went to the Nicholas Chain Bridge, the only stationary bridge across the Dnieper River that ran through Kiev and the countryside, all the way to the Black Sea. Bridges in Kiev, for hundreds of years, had been floating bridges, primitive affairs removed when the winter's ice began to set in. We considered the bridge one of the wonders of the world. It was known for its beauty all over Europe. 'It civilized Kiev,' we used to say, believing it somehow civilized us, too. We loved that river and knew its ancient history. Cossacks lived along it! It had been part of the Amber Road, a main trade route coming in from the Middle East. We thought the river was the most beautiful thing in the city, and the bridge was the second most beautiful. It felt good to become a part of that flow of history."

She's beaming as she tells this story, holding onto my arm as we sit in the sand. I look over at Philip, who has joined us on the sand.

"You mean we jumped from the bridge into the river that night?"

"Yes. We wrapped our arms around each other and jumped from the railing, which was the highest point we could reach. Do you remember?"

"I don't think so. Why is it one of your favorite lives? It ended in tragedy, when we were still young."

"We accomplished many goals in that life. We didn't see ourselves as helpless. We believed we could take care of ourselves. We had fun doing it. We discovered we had strengths and we relied on them. We didn't turn our lives over to anyone else. We did our best, and we were happy."

"But it was suicide. Isn't that wrong?"

"We had gone as far as we could go in that life on our terms, and we knew it. We weren't leaving in defeat and despair. We were making a stand, refusing to bow to someone else's plans for us. That was our intent," she says calmly, "and that was our choice."

I look at Philip. He looks at me. "How do you feel about it?" he asks.

I shouldn't be surprised to see I have suicide in a past life. And this death seems much better than beheadings and battles.

"I feel okay about it. And I'm kind of in awe of the courage those two had." I look at Nika. "That's why you felt like a sister to me when I first saw you." Looking at her, I think of my own sisters, trying to imagine them doing half these things.

"A sister, but closer. I'm so glad I'm here to see you," I tell her.

"And I you," Nika says, smiling. "You know, you still have the courage we had then. You've just jumped again!" And she laughs, causing me to laugh, too.

"This advances us?" I ask, interested to know, wanting that for me and for her. "To have jumped?"

"You'll have a better balance of the spiritual and the physical in life now. You've allowed the infusion of spirit into this vehicle," Nika says, tapping my chest, "for earthly expression, which is what it's all about. You'll find it easier to stay on your purpose."

"How does it help you?"

"A change in your vibration changes mine, by association, because our energies are so connected. It helps everyone in your cohort. Jumping raises your vibration because you've cleared fear in order to do it. Any time we get rid of some of our fear, our vibration is raised because it's no longer as constrained as it was."

"Well! Maybe that's why I feel so wonderful here."

"Everyone feels better here!" Nika says.

"We need to go," Philip says. "There's a man in town for you to meet."

Another woman comes through the small crowd around Philip and me, and I begin to wonder if my whole cohort is women. She has grey hair pulled back in a double bun on the back of her head. She's dressed in a mid-calf length skirt, with blouse belted over it. She wears soft moccasin boots.

She's Navajo, I think, because I've seen women like this when I've visited my sister Kelly in New Mexico. I feel an immense love for this woman, just as I do for Nika.

"I was your husband in our last life together," the woman says, taking my hands in hers. "I'm someone else's granny in this life that we share. But I'm there for you, too."

My mind is reeling. This woman is in my life now!

"We live within each other—that's what a cohort is. You can see that now?" the woman asks. "We had a deep kind of experience together—a life and death one. In that existence we successfully piloted a group project to a kind of cosmic completion. That's rare. Things like that get planned often but seldom completed. So many things have to come together—people have to hold firm in their resolve to maintain authenticity of self and purpose. When we succeed, it's like every holiday and celebration rolled into one, like finding your lost parents, or reaching the top of a mountain you never expected to be able to climb. The success is felt by your whole cohort, and beyond. It's an extreme exercise in service, so it produces an extreme euphoria. You and I worked hard to do that. Do you remember?"

I stop to think, and the memory starts to surface. We didn't intervene in something—someone died. I remember. It's a small story, really, so I would never have realized the size of its effect. We were children, not more than eight or nine. We let our friend drown. We could have saved him, but we didn't. Somehow, we knew we weren't supposed to. He had to die in order for his family to learn compassion. He was supposed to be here for only a short while, and he knew this. If we intervened, all of the plans everyone had for this life would be put to waste, and some of those plans were important for the country and the world. So we let him drown and then we took his body home to his parents, after getting it onto our sled. Back then, I only knew I was confused and paralyzed by fear the whole time.

"It's the *not* intervening," the woman says. "It's almost impossible for us when we're on Earth, especially in life-and-death situations. We tend to follow rote behaviors for any given situation, but especially those. In truth, all situations are different and require our intuition. But usually we can't see that when we're on Earth. When it's life or death, we think we're supposed to intervene on the side of life. But that time, seeing death approaching for the first time in our young lives, we still listened to our own intuitive knowing and watched him die. We cried, but we held on to each other and stood firm, supported by every ounce of energy our cohort could send our way. And then we still had to witness his parents' grief, knowing that on some level they did blame us, even though they said they didn't. It was quite traumatic for everyone concerned, and it followed us for the rest of those lives. But there was a way we did have peace on it, and we helped each other maintain that."

"What are we to each other in this present life?" I have to ask.

"That's still to unfold," the woman says, "though *not* intervening is still a theme for me, as are lost children." She looks down for a moment. "I just wanted to plant this awareness for you, for you to know I'm there for you, whether or not we ever meet."

We hug, and I feel this woman's power and again feel the sensation of being one. "Go and finish your journeying," the woman says, smiling. "We're proud of you. You're clearing the path for so many others."

I blow her a kiss as I move up the beach again with Philip. I think about how different my journey is from Duncan Robert's. He met one group of people and stayed in one place, listening to stories that told him of his larger identity. He was transformed by hearing what he had done in other lives and learning what he could do in this life. Maybe I'm learning the same things in a different way. Philip is quiet while I ruminate.

Two people are walking next to me, on my left, and suddenly I'm aware they are my mother and father from my current life. I am face-to-face with my abuser, a man I have always feared. As we walk, I feel my father's courage, and it's an incredible realization to me. I resist, but the information comes to me (as it does in the Void) with its heightened energy, and I can't avoid the knowledge of what made the abuse possible. Because I'm in the Void, this knowledge neither outrages nor sickens me. My name is on the things that led to the abuse, too.

First thing I know?

Only someone as close to you as your cohort would engage in this kind of advancement with you. I've had a buried idea that I was experiencing abuse in retribution—because I had engaged in it in another life. Engaged in it maybe with the entity who is now my father. We took on something incredibly difficult, together. We were partners in it. Now I realize that just wasn't the case. The three of us—my mother, too—agreed to take this on out of love, to help each other through a complicated skein of generational relationships that had gone from bad to worse.

This is the second thing I know: we can carry wounds of the spirit from lifetime to lifetime. Times when we were made to feel less than or others were, times we tried to right a wrong and failed. Times we failed in some way—failed ourselves or others. We want to keep trying until we've righted it, so we carry it along.

In our cohort, we had occupied various roles over various lives—first helping to create grudges and resentments that had become deeply embedded, and then trying to work to alleviate them. We created this situation as a group and we had to resolve it as a group. These grudges and resentments had constrained all of us, dooming us to life after life in which we strove to ease them, heal them. It was slow, laborious work. Progress was incremental, and it kept us from other pursuits.

So, my father proposed the most courageous resolution—it called for something beyond everything we had been trying. He wanted to settle it once and for all. It required something transcendent, that we wouldn't be able to deny had changed us profoundly. Incest.

He proposed this scenario to give everyone a chance for a purge of the negative energy that constrained us all. It was a drastic proposal, extremely difficult for everyone involved and could only be carried off by those with impeccable motivation and dedication. His courage and love had inspired me to offer my partnership in the scenario.

The third thing I know is that lives are for trying things, taking risks, for the right reasons, under the right conditions, so progress can be made. Because I did, my mother did. My mother and I had had many other lives together. We all trusted each other to stay true to purpose, in order to achieve the larger healing.

We stand face-to-face now. No one takes anyone's hands.

I realize how long I've been carrying buried hatred, fear, and confusion about my father. I see the harm that does to my current life—this is the stuff of illness, how it starts, where it starts, how it gains hold. It takes up residence in a corner of an essential organ in your body and eats away at it—the unresolved anxiety of it always with you, like a piece of leather rubbing at your skin until it reaches bone. It can do this because you have weakened your own spirit enough by this negativity to create a permanent home for it. I know I have worked hard on Earth to be able to manage my understanding of the abuse and make a kind of peace with it. I realize now only my father can heal me or help me heal myself at the level of spirit. But it's for me to do, to allow, not him.

I have to love him, and my mother, the way I love Philip.

This would have seemed impossible, unthinkable before. I can do it now because I know this is how the healing of the whole cohort happens—they find their way to love, out of the place of grudges and resentment and pain. If I permit the healing, they can all heal and move forward. We all play a very real part.

Healing is an action, a choice, a stepping out of the old and into a new way of seeing the situation. What has made me hold onto the old? To prefer it over healing? Well, you have to be ready or letting go to heal can feel like further victimization, creating more resentment. It's such a worn-out platitude to say "you have to be ready" to let go. But it had been so hard to get hold of an awareness and even limited understanding of the abuse, that letting go of it seemed wrong at first. My understanding of it had seemed so hard won that I thought letting go of it meant I would lose that part of myself again, would lose all that understanding, and go back to being that unprotected child.

If you're ready, it feels like becoming whole, reclaiming every piece of yourself ever given up to damage. And I find I'm ready because I've looked at it, as completely as I could. I went back and looked at it as the adult I am, putting it on the playing field of adults. So it has become integrated into who I am, a permanent part of myself.

Being here, in the Void, has allowed me to then move it into the realm of the spiritual, where such acts usually originate, for the deepest understanding of it—of why anyone would do it, how they could, and what they would achieve through the doing of it. I didn't know it at the time, but engaging in therapy, entering the world of counseling, as I had done in self-defense for a number of years, was a spiritual act that put me on the path to a spiritual understanding. These things are not separate. Each works to make you whole, through an understanding of yourself. Each works to give you yourself back.

I look at them both as they stand facing me, my mother and my father. Almost immediately I know I can do this. Not only am I ready; I am able. In fact, none of this would have happened if everyone here hadn't known I was ready. They knew it before I did. I shake my head in awe at it all. We are all equals now. We have come full circle and can thank each other for the partnership. We have been able to accomplish our healing. I had been the only piece holding it back.

Now we hold hands, looking into each other's faces. I feel that we are finished. We have done what we needed to do. We will part now, with much love and respect for each other, and we will probably not have any more lives together. They will move on to other challenges, able to do that because of the help we have provided each other. I hold their hands tightly now, feeling the largeness of the moment, thanking them. My father says, "It's a wonderful thing we have done. Harder to do than most things, but with a greater reward, too. I thank you, always." Tears come to my eyes. "I thank you," I say, having difficulty speaking.

My mother says, "You always were my favorite!" And we both laugh. "You kept me going through it, Babe. It was so hard for all of us. I am so glad not to have to do that again."

"Me, too," I say and I kiss their hands in gratitude. We part, my parents walking off to the east, away from the water. I stand there crying, feeling the warmth of their hands lingering on mine.

Philip takes my hand and asks me how I'm doing. I give him a reflective smile. "Never better." I wipe the tears on my sleeve. "I guess I'm healing from the inside out." He puts his arm around me. "Some lives run deeper than others." I lean into him, and we continue up the beach. Though emotionally depleted, I feel capable of anything. Which is a good thing, since I know we're not done yet.

We go up the beach to the town we see in the distance, with high adobe-like walls, huge windowless expanses of them beneath a blue, blue cloudless sky. I know there has just been the call to morning prayer and some part of someone within these walls is present to me, someone who has opened to prayer. I suddenly realize he might be thinking of me as God! I mean Mohammad, peace be upon him, because this man is Muslim. We're going to visit him.

I turn to Philip. "This experience tells me that the veil that separates all our worlds is rapidly shredding. We can have access to each other, through conscious contact, such as I'm getting ready to have with this man. It's not something invasive or intrusive, but presence, as if I was sitting there next to or across from him, quietly, respectfully waiting for him to join me with his attention, extending my positive regard to him. Is this right?"

Philip nods. "Yes, access, to see each other as gods. Because that's what we are. It's important that we see that now, for the well-being of the world."

I look at him with a sudden realization of the significance of what I'm doing.

I ruminate as we walk. I'll be a god to a guy in town, because we all are gods. But this concept of gods shifts from dimension to dimension, and can get tied into worship and dogma. Activities normal to us in one dimension can appear supernatural to those in another dimension—it can freak out anyone who is confused, lost, lonely. Take a few of those people in a hard place, looking to be rescued or led rather than lead themselves, and boom, religions are born.

I'm somehow being filled with knowledge as I walk with Phillip and the group to this town. It's like being in their presence is information. I know that all of this is about being able to see myself as one, with my team and my cohort and everyone and everything else. A tall order, because to do that you have to see yourself as large as you see them, not as small as the world has made you believe you are. There's a real equality, of spirit and self, that requires some stepping up from where I've been living. This is the real key to the thinning of the veil—to see who you are in all of your expansiveness, across all time and space, all Universes.

We get to the town, Philip leading us through the gates in the wall, down a crooked trail of dirt roads, directly to the man's house. It's a narrow house on a narrow winding dirt road. The front door, which is unlocked, opens onto a long narrow hallway. At the back of the hallway is a small room, its floor layered with rugs, its large wooden back door open onto a small green courtyard, to receive the morning sun. A goat grazes peacefully. The man is prostrate on the floor of the room, saying his prayers towards the rising sun. I go to sit on the floor in front of him, wondering what I'll do. He knows I'm there—I can tell by the change in his awareness, the tension in his demeanor. He sits up and we look at each other.

I know immediately that he is of my cohort. Tears begin to course down his face, and I have tears in my eyes. I don't know what he sees, but I imagine he is seeing something greater than me sitting there in my matching outdoor wear, with my hair pulled back in a ponytail. True, I do have everything covered but face and hands, like any good Muslim woman, but I have pants on, which wouldn't be good. I can't imagine he'd be having such a reaction to seeing a woman, period, given his beliefs. True, Mohammad, peace be upon him, was guided by significant relationships with women all his life and even said men and women are equal before God, and things like "Heaven lies at the feet of mothers," but much of that ideology can be lost in patriarchal or tribal law, as is evidenced by the continuing restrictions on women and their activities in Muslim countries—something else I have reported on for the paper.

What I see is a man, small in stature, looking at me with such genuine love and devotion that I am moved. I take his hands in mine, in that singular gesture of love and acceptance, and begin to talk.

"Rise and be of service to your people, especially the women and children and those of limited physical or economic means. You are to lead the way for the men of this village in that regard. Your existence will be a constant reminder of the Prophet's highest values, of the highest expression of all five pillars of Islam—faith, prayer, charity, the fast, and the pilgrimage. Mohammad, peace be upon him, noted the importance of even a smile, and you are to live your life with a smile for all, those like you as well as those different, whether in faith or appearance or means. Your job is to love all."

I have to smile at these lofty words coming from my own mouth and watch the effect they have on him. The man touches his forehead to our joined hands, and I hear him, in a choked voice, hardly coherent, pledge his allegiance to my words. I guess I've been his burning bush, and I'm astonished at the whole thing. The man continues to sob and profess his belief in it all. He offers every evidence that the experience has been transformative for him. I look up at Philip, our witness, and he nods at me. It's time to go. I bend my head and kiss the top of the man's still-bent head, removing my hands from his. He stays in the same position, quietly sobbing.

I rise, and Philip and I leave the house. The others wait outside. Morning prayer is over and people are moving into their daily routines. Our group heads back to the beach. As we move through the growing crowds of people on the streets, I am aware that the people don't seem able to see us. Some people do have a limited awareness, moving slightly out of our way without actually looking at us. As we walk, I ask Philip why the meeting was necessary for the man.

"Because he was in need of such a meeting. He has lost his wife, and with her has gone much of his interest for life.

He couldn't see his way, his purpose, what he could contribute that had any value. You're his cohort—you had been his wife. He would respond to your words, as he always had in this life. You were the bridge."

Hardly anything surprises me anymore, I think, shaking my head and laughing. "Why not just have me appear as her?"

"His purpose is greater than that of a husband. We wanted to remind him of that and not have him just think he needed to replace you. This man can do much good in the life he has left, positively directing many others away from greed and meanness and self-service. He can save the lives of others suffering from hunger and ill health. He can become a force for the good in his village. In past lives, he has not stepped up to such a role, leaving it instead for others. In fact, he has often engaged in the reverse."

Okay, I get the picture. "So you believe things will be different for him now?"

"What do you think?" Philip glances at me sideways.

"I think yes," I say, remembering the man's tears.

"I, too. This is what we do for each other, and when your cohort does it for you, you can hardly remain unchanged by it. After all . . . "

"Yes, I know. A bond stronger than life."

As we walk, I try to sort what I'm learning here. I can feel that my time is coming to a close, and I really want to consciously capture what I can of its meaning while I'm in this place of heightened energy. What's been the purpose in meeting them all? Further enlightenment about our situation, our greater spiritual situation? Sure. This experience in the Void is what spiritual people refer to as an activation—it activates something in you that was dormant before, brings it to life, and then this thing brought to life serves you and your purpose. This bond that is stronger than life is an activation.

The end of my jump unfolds at night, on the beach, with the stars, the wind, a warm fire. Philip and I sit, talking, a small distance from the others, who are around other small fires on the beach. He wants to make sure I know my purpose, because isn't that what I've come here for? He surprises me by talking of two primary things: first, books. He tells me I have my books to write. And second, he talks about my relationship with Miles, and going wherever that leads me. He shares that it signifies my openness, my willingness to engage with life, which leads to progress for all, not only for me. All of this will help my cohort, because I'll be engaged in being my best self—having courage, to share with them; health, to share with them; happiness, to share with them. All are in hard situations from time to time.

"Your help is necessary," he tells me. "All of us are starting to do that now—not just help when we're between lives, but help consciously now, within lives," he tells me. "Seek contact with each other."

Philip's words hit me deep in my core. I've spent my life avoiding my real purpose—dancing around its edges, skirting it, out of fear, taking small sips of it only. I've been led by my editor, directing my writing topic-by-topic, rather than pursuing my own interests and intuitions. But no more. My purpose is greater than that and won't be denied, Philip tells me. This is what I have felt knocking at my door, shaking me awake at night, leaving me sleepless. I have work to do! I'm to write a book about what has interested me since childhood—the Void—a whole book. Not just an article. I'm to commit to something bigger, with my name on it. I need to take this risk. We all do; we can't be afraid of our own success forever, which I know I have been. So I'm just going to do it.

I realize, too, that part of my job in writing is to keep magic in the world—the same kind of magic that's here on this beach now. Magic has held the truth for the world a long time, Philip tells me. We read magical books to our children, but then we stop. Then our interest in it moves underground, into adolescent fiction. Adults keep a fringe interest going in fantasy and science fiction, interest in astrology, and having their fortunes read. On some level, their deeper truth seeks an outlet in this way. My book, my books, will be part of that tradition. They will reinforce the existence of magic in the world. They'll be categorized as fantasy or fiction, but I'll know them as *truth*. I'll give them this widest latitude of being.

We cover a lot in this talk. All of my usual faults and foibles are things of the past, he tells me. I have claimed them as my humanness, my lack of perfection, but he tells me that this so-called lack of perfection has no effect whatsoever on the size and scope of my spiritual being, which is as immense as anyone's. Yes, as immense as his, he says, reading my mind. Accepting that puts us in our full energy. Then we're no longer buffeted by the things, events, and people of our lives.

"You'll know when the phone's going to ring and who's on it," he says with a smile. "You'll remember your dreams more often. You'll trust more. You'll be more open to everything."

I smile back, thinking, "Okay! I'll be psychic."

Philip laughs, saying, "Yes, you will."

Then he's telling me good bye. We embrace by the fire, and again I feel so enveloped by a complete love that I'm lost and renewed at the same time. We start walking toward the tunnel I came in by, just up the beach, in the rocks. The wind refreshes me as we walk, and I see the phosphorescence of the waves as they ripple onto the beach. Countless stars twinkle in the moonless sky. It's a perfect evening. The others leave their fires to walk with us, and I am happy in their companionship.

I know I am coming out of the Void and will wait for Miles. I go back into the tunnel, from the beach, turning around once to raise my arm to the group who's stopped to stand at the tunnel's opening. Tears are streaming down my face again, and I let them. The old ways don't fit me anymore. I'm not the same Babe I was.

Universal energies have been at work.

I go to the edge of the Void, ruminating as I sit, leaning against the rock wall, feeling the murmur of the winds from above and below. I relax into the sound and the Void's constant twilight, lulled into sleep.

CHAPTER TWENTY

Miles's Jump

WE'RE HOLDING HANDS, then we're not. I feel myself falling past her, falling below her. I feel a catch in my throat, an urge to grab her. It doesn't seem right. I should be there to help her, not leave her on her own. But there's nothing I can do. It's like with Duncan Robert. I didn't know how much I cared about him until he wasn't there anymore. It's a while before I get hold of myself again and take note of my own fall.

The light is dim, but I see the walls of the Void around me, rocky, unchanging. Every now and then there is a cave-like opening in one side of the wall. I see into it for a moment. Sometimes I look into a cave and it opens onto another space that feels like another Void. Sometimes I see something fall past quickly in that other Void, so fast I can't be sure what it was. Sometimes the shape suggests a person, sometimes an animal.

Once—and I'm sure no one would ever believe this—I fall past a crevice, an opening in the wall that provides me a narrow view of another void-like space for the length of a few hundred feet. Before I know what I'm seeing, there are objects falling past over there—horses! A herd of horses! I hear them snorting, I see their legs flash by, their tails streaming. They're falling head first, as if they're running down the middle of the Void, manes blown back, legs flashing, tails stretched behind them.

It's a magnificent sight in the twilight of the Void.

A whole herd, for god's sake. Why? Where are they going? What could be the reason? I sensed no fear or panic from them—they were just falling. Like me, but not like me. They were hurtling down, as if they had taken the fall on, not just surrendered to it. As if they had charged into it. I could feel their absolute empowerment, intact through the fall, almost as if they weren't falling and were just running, full out, for the joy of running.

The fall, in a crazy way, does give you time to think of things like this. It's as if I've stepped outside myself and am watching this thing I'm doing. I can't think of another time in my life when I have surrendered to anything the way I have surrendered to this fall. Everything is out of my management, control, direction, planning, and organization. I don't know where I'm going or what the outcome will be. My life has been all about knowing those things. I hadn't realized how much—again, until it was gone.

That seems to be a pattern for me. I seem to pledge allegiance to the pattern, not the people. When you teach, as I do, you have to be prepared, have your semester planned, be on top of your grading, and have the administrative side under control. You're the one they all look to if something's not in order. I've spent my life holding firm—the opposite of surrendering. I hadn't known I could surrender, that I was capable of it. I'm not like the horses.

All of a sudden, I feel the wind in the Void shift, and I'm literally pushed by it, quickly, into an opening in the wall. I land on my feet with sort of a double jump, pushed abruptly into a side cave, as Duncan Robert had been. There are five robed figures standing in the center who seem to be waiting for me. At first, I'm taken aback. All I can do is stand and stare. They stand, watching me land and collect myself, and then they move forward to take my hands. They surround me, and I think every one of them is touching me, on my hands, my arms, my shoulders. I'm overwhelmed with the warmth of their reception, their kindness, their openness.

"Welcome, welcome, Miles," they say. "We've waited so long!" I'm immediately comforted. They introduce them-selves, shaking hands with me one by one, but I don't get all their names—they're foreign sounding to me. I find it hard to distinguish among them in the dim light. They look alike. They seem older than I am, with long hair and beards.

I ask where we are, and one of them says, "Come with us. We'll show you."

Smiling, still surrounding me, they steer me to the back of the cave. The back of the cave narrows into a tunnel, which then curves and opens out onto a hillside at twilight. The hillside extends up and away from the base of the hill where we stand. It's a beautiful sight—like something out of a movie. There are small fires scattered up the hill and people gathered around them, maybe a couple of hundred people of all shapes and sizes.

There's much talking and laughing, and children run-ning around, calling to each other in fun. I can smell food cooking, too, and I realize I'm hungry. I didn't eat anything before the jump, figuring it wasn't a good idea to jump into a Void with a full stomach. My companions steer me to some blankets and cushions on the ground nearby, and I sink gratefully into them.

Some men and women are tending a large round skil-let without a handle, resting atop a large narrow barrel that apparently has hot coals in it, just under the skillet. A mixture of chopped things cooks on the skillet, stirred and tossed by two men with tongs. Small ebony bowls wait on a small table at their side. Several children on the blankets have already been served and are eating with their fingers, helped with pieces of bread that the women pass around.

I go over to the blankets and sit with my new compan-ions, smiling and nodding at the other people as they smile and nod at me. They are dressed like tribal people every-where—in colorful cloths, wrapped artfully around their bodies and heads. Their feet are bare and their hair and eyes, dark. They look fierce and beautiful. Someone brings me a bowl of the food, with bread and a mug of water. I eat hungrily, and it's very good—I can taste garlic and oil and think the meat is probably goat, which I've had before. I can taste spices—turmeric, I think, onion and chilies—and there are root vegetables as well.

My companions don't eat. They sit next to me and watch everything. Ran, who seems to be the leader, does most of the talking. He tells me that I was once with them, on Sirius B, a ghost planet now. They were engaged in the populating of Earth, the seeding of it with early versions of humans, created of the DNA of animals already there on Earth and of star seed, from them. This was how the human race began.

Ran tells me of my origins, why I teach writing, to create record keepers. "You do it now because you did it then," he says. "It's in your DNA. Our job, as storytellers, is to unite and honor all ways and all races, so all can know and appreciate them," he says, in his soothing, almost monotone, voice.

My chewing slows, but my mind races.

"Now it's time to use the stored records," he says.

I'm not sure what he means by that. Some of the people on the hill are unwrapping their drums, which were stored carefully in animal hides and blankets, and beginning to tap them lightly, rhythmically. They're becoming a drumming circle—a huge one—as they start to face each other.

"These are the sounds we use to unite and heal—by aligning with the universal heartbeat. Our origins are in unity, not divisiveness," he says.

I think about my own work and its deep roots in my history of being. Ran is giving me the bigger, truer story of myself.

I know I want everyone to use their own voice to find their uniqueness. Students show up in my classes, which means they have a desire to know. Writing gives them a tool to find themselves, so they can provide their own direction. They think they're there by accident of scheduling or requirement, but they've come for the stories. I help them find their *own* stories.

"Go and join them," Ran says with a faint smile. He has seen me watching the drummers, moving my hands in time to their rhythm.

"Here's a drum," he says. One of the cooks has handed a small drum with a handle on each side to him, gesturing with his head towards me. He hands it to me, along with the small drumstick that goes with it. I nod my thanks to the man.

"There are open spots in the circle. You are free to take one of them."

I move through the people still eating, standing, and on blankets, and get to the base of the hill. I climb part way up until I see an opening in the circle and settle onto the blanket. I don't think I've done this since Silvia and I drummed at protest rallies years ago, but it feels good as I listen to the rhythms talking to each other across the circle. I join in.

I settle into my own rhythm, as background to the main rhythm, and look around, at the night, at the other drummers. It's so peaceful. I think of the welcome they've extended to me. How is it that any of us end up fighting each other? But I know that people like these have waged war and had war waged upon them, time and again. I look down at the five leaders, standing to the side observing it all. Usually war is at the instigation of men like that, who don't participate in or appreciate the shared culture. It's fought for their gain. Suddenly, I'm feeling a little uneasy.

The man on my left has been staring at me intently, I realize with a jolt. I look over at him. He's a mutant, a cripple, his body twisted and hunchbacked. He holds a small drum, like mine, in his gnarled hands, keeping the same rhythm I'm keeping, while he stares. I smile. The man smiles, too, a gap-toothed smile. He stops drumming and extends his hand. I take it.

He shakes with a surprisingly strong grip, looks straight into my eyes. "A bond stronger than life."

I stop breathing for an instant. Tears come to my eyes. I grasp the man's hand with both of mine and hold on, holding onto the feeling of intense joy that our contact brings. This man is my cohort, my team!

As I realize this, I realize instantly the five elderly men are not. There's something else going on here.

I look at the man, who nods his head. "That's why I'm here. To tell you what a mistake this all is—it's all for show, like people having their dog show you his tricks. That's why they look alike. They see themselves as vehicles for entrapment, so they have sculpted their own appearances for maximum reassurance. Look who you were comparing them to—all beloved father figures, figures of trusted authority. It's all a situational projection, created by those five beings, to ensnare you. Yes, you were a part of the storytelling of this group of Syrians; yes, you have a history with them. That's why they've drawn you to them. But that's not the whole story. You were part of creating a controlling group of stories, manufactured stories, designed to mold the people who heard them in a very specific way."

I look at the elders. The man says, "Don't give them your attention. It's harder for them to know what you're thinking that way. As long as you focus on our conversation and the drumming, they can't get in." I immediately look back at the man. "My name is Leonid. Having my name will help you stay focused on me. Let's keep drumming, too." We resume keeping a simple beat, in time together. Happiness in finding him keeps my fingers moving.

"Think about it," he said. "Think about good stories that build good cultures. In the old days, you'd have an itinerant storyteller, earning his keep by telling good stories. Where did he get them? He didn't make them up. He got them from observing the lives and behaviors of others— a village rescuing a goat from a well, an old woman dying and her husband following her in death days later, a farmer figuring out how to grow his best crop, all the magic of nature—this was the stuff of his stories.

"So everyone contributed to the stories—they didn't come from one source with its own agenda. Stories are powerful things. You know that. Stories are how we hypnotize," he said. "Think about it. The storyteller is a powerful person to the people—he travels in ways they don't, knows people they don't, sees things they don't. When he tells, people listen, suspending their disbelief until his story is done. His stories get repeated, within families, within villages, within the regions he travels, and repetition is a powerful force for molding people—we structure education and learning around repetition. You know that.

"These people used manufactured stories to isolate people from each other, making them easier to lead and ensuring they remained mistrustful of each other. The idea was that they would only trust the storyteller and whomever he told them to trust. Sure, any itinerant storyteller chooses what to tell and tells it in his own way, but his motivation came from his audience—his job was to entertain his listeners. He did so with integrity, and his listeners knew that. He wasn't looking to control them for his own purposes. He entertained them for the joy of it. It made him happy, and he hoped it made them happy, too.

"If you're a manufacturer of stories, you're not making anyone happy. Stories that lack truth will ultimately destroy the teller, as well as the listener. The stories need to belong to the people—they need to be able to question them, test them based on their own experience, share them or not—they decide if the stories become theirs. These are the stories that endure. You've been part of the manufactured stories, and that's what you saw here tonight."

I look around and feel the truth of what Leonid tells me. Everything feels wrong, and I have to leave and not get caught up in this whatever-it-is.

Leonid says, "Yes. Head down the hill, slowly, and I'll help hold the attention on drumming. That will slow them down a little. Don't stop to talk to them. They're pretty good at hypnosis." He looks at me and I look back. "Just get yourself back to the Void. We'll meet again. Don't shake hands. Just go." Leonid goes back to his drumming intently.

I whisper, "Thanks." Leonid doesn't look up but nods his head toward the tunnel. I pause a moment, and look back at Leonid, not sure I'll see him again. Leonid looks up. "The horses?" I ask.

"They were showing you the way," Leonid says with a smile.

I take a deep breath and start moving down the hill, not running. The elders sit at the bottom, near where they came out of the cave. They watch me. I finally get to the bottom of the hill and move through the people still sitting in groups there, with their families. I'm nodding and smiling, and they are, too.

When I'm nearest the elders, I stop to talk to the people I ate with, thanking them and bowing. They're nodding and bowing. Then I grit my teeth and move up to the elders, who regard my movements with curiosity. I bow, thanking them, telling them I have to go. They get up, try to talk. I just keep moving, quickly, moving toward the opening.

I glance back. The elders continue towards me. I look at the hill beyond them. It's starting to disappear, along with the people, the drums, the fires, the food, to just fade out around the edges. I look again at the elders and I see their faces are disappearing.

Then I'm running, frightened, through the tunnel, back to the cave. I don't look back again. I'm sure I could disappear, too, never to be heard from again. It hadn't occurred to me that I might not come out of the Void. I get back to the Void's edge and stop a moment, to catch my breath, to settle myself, before I try to hurl myself into it again.

I can't believe what I'm about to do—to jump again into the Void. This is very different than the first time. That makes me think of Babe, and I wonder if she has run into any trouble, if she's okay. I picture her smiling, joking face. Then I hear noise in the tunnel behind me. People coming! Thinking of Babe has centered me. I take a deep breath and jump. And fall again.

CHAPTER TWENTY-ONE

Miles's Second Jump

I DON'T KNOW HOW long I've been falling. It's taken me a few minutes to settle into it, wondering if they would come after me somehow. I work to calm my breathing so I can relax into the fall. Gradually it dawns on me that falling feels safer than being back on that hillside. How I feel about the Void is changing. I have to laugh, with a kind of euphoria. Good old Void! Always there when you need it.

I think of Babe again. On an impulse, I close my eyes and call to her. Her smiling face appears in front of me. "Babe!" I shout, smiling, too. "Can you hear me?"

"Of course I can hear you! You don't need to yell."

"We've never done this before," I say, referring to our telepathic communication.

"We've never been in the Void before," she says drily.

I laugh at the humor that I know and love. "I love it!" I say, meaning her and being in the Void.

"You're falling again?"

"Yes! Can you believe it? I was caught in something back there, snared by it. But a member of my cohort saved me. Where are you?"

"I'm on a beach near a desert, and we're heading for a town, where there's a guy who thinks I'm God!" she says, laughing. "I have to go! We're almost there. Stay in touch!"

"Yes! I'm glad we can do this. I'll call you!"

We laugh, and she's gone, and the Void seems a little brighter for my having connected with her. That's something I know as truth, whether or not I can always tell truth, I think, looking back at that hillside. I know it from my own experience—Babe brightens my existence. But I'm shaken by the fact that I fell right into that projection, without questioning it, without noticing anything. It chills me to think I could have stayed there! I have to hold onto the things that Leonid said to me. If we value the uniqueness of each of us, we'll always want to honor and protect that. That feels like a necessary truth to me, and the main one that wasn't acknowledged back there. I think about every baby, every child I've ever known, each destined for its own greatness, each a necessary contributor to the world, each with a full potential to live up to, made up of its own talents and abilities. These thoughts give me comfort, as I try to shed the effects of being in that situational projection.

It's not that we can't get truths from others or from our 'higher' sources. But I need to determine the validity and resonance of the information and not be hypnotized by it. That's the difference between the world I believe in and the one "they" created back there.

I'm still falling, but the air seems to be changing. It starts to feel denser. I shift my head to look down and get a jolt when I do. Far, far down I can see pinpoints of light, floating and moving. There must be a bottom! Uh-oh. I always thought it was bottomless. I can't think "bottom" when I think "Void." If there's a bottom, will the fall kill me? No, because I still believe the Void isn't a place of death. It's a place of life. But what do those lights mean?

As I get closer, I see the moving lights are torches. They're held by people, all moving across the ground at the bottom. They're moving rapidly, single mindedly, in the same direction, and they don't seem to notice me. There are a lot of them. They're mainly men, but I see some women interspersed. They're sort of nondescript in their appearance, but they remind me of depictions I've seen of people in the Middle Ages, sort of roughhewn—clothes and matted hair and stocky builds. I wonder if I'm going to land on top of them.

Just then I feel the wind pick up, and I feel myself buffeted, as if a hand came under me and gently shifted me to the side of the Void. Not a real push, like last time. The wind deposits me on a ledge a little above the crowd. I land on my feet, up against the rock wall behind me. I lean there a moment, getting my bearings, savoring the ground beneath my feet, as the crowd with torches moves below me.

I'm closer to them but they don't seem able to see me. They're all looking forward intently. They're not talking. I just hear the sound of all those feet moving across the ground. But it doesn't feel good to me. It makes me think of the hillside. It's as if they've become mindless, or of one mind, without individual thought. I don't know what force could be moving them or where they could be going. I don't feel pulled to join them. In fact, I feel the opposite and stay next to my wall. Finally, they're past me.

As the last of them goes by, however, I see three people at the end of the crowd stop and turn towards me. I'm startled. One of them is Leonid. I look at my ledge, wanting to get down there. There are rocks I can step down, to the ground, and I do quickly.

"Leonid!" I call, waving wildly to him. I'm so glad to see him! Leonid is smiling as he limps to me, with arms open. The other two follow. He and I embrace. Leonid looks much like the people in the crowd, roughly dressed with thick chopped hair. His curved spine makes him a full head shorter than I am. His face is the liveliest thing about him. His dark eyes sparkle, his gap-toothed smile is constant, he projects a continuous warm welcome. He's the opposite of the five elders.

"God, it's good to see you!" I tell him. "How did you get out?"

"Oh, they weren't interested in me. And the projection just faded. Kind of like that one." He points to the group that just passed. "They were a projection, too."

"What do you mean? How could you tell? They seemed pretty real. But so did the hillside." I'm a little alarmed.

"A projection is a temporary scene created in space, which is malleable energy with just the right flex to take on individual or group projections," Leonid explains. "People project out into their immediate space as a kind of experiment, to work on emotional and psychological issues they want to master. Like in dreams. They create scenes that allow them to examine the issue and their own response to it. But make no mistake, Miles, they're as real as you want them to be. They have power, too. They provide direct experience of an issue, which can be transformative."

"How can you tell when you're in it, that they're projections?" I ask. "I almost became a permanent part of the one on the hillside! Is it like mass hypnosis?"

"Yes! You could have stayed on that hillside. But it's a choice if you keep hold of your own consciousness," Leonid says seriously. "You stay yourself wherever you go in the Universe, you know. Think about it. You were able to step out of it, as soon as you no longer thought of yourself as part of it. This one," he says, referring to the torch bearers, "you didn't even think of stepping into. But you could have. You could have gone with them, for as long as you needed to. But you didn't. So you can trust yourself on that."

"What do you mean, for as long as I needed to?"

"These projections are always opportunities for healing," Leonid says, looking up at me earnestly. "If you needed the healing, you'd be drawn to the projection, to participate. You entered the hillside because you'd just fallen through a Void, and the hillside seemed the perfect place to collect yourself, to feel safe, to be welcomed. It was along the lines of what you expected to find—something warm that feels like home. Right? Think about it. It was what Duncan

Robert found—his people. Those elders resonated with what you thought you'd find—wisdom personified."

I have to agree with that. But then I look at him shrewdly. "Listen to you! You're the wise one."

"Yes, and don't I look like it?" he says, mischievously, looking up at me.

"Well," I say, feeling slightly embarrassed at where this conversation seems to be going. I don't want to talk about the fact that he's a mutant.

Leonid laughs. "It's a projection!"

"What?"

"It's a projection! I project this image of —what did you call it—a mutant. I carry this, as a tool for healing."

"Explain that!" I say, confounded.

Leonid laughs again. "Think about it. Projections can be individual or group, any setting imaginable. Why not a projection onto the arena of ourselves? You can use space to do that."

"But why would you?"

"As I said. For healing." I look at him, still confused, and he says, "It can be healing for the person who carries it, because he may have mistreated deformed people before, and by wearing the deformity, he learns they are the same as he is. It can be healing for the people who witness it because they are reminded to hold onto their compassion, which they may not have done before, when confronted with a deformed person.

"I wear it because I inflicted this kind of deformity on someone else. Before the lesson can be completed, though, there has to be complete forgiveness. I have to forgive myself for doing such a thing, especially if I did it with intent, or with relish. Otherwise it becomes part of what gets carried down to other generations, other lifetimes, through bloodlines. But I can't forgive completely without fully knowing what I inflicted. It's completed when we come full circle and are made whole again, without anger or guilt or shame, by walking through the experience of it." He looks at me seriously.

"Wait a minute. You inflicted this kind of harm on someone else? I find that hard to believe. You're one of the kindest people I've ever met. I know that, right down to my core."

He looks up at me. "I did it to *you*. In another life. That's why I wanted you to see it. That's why I was the first cohort member you met. The healing is for you, too, so you can forgive me."

I just look at him, stricken by what he has said. But I feel the truth of it, just as I felt his truth on the hillside.

"Wait a minute! I'm forgetting my manners!" He points to the two people we both seem to have forgotten, standing a few steps behind him. "I want you to meet two other members of our cohort!" He steps aside to signal them forward, and I stand there stunned and overjoyed. Now we're cooking! Cohort members!

One of them steps forward, hands extended, smiling broadly. It's a woman! She's a woman, I correct myself. Her height and her short hair and all this loose, non-descript clothing fooled me for a minute. She grips my hands, and I feel her strength. She's like an Amazon, exuding an energy of confidence and toughness and kindness. As we grip hands, I feel solidly connected to her, heart to heart. We look at each other, and I love her! This sensation overwhelms me, and it feels absolutely new to me. I don't think there's ever been a time when I felt this strongly this instantly for anyone.

She laughs uproariously, reading my thoughts. "Why do you think you jumped? Because you've always felt this! You've been our role model!"

I look confusedly at Leonid. "It's true, Miles. You're good at feeling things and allowing that to guide your behaviors." He smiles and adds, "Jumping isn't a head decision, you know."

I shake my head and look back at the woman. I still feel drawn to her.

"I'm Norwenna," she says, "and we've known each other forever, practically. Mainly, we've fought together, over and over, because our cohort has done a lot of that. It's why we feel so close. Being shoulder-to-shoulder in life and death situations does bind you." She laughs again. "It's why you're so anti-war now. You've had too much of it. You'll get there!" She punches my shoulder and steps aside to allow the other person to step forward.

This one is a man—I can tell by his short, well-trimmed beard. He's tall and thin and reminds me of the five elders back on the hillside, only younger. The man hesitates, sensing my thoughts, and Leonid says, "Miles, this is Keilor. He's an intergalactic being, yes, but he's also a very powerful healer. He's here to learn from us, as he helps us heal. He's always been a part of our cohort, and he's not our only intergalactic member."

I look at Keilor. His eyes are his most striking feature. They're large and they're a golden green. They seem to hold a deep knowing. He looks at me and smiles. I feel so warmed by his smile that I smile back, extending my hands to him. He takes them immediately in both of his, and I feel tears prickling my eyes. I discover that I love this man, too.

"I'm here to learn more about how and why you battle and to help you heal from it," he says. "It can be hard to heal from, but your planet desperately needs to do this."

His accent sounds faintly British to me. "How do you do that—help heal a planet?" I ask.

"I help through the energy I carry," he says. "It's different than your energy, because I've never fought."

I look at Leonid, perplexed by Keilor's statement. Leonid says, "It's true. His energy is more pure. It has the power to negate the energy generated by battles and wars. That energy has nothing to attach to with him. So he can heal by his very presence, if someone is ready to heal."

I hardly know what to make of that, but I'm deeply moved by it. I feel as if I'm in the presence of a holy man. Leonid nods at me in agreement, so I know he's heard my thought.

"Come on. Let's walk," he says and heads up the direction the torch group went. We follow him. I notice the bottom of the Void is vast and there are other seemingly endless passages off of it.

"Where are we going?" I ask him, not wanting to get too close to that torch-bearing projection.

"Let's go see if we can find Ethelred, then you can get the whole story." He looks at me. "You have the opportunity to experience the story directly, for yourself, for your own healing. If you want."

"Ethelred?" I vaguely remember that name. From medieval history. "Do you mean the Ethelred who was a king of England?"

"Yes, he was," Norwenna says. "I remember him well—Ethelred the Unready, to some. His reign was marked by lots of military crises, for which he wasn't unready—in fact he was quite forceful. He was just so burdened by how his reign began."

"Say more," I say to her. "Wasn't there something about brother killing brother?"

"Yes, sort of. His half-brother, Edward, was murdered at sixteen, after being king only three years, which gave Ethelred the throne when he was only ten. Clearly these children were pawns for larger forces. It was all about possessing land, for power. That's what monarchies are still all about today. But they had no way to maintain real control of all that land back then. They just passed it around on paper—I mean parchment."

She pauses a minute, looking off down the tunnel. "Ethelred's mother was believed to have orchestrated the murder. But they were brothers, who played together as children. So Ethelred could never forget that his rule was founded on the blood of his brother. He spent much of his life working to make his murdered brother a saint, which he did."

"Why are we going to see him?" I ask.

"He's part of our cohort," she says. She looks at me somberly. "Knowing your cohort is knowing your full self. Being in battle together makes you really identify with each other. It can be the foundation of a cohort. And often it keeps us choosing male lives, because the male experience is indelibly imprinted on our spirit." She smiles. "That's what I'm trying to balance."

"But I'm against war!" I protest, trying to imagine all of these fighting lives. I've always been against war.

Leonid laughs. "Well, you are now. Because you've learned a few things. Nothing makes a war a good thing, and you found that out. But we're talking about what happens to people within a war, and I suggest they can still find the good, even as they learn the bad. Or maybe because they learn the bad, together." He looks at me and laughs. "Heck, this planet is all about war! There had to be more to war than just war, or you'd all be dead."

Keilor, who has been quiet, nods. "I think the fact you're against war now is a good sign. It means you've experienced some healing."

While I'm pondering that, Leonid stops at the opening to another passage. They all look at me, as if to make sure I want to do this. I nod, not really knowing what we're doing but trusting them all, and we head into the passage, which to me looks like all the others. We walk for a ways, without talking. Slowly the walls gain my attention. There are markings, hieroglyphs. They look like chicken scratch to me, but they're in color and some are repeated. I ask about them.

"They're war stories," Leonid says. "That's what this tunnel is—the War Hall. Warriors have left the tales of heroic battles, whether won or lost. This is part of their healing, to tell the tale."

"Say more about us choosing these lives of war and why we would," I ask, troubled to be in a place that marks the events that meant death, often horrible death, for so many.

"Well, the choosing is all done between lives," Leonid says. "That's when we do the planning. We figure out why now, and with whom. You're making that choice when you're who you really are, your whole, fully knowing self—you're holding all the experience, all the memory, all the history. And you're doing it with your cohort, who have been there every step of the way with you. It gets pretty complicated, as you can imagine, because there's lots of other people, too, on the same purpose. You see how it's different from projections—it has a common, consciously realized purpose for all. We're not re-living something we haven't gotten clear of yet. We're creating something, together."

"But why? Why would we?"

"Well," Norwenna says, thinking about it. "It's done according to contracts, typically. As a contract, it's often done as a favor to a cohort member or to complete your own karma with that person. It works to balance karma, to balance what's been released into the world by war. So, ideally, we would have fought once, like kids fighting over a toy, and we would learn our lesson, never to do it again."

She actually snorts at this.

"But on Earth, we've done it over and over. The irony is that every time we do it, we're all agreeing to fight to end all fighting!" She shakes her head and kicks at a stone on the tunnel floor, sending it flying into the dimness ahead of us. "It just seems to take us a long time to do that, to get that lesson. So, we fight because we're young and ripe for adventure, or we fight because we've been talked into it—to see ourselves as heroes or properly patriotic, or maybe we're branded cowards if we don't."

She looks at me, to see if any of this is ringing a bell for me. Considering all the war experience I've apparently had, I guess it should be. But I'm not feeling it yet.

"Or maybe we're just forced to fight, by somebody more powerful than we are, who holds our lives and our families and our property hostage. Anyway, the idea is we get used to fighting, if we do it enough." She pauses again, thinking. "And it's hard to stop."

She looks at me, and I see a deep sadness in her eyes. "That's what happened to you. And to me."

I don't want to hear this.

"I want to heal," she says. "That's why I'm here. I don't want to carry the blood and gore any more. I want other experiences. But sometimes I think I've stayed too long at the fair."

Her words chill me. I'm not like her, I say to myself, but it carries no conviction.

"No one wins. This is my last piece of work here, and then I can move on. But it's taken its toll. I find I don't make a very good woman." She smiles at me, and I feel the chill to my core. "Too much baby killing, I guess." She turns away from me, saying, as she turns, "You can extinguish your own light before you know it."

I can't speak. Fear has a hold of me.

Leonid goes on talking. He agrees with her. "Think about your own Civil War, right on your own territory. Your own history tells you it was fought in 10,000 places, with three million dead. Think of the battle at Cold Harbor. Your history tells you about that, too. Skeletal remains from the first battle at Cold Harbor were found when they dug in for the second battle. More than 7,000 men died in 20 minutes. Necessary?

"World War II, history tells you, called more than 85 million people into uniform, yet the over-whelming majority of people who perished were civilians. They still say the real number will never be known. And wars are full of stories like that. Yes, that kind of chaos can create fertile space in which to learn some of life's toughest lessons, if you survive. But it's not the only way to learn or even the best. It's just the most expensive way to learn. Somebody pays and somebody profits. Somebody always does."

Norwenna looks at me, her eyes cold and dark. I'm disturbed at seeing the light go out of her this way. "Some people think wars bring out the best and the worst in us. But I think they're designed to bring out the worst, in order to win; the best is only incidental." She looks down.

"You know, things like blood lust can develop in wars."

"I don't really know what that is," I say, wondering if I want to. But this seems important to her. And I have a feeling if it's important to her, it's important to me.

"People consumed by blood lust just want to kill, to feel powerful, maybe because they've gotten attached to their possessions or their people. Or maybe they're too afraid of being killed, so they just kill everything they can, trying to feel safe. Maybe they're even supposed to be killed, and they know it but don't want to be, so they kill instead. Newer, less experienced souls might follow them, caught up in what they see as the glory, the spoils of it." She looks at me, and I have to admit I feel something here, like she is telling my story, too, not just hers.

"And so-called religious wars are the worst!" she says. "Convincing ourselves we're doing it for the highest possible good. It's the highest possible delusion, but it can take a while to work our way out of it. You should know. You've been there, done that," she says, with a short laugh. "So have I."

Seeing the unhappy look on my face, Leonid says, "Think about it, Miles. Ethelred is our cohort. Battle was our cohort's way for millennia."

Norwenna and Keilor nod. I'm thinking about what it means to try to heal from all this. I guess it's possible, because Keilor is here.

We come around a gentle curve in the tunnel, and Leonid points out an opening on our left. This time the markings scrawl across the left side of the opening, indicating some sort of battle associated with the portal. It's dark inside, but the three of them walk right in. I follow and as my eyes adjust to the dark, discover myself in a good-sized room with high ceilings, and a low-burning fire in a fireplace in front of us. By the fire's light, a table is visible with a couple of flickering candles on it. The table stands between us and the fire. A large man sits with head bowed over some papers. Startled by our entrance, he rises up out of his chair. Then his face lights up at the sight of us.

This must be Ethelred. He shouts a greeting and rushes around the table to give each of the others a bear hug that lifts them off the ground and then settles them back down. Tall as Norwenna and Keilor are, they seem dwarfed by this man. They're all talking and laughing.

Ethelred looks over their heads to see who is behind them. All goes still. He stares at me for a long moment. I'm feeling just a little unreal. Who am I to this man? This, after all, is a king.

He comes over to me and takes both my hands in his—a gesture of unquestioned loyalty, even at Ethelred's time in history. "A bond stronger than life," he says, as he looks into my eyes.

Leonid says, "Ethelred, meet Miles. Miles this is Ethelred."

So, I meet Ethelred—inside his castle, in the middle of the night and have to smile. I feel deeply touched by this man. Though I do realize, after all the war talk, that *castle* is just another word for *fortification against war*.

Ethelred looks at me with tears in his eyes, and once again, I have tears in mine. I have never felt as close to anyone as I do to these people.

"So you've come to help us," he says.

"If I can," I say, and mean it, though I have no idea what might be expected of me. He looks at me for a moment, with such love that I finally have to look away, I'm so overwhelmed. He squeezes my hands and then lets go, turning to the others.

We all look at him, and he seems to sense that everybody is ready for whatever it is we're going to do. I think

I've stopped breathing for a moment, the atmosphere seems so heavy with this unnamed purpose. I'm just going with this flow, with these people.

"Let's go," Ethelred says quietly, and we follow him from the room.

Ethelred seems to know clearly why we're here—"to take a look at some significant warfare for our cohort, to heal it." That's what he tells me as we all walk down the dark halls of the castle. Apparently he's used to walking these halls in the dark. Nobody mentions grabbing a torch or a candle. He's trying to give me some background for the battle we're apparently going to witness, as we feel our way down narrow winding stairs in the dark, trying not to bump into each other. Ethelred sees like a cat—he points to engraved words above the door we exit by. The words are in Latin, so he translates them—"If you want peace, prepare for war."

"It's what we live by," he says. We head outside, past the animal pens and out into the fields surrounding the castle, and he talks to us about the work and duty that fill his days.

Once outside, I finally get a real sense of where we are—in another place and time. Everything feels different—the air, the ground, the sky—as if it doesn't fit me but it's allowing me to be here on borrowed time, only because we have work to do. There's a full moon, and by its light I can see the walls of the castle stretching up and up and up behind me. I can't see the top of them. I can't see the extent of their breadth either. The walls go out into the night on both sides of the door we came through, without a visible end. The ivy that grows part way up them undulates with the light wind, adding to the sense of being somewhere other than solid reality. In front of me, land rolls away in every direction as far as I can see. The woods take up part of it, but they go on and on, too. There's such a vastness to it all. Who could rule this? No one could. Yet they try.

And this larger-than-life man in front of me is somehow of two times, as well. His own and ours. And he's got a command of it. I have no trouble believing he's a king. Not only is he tall, he's got a great head of wavy red hair and a beard to match. He's dressed with a simple elegance. He wears an earth-colored, belted tunic over knee-length breeches with matching stockings. He has a short cloak over the whole thing, and his head is bare. He's very muscular and moves with great agility. His presence feels larger than life.

"These are hard times indeed," he says of his legacy of time. "It's a primitive, violent land—not long since a Roman boot trod here. The land is uncultivated and food not easy to come by. People are isolated from each other by the span of countryside and by the amount of work they have to do to just survive. Because they spend so much time alone, they're an independent lot, mistrustful of everything but their own judgment. But we make them fight, for causes they don't care about, on empty stomachs and with homemade weapons. History will say of these people that they lost the will to live, to have children, due to the dreadful toll of prolonged warfare. My heart is not in it, either, but we saw no way out of it. We try to keep the relentless Danes at bay, but there is no constancy in my own men's loyalty. So we fight, and fight again, sometimes each other, sometimes the Danes. There seems no other way."

The moon helps us see our away across the fields of grass to the top of a low hill in the distance and the mild wind moves with us. There's mist in the low areas and it comes alive with the wind. The land has a fairytale feel to it, as if any inanimate thing could come to life.

"We're all in the same place," he says, looking at me. "You, me, and Norwenna. We've had our fill of warfare. And tonight we'll put an end to our part in it." He's silent for a moment as we continue to walk towards the hill.

"I'd rather be doing the things that hold the land—clearing and irrigating, building communities, ensuring wealth this way, in the things that root the land in the people's hearts. Then they will feel loyalty to the land as well as to me, because I gave it to them. They will defend it when I'm not there, because they know it is theirs to defend.

"My brother was better at battle than I am, even as a boy. I wish he was still here. He'd manage all this. I'm better at statesmanship—holding things together—not ripping them apart.

"I do love this land and the people. The land may isolate them, but when they come together, their isolation is the commonality that binds them. And it breeds an independence of thought and spirit that's good for the development of the land." We're moving through mist now, at the base of the hill.

His people might be taciturn, but Ethelred can talk—maybe all royal people can, by nature or because they are expected to. Maybe, though, it's because he has things to be healed, and talk is one way to do that. He has high energy, too—as maybe all royal people do, because don't they have to, to lead? I find it infectious and like Ethelred for it. He is a leader whom others naturally follow, as we do.

Leonid has been quiet as Ethelred talked, but now he speaks. "Do you know this place?" he asks me.

We've crested the hill, and I look out over the larger clearing in front of us, silvered by the moonlight. I see the dark woods just beyond the clearing. It's the same as all the land around it, but it's not, in a way I can't describe. Suddenly, I feel the hair stand up on the back of my neck. That's a first for me. I know this place, on a visceral level, and it's not good. I want to go back to the safety and warmth of the castle.

"I do know this place," I say quietly, really afraid now, in the pit of my stomach.

"We all do," says Ethelred, tense beside me.

Norwenna and Keilor, standing to the left of me, are looking around them uneasily, too. Norwenna has gone pale. She looks at me with fear and sorrow. But she's determined, too, and I align myself with her determination. Otherwise, I feel as if I could crumple into a boneless heap right here. Leonid has that same determination, as he stands still, staring ahead of him. Keilor is a tower of strength. He is actually serene. I guess that's what comes from never having fought. You don't know to be afraid. I take a breath. We are as ready as we ever will be, for whatever comes.

All of a sudden, we all turn our heads to the clearing in front of us, as if there's been a signal. I know the clearing is going to come alive. And it does. I feel it change. There's a ripple of energy that comes from the clearing and passes through us. Apparently it took only our arrival to cue it. With the ripple comes life. Dim shapes that followed the ripple begin to assume human form. I can hear the sound of many voices, of branches breaking, of movement. Out of the mist, I see a contingent of men rushing through the grass toward another group of men who are waiting for them, standing braced, weapons raised.

"This is too quick!" I think, trying to slow the projection with my mind. "I'm not ready!" But we're in it. The five of us are standing there, and it's daylight, and the battle has already begun. The two groups of men are shouting at each other, enraged. The first group is shouting, "Ethelred, Ethelred!" The second group shouts something back that I can't understand. Then they are on each other, and the sounds are awful, like nothing I've ever heard.

The thuds and clangs of weapons on weapons and on shields are everywhere, but underneath that are the muffled thumps of blunt trauma, weapon landing heavily on human flesh and the flesh absorbing the blow. Screams and groans and guttural sounds follow. It's a cacophony from hell, with no beginning and no end.

The scene is so chaotic—not a leader in sight, no battle lines in evidence, just men brutally attacking men. I'm almost paralyzed with fear, and I shout to Leonid, wanting to know it's not real.

"It's a projection?!" I scream.

"Not for us!" Leonid shouts back. "We've created it, and we've chosen to be in it!"

He moves forward, and I follow. The five of us have become separated by the battle, in the midst of it, but not a part of it. I lose sight of Ethelred and Keilor. Norwenna stays to one side of me, Leonid on the other. We move into the midst of the fighting. Leonid is looking for something, but I don't know what. It's awful to see what we're seeing, to witness it. I flinch and crouch, trying not to lose sight of Leonid, as men swing their weapons over me. Leonid just keeps walking forward. Crazed, unseeing faces are all around me. Men mindlessly climb over each other, falling, slipping in the blood and sweat and mud, trying to stand to deliver another blow to whoever is standing next to them, whoever is trying to do the same thing to them.

I can hardly comprehend the array of strange, vicious weapons the men are using against each other. They have turned the equipment of their everyday lives—hoes and meat hooks and hammers and axes and pitchforks—into the tools of war. They wield them with particular aim and steadiness, to great effect. I cannot imagine the men who have been struck down rising again after blows delivered by these men with these weapons. The fallen men are mangled such that they resemble slaughtered animals more than men. Their blood has made the ground molten. Many of the fallen men scream in agony, but some are silent.

In the distance, the women, who have traveled with the men to this place and have an encampment further into the woods, are watching at the edge of the woods, apparently ready to help, if they can. I can hardly stop myself from screaming at them to get back, to leave.

"What are they thinking? Where are their children? Get yourselves to safety!"

I must have screamed this out loud, because Norwenna has hold of my arm. "Steady, Miles. We can do this." I look at her, seeing the tears coursing down her face, not knowing what she's talking about. Can't she see these women and children are in danger? All I can see and know at that moment is battle.

I throw her off me and run for the woods. I can't help myself. I can't just stand by and watch. Norwenna and Leonid are running behind me. The women ahead of me are running, too, trying to get back further into the woods. Some do have their children with them, and the children are screaming and crying uncontrollably. None of them are able to move very fast, which makes them easy prey.

Suddenly, a few of the fighting men have come after them. They begin to slay them, helpless women and children, and the women are begging for mercy for their children. The men hit the women with their clubs, split them open with swords, and kill the children, too. Their screams are more than I can bear.

"Stop it!" I scream at them. "Stop it! Stop it!"

But I can do nothing. We might be in the projection but we are definitely not of it. I fling myself on the men anyway, shouting over and over for them to stop. I see Leonid watching from the trees, stricken. Norwenna crouches over the bodies of the women, her eyes blank, tears still streaming. I don't know where Ethelred or Keilor are. It's a nightmare that won't end.

The man directly in front of me hits a woman from behind with his club, knocking her senseless to the ground. The woman looks dead but is still clutching a small child, who is crying without pause for breath. The man bends over and pulls the child from its mother's grip by its legs. He stands upright and then turns and bashes the baby's body against a tree, all in one movement. The baby's crying stops instantly.

I know I will never be able to get the sound of the baby's body hitting the tree out of my mind. I can't scream, I can't breathe, I can't move. I stand there and watch the man toss the baby's body into the woods behind him, without looking. I'm beside myself now, shocked into stillness.

The killer is standing next to me, surveying the dead women and children scattered around him on the ground. He doesn't see any standing, living people and starts to turn back to the clearing, as the other men are doing. As the man turns, he pauses, as if looking at me. We stand only a few feet apart and are almost the same height. The man looks directly at me, and I see that the man's eyes are dead eyes, without any light. He seems more like a thing than a man. I look at him, and in that instant, my heart stops.

In that instant, I know I am this man. He is me! This was my life. This is what we came to see. I reel from it, unable to hold myself up. Then Leonid has hold of me. Norwenna is with him, on my other side.

"When you heal for you, you heal for all of us!" she shouts to me. "This will not be, cannot be, done again. Have the courage to heal it!"

I look at her as she shouts at me, knowing she's asking for help, too. But I can't do any more. Tears are streaming down my face. I know I can't see or hear any more of this. I can only feel the horror of what I've done. I lean over and vomit for what feels like a long time, feeling Leonid support me, wanting to rid myself of those images, the realization of what I've done.

I can't help but be swallowed in the shame of it, the horror of realizing I'm the kind of person who could do such things. I've always known of these kinds of horrors. This is everything I've spent my life protesting against. But I had classified the people who did them with the Hitlers, the crazed, those beyond saving. The lowest of the low. And I'm one of them. How do I live with that?

"By realizing you're not beyond saving. No one is. You're one of the saved," Leonid says.

"And don't kid yourself!" Norwenna says fiercely. "We're all that kind of people. Why do you think I'm here today? I'm that kind of person, too! If this planet is about war, who do you think has been fighting them for thousands of years? We all have! Do you think all your lives were about being a good person? What would be the point of that? And wouldn't there be more signs of that in the world?" She cries as she talks to me, gripping my arm hard, her face close to mine, so I can't look away.

"Lives usually lead people to the hard places. Then people have the chance to lead themselves out, if they will. That's what cleanses the person and the place. That's what you are doing today. And don't forget, you're healing all of us, you know? This is what we're meant to do—heal ourselves and each other."

We look at each other. I continue to cry—*like a baby*, I think. When I watched myself pick up that baby, I remember that I had the baby's perspective for just a moment. The world was spinning dizzily around me before there was an explosion of darkness. I felt no pain, but I felt extreme fear and loss. I think about the comfort I am getting right now, holding onto Leonid, and realize that's part of what I took from the baby—the hope of any future comfort from its mother. I'm also taken by the unexpectedness of Leonid, a cohort member who knows everything about me and is still willing to hold onto me while I vomit and cry. Have I ever done that for anybody?

After some time, the three of us settle to the ground, and Leonid has gotten us some water in a kind of leather bag. I thankfully drink and so does Norwenna, while we lean back against a giant tree. The battle projection is gone, I think, but the trees remain as reminders. I look up at them, and I see how beautiful they are. They are ever-constant witnesses, reminding us of what can be survived. The fading sun creates shadows through their leaves, turning everything on the ground gold. The beauty they create takes my breath for a moment, as I discover I can still appreciate beauty. The beauty gives me hope.

Then I doze or lose consciousness. Some time passes— as when I was falling in the Void. When I look up again at Leonid, I'm still on the ground, leaning against the same tree with Norwenna. It's quiet in the woods, the light now moving into twilight. I hear no bird or insect sounds.

Leonid says, crouching down next to us, "Let's finish the healing, Miles. Let's think about the baby a minute, to come full circle. Let's honor the baby a minute." He touches my face gently. "Look at me, Miles." I look away from the battlefield into his kind face.

"There are no babies, you know. We're all the same age." He smiles, and I look at him numbly.

"So, the baby made a choice, too, in between lives. Made that choice for you. To get the lesson. To help everyone to never do it again. To help us heal. So, think about the baby a minute, not yourself. Let's thank the baby."

"Wait a minute! What lesson?" I ask, barely able to get words out. "What lesson could there be in this? Help me see that."

"Fighting over land is one thing. Killing children is another. It's after a different kind of power, isn't it? Those who take the lives of children want the power of God, don't they? Then they're the indisputable winners, land or no land. Who can compete with that? If you've taken away what God has begotten, then you can call yourselves gods and you can demand to be worshipped as gods. So, you get all kinds of added value from killing children. You begin to see it as a useful, even necessary, part of warfare. But tampering with children brings an early and harsh darkness to the world. We're forced to see that something like that is possible. Children are supposed to be protected and given a chance at life. What's the purpose of anything if this isn't true? Who wants to be in a world like this? Everyone's spirit is drained, weakened by such acts. So, it's the ultimate warfare, isn't it? A kind of total defeat—physically, emotionally, and spiritually. What would be left that you could do to people that would matter more? Why would they want to go on?"

"Agreed!" I shout at him, demoralized by his words. "Agreed! So what's the lesson?"

"Something has to bring us back from that self-annihilating edge," Leonid says. "The baby is an example of someone willing to try to find a way."

I'm stunned into silence. The baby, who had seemed to be the embodiment of victim, turns out to be the embodiment of hero instead.

"Remember, it's not a baby. It's a spiritual entity, just like you, on an earthly journey—a journey that's supposed to make a difference, for the good in the world. That's what we spend our lives for. So, that baby gave its life for you, to stop you from doing such a thing again. It gave its life for everyone who witnessed it, so they'd never forget and the generations of warfare could end. And it gave its life for itself, too, to experience the growth in understanding and compassion that such an act begets." He smiles again at me. I'm still stunned by it all.

"We witnessed a great thing today," he says to me and to Norwenna, who has been listening intently. "Every day people on Earth give themselves and their lives for each other. Like Jesus did. We all do have a chance at emulating the model he laid before us." He sees my still-stupefied look and says, "Just remember that the things babies do are usually the best lessons. Not the things men do." He smiles at his own comparison, nodding.

Norwenna, like me, sits and stares into the distance, with her own thoughts. I take her hand, and she squeezes mine back. I sit there, remembering the baby. I can hardly imagine such courage. The woods are still quiet around us.

"How do we thank the baby?" Norwenna asks, remembering Leonid's suggestion.

"From our hearts," Leonid says, looking at us both.

I bow my head and Norwenna and Leonid do, too. I fervently thank the baby for its incredible act of service, as tears flow from my eyes. I haven't words for it, I just emanate a feeling of gratitude from my heart, focused on the baby. I am engulfed by my love for the baby.

Suddenly, I know who the baby is. It comes to me. It's Silvia, my sister in this life! Duncan Robert's mother. I see her smiling image in front of me. Silvia, whose one wish would have been to end all war.

"That's who would do such a thing for you, to heal you and all concerned. She wasn't doing it because it was karmic payback for her. She was doing it to learn higher service through you. Now, that's love!" Leonid says with a laugh. "But then, what isn't?"

"Is she our cohort?" I ask, in wonderment.

"No, she's a neighboring cohort, one that works with us regularly, depending on common purposes," Leonid says. "That's why you feel such a connection to her. You know her."

I shake my head. "But who would ever think that we shared such a thing? How do you pay back things like that?"

"That's the kind of thing we work out as a group. I mean, think about it. How many people were involved in this battle today? Lots. And all were in on the planning, between lives. You never deal with these things alone. Things like battles involve a lot of karma, a lot of opportunities, a lot of specific activities to be orchestrated. They're taken very seriously, believe me. We're trying to see that these things don't happen again."

"But, my god, you plan killing babies?" I ask, and I can hear the anguish and accusation in my voice.

"No, we don't plan killing babies," Leonid says, unperturbed, "but we know it's a possibility. We know where all this battling can lead, you remember, because we've experienced it many times before. So we're ready for most things. That's how Silvia could have chosen her role—because she knew how yours might play out. All of us wanted you to get the lesson, to be saved, to help us end the killings, rather than continue to be a part of perpetuating them, by leaving them unpurged."

I'm dumbfounded into silence once again. Leonid says, "As Norwenna said, this is what a string of lives looks like in our cohort. It's a lot to try to heal from, a lot of people to be healed. That's why we did what we did today. And what you did today has reversed that string of lives for us. I wish you could understand the significance of that." He gives my shoulder a little shake, smiling at me again.

Norwenna squeezes my hand. "I needed it, Miles. You know that. Thanks for helping provide it."

"Where's Ethelred?" I ask, suddenly remembering this was Ethelred's battle, too.

"He'll meet us back at the castle. He lost sons in this battle, you know, so he always gets a little melancholy. He had to do his own healing around that. He knew this was yours to do, or not. He didn't want to influence it one way or the other. Your choice, always."

Norwenna says, "You know, this battle was in a particular time, a time before rules of warfare emerged. Rules came with Arthur and the Knights of the Round Table, later. This battle reminded me how important the rules are. They provided the first formal recognition of the difference between soldiers and civilians—women and children and older persons—helping to ensure terrible killings like we saw today couldn't happen again. They provided a space for justice and fairness within the bloodshed." She pauses to look at me. "And I fought them! I didn't want any reason not to kill."

We look at each other, holding each other's hands, forgiving each other.

Leonid nods his head towards the castle, and we get up from our spot under the tree. I dust off the seat of my pants, feeling stiff and bone weary. The light has almost faded from the sky, and I see our rising has startled a large flock of ravens into rising up from the field in front of us, where the battle was. The ravens head into the woods, and I remember that ravens were regular battle field scavengers, to the degree that myths grew up around their being the bringers of death, not just the scavengers of it. I shake my head at that, thinking about how often we've shifted blame to animals and other aspects of nature for anything bad that happens, rather than see ourselves as the cause.

As we walk, I can see by the soft glow over the far hill to the east that a moon will be rising soon. "Isn't this where we were just a short while ago," I think, "walking with Ethelred across this field in the moonlight?"

Leonid, who has heard my thought, says, "And it's still beautiful, isn't it? The field."

"Yes, it is," I agree, "but I wouldn't want to return to those woods."

"Neither would I," Leonid says. "And now you don't ever have to. None of us do. Thank you."

"Stop it, now, or you'll make me cry again," I say wearily. "Thank you."

"We've helped a lot of people today," Leonid says, thoughtfully.

We walk back across the field, through the knee-high grass, back to the castle, and I think of this thing between us, this thing that is "a bond stronger than life." I sigh. I had had no idea.

Ethelred is waiting for us at the castle, at the small outside door that we exited by, just the other side of the animal pens. He gives me the same kind of bear hug he greeted the others with, and I have the breath crushed out of me while I feel my feet leave the ground. It's not altogether unpleasant. We go back up the winding stairs and into Ethelred's large room, where Keilor is sitting by the fire and a feast waits by candlelight. There's a tart red wine, good bread, plain roasted meat with a few roasted vegetables. We fall to it, surprising ourselves with our hunger.

The food tastes wonderful. Rosemary and fennel and onion flavor the meat and vegetables. I still get pleasure from sitting in a castle, at night, with a king, savoring a meal.

At the end of the meal, we talk about my return to my life. The rest of them are going back to their between-lives pursuits. They tell me I will fall asleep here and awaken back at the edge of the Void, in my world. I wonder about my life back there and how it will change because of what I know now.

"It will come to you. You will know what to do," Leonid says. "You have your place back there, your work, your life. You did not come to the Void searching for those things. You came to deepen your own understanding through the lifting of the negativity that has haunted you." He smiles at me. "You would never have been a war protester without these wars to protest. You now have a real compassion you didn't have. Your heart is different now."

The Void was calling to me for a long time, and I resisted. I see why.

Leonid just smiles at that. "You are a story teller and a keeper of stories. You've always kept the stories that do the most healing. Keep teaching, Miles. Keep speaking out. And keep your students reading their stories out loud! No matter how much they object!" Leonid laughs.

"You've done a good job. Now you can relax a little. Deep down, you can believe you are a good man, worthy of anything. Or anyone." He smiles mischievously at this. I blush, thinking of Babe, despite trying to hide it from Leonid, who knows all.

As I prepare to sleep on the low straw berth up against the wall, near the fire, Ethelred, Leonid, Norwenna, and Keilor come to say good bye. I get another bear hug from Ethelred—a long one. When Ethelred puts me back down on the ground, I can see the gleam of tears in his eyes.

"You helped my sons today, you know," he says. "They've gone Home, to be with their mother." He looks at me.

He brings tears to my eyes.

"We released all today that was holding us back from wholeness of spirit—guilt, shame, regret. We let down our borders and defenses and made ourselves vulnerable to the scene from our heart's perspective. We won't kill in these ways again." He, a king, stands and moves into a deep bow to me. Before I can stand, he has moved back into the shadow. "Until next time!" he says as he goes.

Leonid steps out of the shadows. I stand, and as we hug, I realize Leonid is no longer a mutant. He is no longer deformed. He's almost eye-to-eye with me now. His body is straight and strong, his teeth are restored, he shines with good health and well-being. I have to laugh.

"You're yourself again, you handsome devil!"

We both laugh and hug again. Leonid says, "You'll never know all the ways you've helped. We never do."

"Does it always take such an ordeal to heal?" I'm thinking of the dark, dark space I went after the battle.

"No. It's only the resistance to look at it that makes it hard."

"I feel scoured clean by it." I take his hands in mine. "Thank you for guiding it." We hug one last time. As he walks away, I declare, "And you are a handsome devil!"

He laughs as he moves back into the shadows.

Norwenna steps forward and takes my hands. I grip her hands and smile at her.

"We were in lots of fighting lives together," she says, "laying waste to everything around us, known for it, even proud of it." She pauses, looking at me. "I found it harder to leave than you did. I didn't have that storytelling thing that you do." She smiles. "Even back then, you used to be the one who wove the battle stories together at night, around the fire. I look back on the singing and dancing and storytelling around the fire and wonder if that was us at our best." She looks back at me. "Even then, you had more than just fighting energy.

"I never felt I had any other skill. For the longest time, war was all I knew to do, so I kept going back to it, thinking I could heal it from within. But I hadn't built the resources to do that. I see that now. I can see that being a woman for a few lives builds a wealth of resources."

She smiles sadly at me. "A woman wouldn't do what we did on that battlefield. And she'd know why, because she knows what she values." She pauses to stare into my eyes.

"I just think I need to consider the woman's perspective for a while." She laughs.

She stands and we hug. As she walks away, she turns to blow me a kiss with both hands, a very womanly thing to do. "You're getting better at the woman stuff!" I call after her. She laughs and waves over her shoulder and moves off into the shadows.

I'm too keyed up to sleep, so I'm glad to see Keilor come and sit on the edge of the berth with me. I want to hear what the day was like for him.

"Tell me what you did today," I say. "I didn't see you, but I felt you around."

"Yes, that would be right," he says, "because I wasn't there to be seen." He smiles at me. "I dissipated my physical form into pure energy. I did this to provide protection, direction, and guidance to all of us who were there trying to heal that battlefield. As energy, I could see where I was needed the most.

"You remember my energy holds steady and constant. It does not waver. When I bring my energy into a space, like this battlefield, it can re-align all the positive energy that's there. It will then follow the highest intent present. And we had of course set the intent to heal. The energy of the trees, the rocks, the water, the wind, the animals, can all be called on, as well as the other natural forces, the ancestors, galactic forces, light beings, and so forth. All the forces indigenous peoples have always called on." He smiles.

I stand to hug him, but he stands and takes my hands in both of his instead. Then he drops to one knee and places his forehead on our joined hands. After a moment, he looks up and smiles. "This is how we do it where I'm from."

I laugh, charmed and moved by his gesture. Then I drop to one knee, too, and he laughs. We look at each other and then touch foreheads. I know I will never forget this moment. "Neither will I," he says. We rise together, and he turns to walk into the shadows, looking back once, raising his hand. I raise mine, and he's gone.

I sit and remember all the horrors we saw this day. How often during the day I believed "I can't," or "It's more than I can bear," or "I don't want to do this!" How I was weakened by horror and shame and self-loathing. I was never sure I wanted to, or could, go on. Through it all, Keilor's energy remained constant.

As I lay down to sleep, covering myself with a rough blanket, I watch the coals of the fire glow. I feel a greater peace than I've known before, because I know now who is in the world with me, working for the good. I think of home and Babe and fall sound asleep.

CHAPTER TWENTY-TWO

Carrie Jean

THE MORNING OF MILES and Babe's jump, I sit at the Void, in the grass, thinking about what I just witnessed.

Why am I around so much jumping? Duncan Robert. Babe and Miles. Our mom, they say. And my brother, even if he didn't jump into the Void. I can't help but feel destiny pushing me.

I look at the waving grass, the wind bending it to the Void. Tribal lore tells of the people the Void has caught over the years. There weren't that many—a young man who felt called to jump as part of his vision quest, another young man who was said to have jumped from a broken heart, a woman who dreamed it first, and a few others. Who knows how many, or even if any of the stories are true? After all it's all oral history, as they say. Still, the stories of those individual jumps have created a master story to describe the purpose and meaning of the Void, if I could just put it together. Then maybe I could understand it.

All those jumpers made it a place of jumping. But it was there before them. It had its own story to start with. What was it? I know all of this jumping has triggered my own buried stories, and I'm uneasy with it.

Am I a jumper, too? I have to laugh. I don't even know if I'm an Indian! I've hardly thought of myself that way, except for my connection to Granny. Is blood the only determiner, or are we Indian because we live with one, or because we participate in some Indian practices, like eating frybread or going to pow-wows? Would we be Indian if we didn't do those things? Does it matter how a person feels about it? Could we opt out of it? Or maybe we are all part-time Indians, like Sherman Alexie says. We have the blood, whether or not we have much else.

Another Indian, John Trudell, one of the founders of the American Indian Movement, is one of my heroes, too. He said he felt as if he had been knocked unconscious when he was born and has been trying to gain consciousness ever since. That's exactly how I feel. I study our history, but it doesn't give me answers.

Wounded Knee, John Trudell, Leonard Peltier, the American Indian Movement, these are the stories I collect, to see if I can build an understanding of myself out of them.

We're a seriously oppressed people, generally dirt poor, with high rates of alcoholism and suicide. No one expects much of us, and generally, we live up to that. Add to that my own family stories—not knowing my parents, losing my brother, rumors of my mother's jump—and where does that leave me? Nowhere to go but the Void? How do I build my own story?

I think about Granny. She's the only person I know who built her own story. You never can forget Granny is Navajo because she still dresses in the traditional Navaho way—long gathered skirt, stopping just past the tops of her knee-high moccasins, blue work shirt loose over her skirt, buttoned up all the way and cinched with a sash at her waist, purple shawl. Silver jewelry, when she dresses up. Long gray hair in the trademark Navajo double bun, every day of her life, since she reached puberty.

She's unlike anyone else I know. She's got that fierce, frowning hawk visage and is all business. She acts on and speaks her truth when she has a mind to, to anyone, anywhere, any time. She's fearless, which makes her seem powerful and dangerous. She was always larger than life to me and Jimmy Lynn. There is no doubt that she's an Indian.

I look up, gauging the sun's progress and stand up stiffly, realizing the sun is now much lower in the sky. I laugh at what being near the Void always does to time, brushing off my jeans and walking home through the field between Granny's bungalow and the Void.

At home, I watch Granny now, as she moves in the kitchen, wondering what she knows of all that's happened at the Void. I'm starving and I'm home in time for dinner, not saying anything about what I've seen. We eat bowls of green chili stew from the big pot at the back of the wood-burning stove, with her home-made tortillas, grilled right on top of the stove. As usual, we don't talk, but it's a companionable silence.

Dinner is finished and we have washed up. This is Granny's usual flat bread-making time. The kitchen table is clear for her to set up her makings and spread out. I'm sitting in the old rocker near the little pot-bellied stove in the corner of the tiny living room, legs crossed under me, my American history book open in my lap. As night comes on, a chill comes into the room with the dark, not leaving until the dark does. I'm glad for the warmth from the stove. I'm trying to catch up on my reading for my American history class, but my mind keeps going back to the clearing that morning. Babe and Miles's jump is as much with me as anything in the room.

"I saw them, too," Granny says, as if I had said my thoughts out loud.

I close my book and look at her.

"I saw you, too," she adds, stopping her bread making and looking directly at me.

"Why didn't you say something?"

"We were too filled with it, don't you think? I was. It wasn't the time to talk about it."

"But it is now?" I ask, belligerently, annoyed at her for keeping yet another secret, knowing we are both deeply disturbed by what we've seen.

"Yes," she says, going back to setting out her ingredients—flour, salt, baking powder.

"How did you know?" I ask, knowing I'd said nothing to her earlier to indicate I thought the jump was going to happen.

"I was out there the night before, talking with the Void. I knew I was to wait and watch and not interfere, just like that other time. It was birthing a new story, and I would be part of it. I understood it was transforming itself somehow, and I did what I know to do in such cases. I offered prayers."

"It seems to me your prayers were answered, if more jumps indicate a change in things."

"I hadn't seen anybody jump in a long time. It startled me to see it." She sits in the nearest chair, resting her floured hands on the table. "I knew something was going to happen—there had been so many signs for a watcher to see, and I've been a watcher a long time. The crows were one. More people visiting the Void was another. I could see the animals sensed it, and it made them tense. Even the air held the ancient energy that first made this ground sacred. It made me remember the time of that other jump." She stares into the space in front of her, barely breathing, her hands touching the cloth bag of flour in front of her.

I'm tired of the references to secrets, secrets that harbor my story, too. "I'm part of that change, Granny. I can feel it, too. It called me out there, too. I'm part of this, and now I need the rest of the story, and I know you have it." The anger in my voice startles her.

She looks at me. I see fear and sadness shadow her face, giving it more sharp hollows, aging her. I stop, uncertain if I really want to know. I'm sure she'll tell me of my mother's jump, about which I know nothing, and now I'm scared. I don't know if I can carry more ghost memories. But there's no turning back. It's not just my mother. It's her daughter, too. How have I not remembered that?

Granny pushes the bag of flour away as if it now weighs more than she can lift. She dusts her hands on the towel on her shoulder and comes around the table to sit in the over-stuffed chair across from me—the only other piece of furniture in the living room. Her hands sit open in her lap, bereft of anything to hold.

"Yes, the elders have always known more than they ever say. I think they don't understand it all themselves, so how can they unravel its story? And maybe they're ashamed of it," she says as she looks thoughtfully at the little fire.

"Ashamed?"

"Most of the Tribe has always considered the Void a place of ceremony, and we were comfortable doing that— vision quests, dream interpretation, naming ceremonies, that kind of thing—for as long as anyone could remember. We considered it a doorway to Great Mystery and made many offerings there. But I think the elders have secretly seen the Void as a place that accepts the Tribe's failures, because they see jumping as a failure—a failure to manage life. So they attach shame to the Void. And a jump happens in too public a way—a way that's harder to hide."

She stops a moment. "I think we feel every failure as our own, too, and we're afraid they weaken us, weaken our ability to succeed at life."

"But why did the Void allow suicide jumps?"

"They weren't suicide jumps, Carrie Jean. If they're allowed to jump, we just don't have the complete story. The Void doesn't make mistakes. The Tribe forgets this."

This direct, intense attention from her humbles me. She was always so busy, focused on several tasks at once, herding my brother and me into helping her. Sitting quietly like this, she almost seems like another person.

"Of course, rumors sprang up around it—people had only an incomplete story. They thought it was a story about a woman who jumped, but that wasn't true. The woman had just disappeared. It was a child who jumped."

"A child?" I croak, unable to catch a full breath.

She continues to look at me, unblinking. "It stunned everybody. No one knew what else to do but keep it secret, which was always the Tribe's way for most things. The child—a girl—belonged to the woman everyone thought had jumped."

After a moment, she says, "Your mother."

"Your daughter," I whisper. "My sister jumped?"

Granny nods. "My granddaughter." She pulls her eyes away from me and looks off again into the space in front of her.

"She was a fierce little thing. I thought she was an incarnation of my younger self. I was so proud of her. She was so smart. She comprehended things before I could put them together. I'd see the realization in her eyes and know she had already gone somewhere else, ahead of me." She looks back at me. "A child jumped, but she did it for the adults."

"Wait a minute. What happened? How did such a thing happen?"

"Let me get some water," Granny says, rising stiffly from her chair, as if she's been sitting for hours. It's only been a few minutes.

"Let's make some tea." I feel in need of some sustenance, something to warm the coldness that's now inside me. I'm weary from this day, but I rise, too, moving to the kitchen, glad for something to do. It's too much to sit with.

Granny lights the fire under the kettle on the stove. The kettle always has water in it—that's a habit from the old days, too, when you had to travel to the source to get it. I get the tin of loose tea leaves from the shelf above the sink. I bring it to the kitchen table where Granny has already set out two mugs and the old, chipped Fiestaware tea pot, which is a cheerful yellow. I use the tea ball to scoop tea from the tin, then close the ball and hook it onto the rim of the tea pot. We settle into chairs at the table to wait for the watched pot to boil. The bread makings are still there, unused, which never happens in this kitchen.

"I wish I still used tobacco," Granny says, surprising me. I hadn't known she ever had. "Or drank alcohol," she adds, looking at me with a smile. "Though I never really did."

I find myself smiling back. Why should I be surprised to see that I still love her? Because, she and her secrets have tormented me and my brother for years, leaving us to live with gaps in knowing that made us unable to direct our own lives. Did it cost Jimmy Lynn his life? How much of the responsibility for that belongs to her? I'm unable to ask her that, still wondering how much it might have been my fault. How do any of us hold ourselves blameless?

The kettle whistles, and Granny gets it, turns off the fire, and brings it to the table to fill the pot. "We'll let it steep for a few minutes, to build its strength," she says.

We wait, and as we do, she takes my hands in hers, studying them. This action is so uncommon that it speaks volumes to me—she still wishes she could spare me this telling of the truth, but she knows she can't. It's time—I'm old enough.

We will be equal now, two grown women, moving forward together, no longer separated by age. Girls don't become women when the Tribe celebrates their first menstrual cycle. They become women when life's events make them so.

"Rebecca," she says, "that was her name. She was eight years old. You and Jimmy Lynn would have been three. She had a different father than you two did. His name was Robert. He was what we used to call a half-breed. One of his parents had been white, and he showed it."

She looks at me. "That means he could often pass for white, which he did. He had come down from Canada, looking for work, he said. Probably looking for more than that. He parked cars at the country club. Sometimes he would drive for some of the members when they came out our way to hunt. They always needed a driver because they really came out to party, just like they do nowadays. And those men liked him. He seemed almost one of them—he had some education, manners, charm. They picked him often as a driver, and some of them came out our way for more than just hunting." She stops and pours tea into both our mugs, looking up at me, and I nod to let her know, yes, I get what she's talking about.

"When he was with us, he seemed like one of us. He'd come out by himself and hang out at the Tribal store, meeting people, talking. He spoke native in a way that let you know he'd learned it at home. He was funny. We liked him.

"To this day, I don't know how or when he and your mother met. All I know is that he started pulling up outside the house in his old Buick, and she'd go out to meet him. She was still in high school, but I couldn't do anything with her, short of wrestling her to the ground, which I'd tried a time or two, I can tell you. But I knew it did no good. I will say that I think he was smitten with her, too."

She looks directly at me again, reading me. "Yeah, it's an old story." She shakes her head. "Why do you suppose it keeps happening?"

"It's new to the people it's happening to?" It's all I can think of to say. It's not hard to imagine it happening to me. Don't we want it to happen to us? To have a great, all-consuming love that nothing can stop? Isn't that true of all of us, no matter our origins? Isn't it true of Granny? I look at her and think maybe it is, or at least was, but that's not a story she tells, either.

Granny sips her tea and then says, as if she's heard my thoughts again, "I suppose you're right. I suppose that's how it looks to us when we're caught in it—something not to be denied, something that comes before anything else, something that takes the place of food and water and sleep. We just don't know that it won't stay that way."

She gets up and goes to the breadbox by the stove. She pulls out her secret stash of Girl Scout cookies—her one real weakness. She buys boxes of them by the dozen when the selling season rolls around, and she freezes them for later, so that she'll never be without. The Samoas are her favorite, though they're not called that any more except by her, and she usually hates to share them. Now she puts a few on a plate and puts the plate in the center of the table, near both of us, so I know I'm allowed to have some.

"The rest of it is an old story, too. I bet you could guess it. Girl gets pregnant, boy gets scared and runs. Girl's heart is broken. Boy can't stay away." She nibbles a cookie, though I don't think they're providing much comfort. "Natalie Wood and James Dean—that's who they reminded me of—always battling the grown-up world. Do you remember them?"

I nod, sipping my tea, remembering *Rebel Without a Cause* and all those old movies that would come on just after I got home from school. Maybe my mother used to watch them, too. "Maybe that's how we get brainwashed into trying to make their stories our stories, even if their stories are tragedies," I say.

"This back-and-forth continues until Rebecca is born. Then they decide to settle down. He's working at the feed store, parking cars at night, so they can afford to rent a little two-room house over off Crawford," she says, referring to a two-block street not far from here. "But I don't think settling down is in his nature, or at least it wasn't then. It's a fight he's having with himself, but she's the only visible opponent, so it's with her he fights. There's not much satisfaction in that, and it just drives him to drink." She pauses to add more tea to her mug and then takes the tea ball from the pot and puts it in the sink. She comes back to sit in her chair, picks up her mug and stares into the space in front of her again.

I can't imagine what all these memories dredge up for her. That's another reason these stories don't get told.

"Time passes before the settling-down thing really disagrees with him. It's hard for him to come home every night to the same thing. No adventure. So he starts taking little trips, into the city, sometimes north, sometimes who knows where. What we do know is that he's home less and less, and when he is, they're fighting more and more. Finally he tells her he's taken a job up north. He'll try to make some money and then come back. Of course he'll be back, he says. Meanwhile, she and Rebecca move in with me." She looks at me again. "I love having them here, but the spark has gone out of her."

"She still loves him."

"She still loves him," Granny agrees.

"What happens next?" I ask, feeling as if the story is coming to a close.

"She hears from him less and less—an occasional late-night, drunken love call; occasional checks in the mail and sometimes they bounce. Soon it's been months, and life begins to move on without him. They had never married, so there is no pledge to hold them together. Rebecca is four, in pre-school, though I think she could have taught it, she was that bright. Your mom is waitressing. We've settled into our own routines and life is peaceful.

"Suddenly *your* dad, Benny, is now part of the picture. Brought in by a car—isn't that the way? Girls riding in cars. He gives her rides home from work, where he is a waiter, too. And he lives right here with the Tribe. He's one of us. I have hopes. I like him. They're good together. They come in after their shifts and take over my kitchen. They cook, they serve, they even clean up. And it's good. Little Rebecca laughs like I've never heard her laugh. She's enchanted with him and him with her. They've become a family.

"Soon, once again, your mom is pregnant—with you and your brother. Your mom and dad decide to marry, without telling us. They go to a justice of the peace in the city and come home married. Then they go to live with his parents, who have more room than I do, so I don't see them so much, though I hear things, because their business is more out in the community now. His parents drink and are on welfare, but their hearts seem to be in the right place, and they're peaceful drunks, gradually falling asleep as they drink, hurting no one, except maybe by neglect. They sponsor a traditional ceremony for your parents, and things are done right for the beginning of their lives together. You two are born and again ceremonies are held, to welcome you two and give you your first names and celebrate your first laughs. Rebecca seems right at home with it all, and you two worship her from the start. She has found her place in the world, which is the big sister in the middle of your world, seeing the two of you get raised right. Some time passes. And then what do you think happens?"

"Robert comes back," I say with conviction, knowing it must be so.

"Apparently things didn't go so well for him up north, so he comes back down here, a little the worse for wear, expecting to pick up where he left off. He doesn't like what he finds. And I think he's hardly ever sober now. So, it only takes one night for it all to go to pieces. I can tell you what I heard from others and what I know because I saw it myself. What I heard was that she agreed to meet him, out at the Void, apparently an old favorite place of theirs. I don't know if she agreed to meet him because she still loves him or just to placate him.

"I don't feel good about this and know that I must go out there, too. Benny apparently felt the same way, because he goes out there, before the appointed meeting time. What none of us knew was that Rebecca stowed away in the back of Benny's truck, apparently worried about it all and determined to do her part to preserve the family. Also, this is her father who has come to town, and she must be having some feelings about that, too. She's only eight. What could she be doing with this adult-world melodrama?

"I go out in the morning, doing ceremony at the Void. I go to pray and to seek guidance, offering tobacco, corn, and other things in gratitude for the help I knew would be forthcoming. I had visions during the day and knew someone was going to jump into the Void. I knew I wasn't meant to stop it. I was there to witness so I could be of support to others. I can't think of anything harder—not to try to save the people you care most about, but it's not the first time I've been asked to do this.

"Before I know it, night has come, and I'm sitting in the dark at the edge of the Void. There's a half moon up, and its glow pales the clearing, making it hard to see where things begin and end. I hear a car coming up the dirt road and I move back into the trees, making myself small and invisible. I'm quiet, knowing things are at work here over which I have no control. I pray.

"Robert is out of the car, and I hear him moving through the grass up to the Void. He stands at the edge, and the wind from the Void moves his hair. He pulls a flask from his jacket pocket and takes a deep drink. He puts the flask away and wipes his mouth with his sleeve. Then he turns abruptly and walks back towards his car. As he does so, I see the lights of your mother's car coming up the road. He's there to meet her when she pulls off the road. She gets out of the car and I can hear them exchanging words that I can't make out. She won't let him touch her. I continue to pray, working to surround them with prayer. Soon they're closer to me, between me and the Void. I can hear them clearly now.

"I'm married!" she says. "And that means something to me! There's no place for you in that. It was never what you wanted anyway."

"I always wanted you," he tells her. "That hasn't changed."

"It has for me," she says. "That's what I'm saying."

"I don't believe you," he says and moves to kiss her.

"She's wrestling with him, though I think he gets a kiss or two in. I'll never know if that's what she wanted. All of a sudden, a form comes out of the dark and lands on them. It's your father, Benny, who must have parked down the road and snuck up on them. He's trying to fight Robert, and your mother is caught in the middle of it. The three of them fall to the ground, scuffling.

"Then we all hear a high-pitched scream, a child's scream, and everything stops. It's Rebecca, who has found her way to them. All three of them start to disentangle themselves and get up, to move towards her. Before they can do so, she has moved to the edge of the Void. She stops for a moment and looks back over her shoulder at them. I can't read her expression. By then I've moved out of the woods.

"'Rebecca!'" your mother screams, a terrible sound, and then Rebecca jumps. She's gone. There's only dark at the edge of the Void.

"The shock of it stops even the world for a moment. I feel the trees recoil, and sound and movement in the forest stops. I think of Rebecca falling into the dark of that sacred space. I have a relationship with the Void, built over many ceremonies, many prayers, many talks. Every loss I ever had was shared and healed there. I can't think of it as a bad place to fall. But I know it's bad for those who watched it happen. And I, too, want her back. That was the first time I had ever seen anyone jump.

"Then we start to move. Your mother half crawls, half runs to the Void's edge, and I think would have hurtled herself in after her daughter if both men hadn't stopped her. Robert is making unintelligible sounds or sobs. He and your father look at each other, if they can see each other in the dark, and Robert lets go of your mother. He turns and stumbles back to his car and drives off. He leaves what's left of his spirit there. I never see him again. It was rumored that he drank his way back up north and then finished the job of obliterating his memories and himself when he got there.

"Your father wants to get your mother away from the Void, hoping that will get her away from the worst of her pain, so she can begin to return to herself. Of course she doesn't want to leave. I come out of the woods to help them. I find the old comforting words, and I chant them. These words are unintelligible to them, just sounds, but on a deeper level, I know they hear them. Your mother just collapses. Your father lifts her and takes her to her car. He tells me to take his truck. He realizes I must have walked over there. I follow him, and he brings her here and we put her to bed." She pauses to settle her emotions, taking a sip of her now-cold tea. She looks back up at me, checking. She continues.

"Her life went on after that, but she never returned to inhabit it. She just went through the motions. You and your brother stayed out with your father and his parents. I don't know how Benny managed. I hardly saw him. It seemed his heart had been broken twice. Soon he left, too, supposedly to find work, but I think because he just couldn't bear to live that close to the source of his pain. He believed your mother loved Robert, that that's why she had gone out there that night. She never said otherwise. She never said anything.

"Then one night, not long after Rebecca's jump, your mother jumped," she says, knowing I know that. She looks at me quickly. "But not into the Void, as everybody thinks. I don't think she could have jumped into the Void. It isn't a place of suicide, but also I don't think she felt good enough to follow Rebecca into that sacred space. She must have believed everything was her fault, that she deserved some punishing. She got herself into a place where she thought she was doing you and your brother a service by removing herself from your lives, or she would doom you like she'd doomed Rebecca. She couldn't trust herself not to." She pauses a moment, cradling her mug in her two hands. She looks at me, and I know it's hard for her to do that. I know because it's hard for me to look at her.

"She tied a rope around her neck and jumped from the tree on the north side of the house," she says. "I'm so glad I found her and not any of you. I got the ladder and got her down. I did ceremony for her as best I could and cleaned and dressed her, burying her right away with what possessions I had of hers. She's buried a ways from here. I'll show you where." She looks thoughtful. "It was like her to arrange her death outside so that we could still use the house." She looks at me again. "For Navajo women, suicide isn't unheard of for women grieving the loss of a child, though suicide has always been rare for us. I think she felt cornered by her pain and killing herself was her only defense. Suicide is not so condemned by Navajos as it is by whites. But her rope goes with her."

That stops me, and I look at her. "That's what we believe," she says. "Your weapon for getting there always goes with you to the other side.

"Those were hard days for me," she says. "You'll never know how much having the two of you with me helped. After Benny left, his parents asked if I'd care for you and your brother. They were getting older, and the alcohol was taking its toll. They were both diabetic and not able to get around as well. You two were a blessing to me."

"What do you know of why Rebecca jumped?" I ask, knowing she knows.

"She did come to me in dreams for a while. She still will sometimes." She moves the cookies around on the plate, not looking at me. "She tells me she thinks her mom would have jumped if she hadn't. 'I just knew I was supposed to,' she says." She pushes the cookie plate away from her.

"She thought one of the men might have killed the other, too. She just said she knew she was supposed to jump. She was at peace about it. More than at peace—I could tell that she never questioned that jumping was the right thing to do." She looks up at me. "That's how I got any peace with it. From her."

Then she smiles at me. I'm startled by that unexpected brightness. "What?"

"And from you and your brother."

"What do you mean?" I remember nothing of those things that happened when Jimmy Lynn and I were three. Both of us had no memory of either of our parents or Rebecca, even when shown pictures. I know we believed we loved them and they loved us, but that things had happened to carry us apart from each other. It probably helped that most kids we knew had lost family members and many didn't have either or both parents. It was the way things were. You were raised by whoever was handy, often one or both grandparents.

"You two never said a word about any of it—your big sister gone, your mother gone, your father leaving shortly after, and moving from your grandparents. So I never talked of it either. You were the best-natured little things! You made me laugh a lot. I think having each other helped. I know it helped me. You two were pretty inseparable."

That made me think of what makes it possible for anyone to survive. I look back at Granny.

"We were lucky you were there for us."

Granny has tears in her eyes, but they don't fall. "I think that's the hardest thing I ever learned from the Void." She speaks slowly and deliberately. "You can't change the lives of others. You can only witness." She looks at me and laughs a dry laugh. "It's still a hard lesson for an interfering old woman like me to learn! I do think I've gotten better, though, because there have been lots of lessons."

We're quiet for a few moments. I'm saying goodbye to my mother in a new way now, saying hello to my sister for the first time, and looking at what the Void holds differently now.

Granny is still clearly in the mind-reading business. "So. Look who is jumping now. White people. Duncan Robert. Babe. Miles. Who's next." It's not a question. She looks at me intently. I can't answer her, but not because I'm resisting the question. Something else has occurred to me.

"They all come out." I know this to be true. "I mean, Duncan Robert has. And I believe Babe and Miles will, too. I don't know about the ones before them."

We look at each other.

"Where's Rebecca?"

"I don't know," Granny answers. "And I don't know about any of the others. If they came out, they didn't stay around here. Their stories end with their jumps."

We look at each other again.

"I do know that the Void is changing itself," Granny says, "to be of better service. It's not the only sacred spot that's changing in the world. I think they're all changing. But it takes people to change them. A hole in the ground, powerful as it is, can't do as much by itself."

She looks at me. I'm startled for a moment. Now I'm reading her mind! She's thinking me and my friends from Miles's class are going to be part of the change—we're going to jump. And she thinks it's good.

I shake my head. All of this jumping in our family, and now I'm going to jump?

CHAPTER TWENTY-THREE

The Students

"They jumped. I saw them. Without a sound, holding hands, they jumped."

I pause from the force of telling the five of them. I recover my breath as they stare at me. "I was at the Void this morning."

I look at them, and I know they're all going to jump, too. They just don't know it yet.

Donal shifts his gaze to the window beyond me. "I would have, too." He's remembering that night when we were all at the Void, when he wanted to jump with his little brother.

"They're not back yet, but we know they will be. We just don't know how they might or might not be changed."

From the front of class, as I lean on Miles's desk, I survey them. Kevin gets up from his seat in the back of the room, to pace. Monica doodles in her notebook, head hung low over it. Nathan goes to stand at the window, hands in his pockets. Donal hasn't moved. Lonnie sits next to him, flipping his pencil in the air over and over.

Spring break has just officially started this morning, but none of us plans to leave town. We all live in town or close by, and most of us will be working over spring break, not having some mad, all-out fling somewhere south and warm. We're sitting in the classroom where we always have our writing class with Miles, at the time we always have it.

Everyone came. I texted them to be there if they could, and they all came, knowing it must be important.

"How did you know they were going to do it?" Monica asks.

"First, I just felt called to go to the Void. I woke up really early, and I just had to go. It was a clear, no-excuses kind of feeling. It started the day before and then just got stronger and stronger. I hardly slept."

I look at them and then can't help saying, with a little pride, "It's an Indian thing." Then I blush. "My Granny knew, too." They nod.

"So, I walked over there this morning, early, just before dawn. I came through the field by my house and through the woods and stood at the edge of the trees, just back from the Void. And as I stood there, I knew. First, that someone was going to jump. Second, who it was. I was hot and cold, as if my blood pressure was up. I didn't know if I could watch, and if I did watch, if I would do something."

"Like what?" Kevin has stopped pacing, and beads of sweat line his forehead. He's half-nauseated by the thought of their jumping.

"I don't know. Jump myself? Scream? Try to stop them?" I rub my hands together absent mindedly, like Granny sometimes does. "But I didn't do any of those things, because I knew I couldn't interfere with their jump. This was their decision to make. My job was to keep it that way. They came just a few minutes later, together."

"How were they? Happy? Sad? Scared? Did they say anything?" Monica looks up at me, and I know she's seeing it as a love story, the kind of love story Monica would like to be part of someday. I guess I could see it that way, too, if I tried.

"I'd say they were quietly happy. I saw no tension, no nervousness, no worry. They just went about their business. They said something to each other, but I couldn't hear it. They were very calm."

"Oh my god," Lonnie says. He gets up from his chair and starts pacing in the front of the room, having left the back of the room to Kevin. "Oh my god. I can't believe it. I couldn't have stood watching them. I don't know if I can stand hearing about it now."

Lonnie is still feeling the after-effects of his recently departed fear of falling.

"It wasn't for them what it would be for you. They'd planned it for quite a while. You could see that in their calmness. They came ready to do it. You all know that. You know how well they know the Void, how much they've studied it, what Duncan Robert told them. They were prepared. They were not afraid."

"But, why? Really?" Donal asks. "Why did they do it?"

"You know that, too."

"What happens now?" Donal asks. "Do we do anything, notify anyone, get any help?"

I look at them, wondering if I've been expecting too much of them, wondering if I shouldn't have told them. They look back.

Then Nathan says, back to staring out the window, "No, there's nothing for us to do. Except wait."

I sigh with relief inside.

"Well, I know of one more thing we can do." We look at Kevin, surprised. "Think about it. What would he tell us to do?"

Lonnie sighs and nods, thinking of Miles. "Write about it. While it's still fresh."

I wait, wondering.

They look at each other.

"We need to go there to do it, don't we?" Lonnie shivers.

"Yes, we do." Nathan, turning from the window, says it firmly.

I feel a new tension in the room. This isn't about what somebody else did now. It's about what we'll do. They know it, too. They shift uncomfortably.

"Well, okay," Donal says, stepping up, as he always does. "Let's do it."

"Now?" A note of anxiety cracks Lonnie's voice.

They break into a discussion of the reasons they can't do it now—too late to plan it, other responsibilities, no writing gear or any other gear, not ready to write. Only Nathan and I remain quiet.

"Okay." Donal stops their noise. "Tomorrow."

They quiet immediately, most of them looking down, at their hands or shoes or the floor.

"Do you think they're dead?" Kevin breaks the silence again.

"No, I don't," Donal says, "but that's something you can write about—why you think they are."

"I don't think they are," protests Kevin. "I just don't know what to think."

"I know." Monica now has a catch in her voice. "Even though I didn't know them that well, I miss them."

"Me, too." Nathan smiles and adds, "At least we've got each other," in a fake-sincere voice, though I know he means it.

They laugh. Kevin throws a wad of paper at him, which he easily catches and lobs back. It's a nice moment, and I'm grateful to Nathan.

Donal gets them to talk about what time to go, where to meet, what to bring. They make their arrangements, gather up their things, and head for the exit.

"I'm not going to sleep tonight!" Kevin says, as he goes to the door with Monica.

"Come stay at my place. I'm not going to be sleeping, either. We can watch reality shows." She moves through the door ahead of him.

"Have you got room for one more?" Lonnie asks. "I'll spring for pizza. I don't want to be alone thinking about this."

"Sure." The three of them go out into the hallway.

"I've got to get home," Donal says to me. He smiles. "Brogan's waiting for me to read to him."

He turns to me at the door. "You'll be there tomorrow, right?"

"Yes, I'll be there. I wouldn't miss it. Thanks for doing the arranging."

"Thanks for telling us. I wouldn't miss it, either." He lifts his hand as he goes out the door.

Nathan moves from the window and comes up to the desk, where I'm still leaning. He stands in front of me and takes both my hands in his, surprising me. I look up at him, eyebrows raised.

"You're an interesting woman, Carrie Jean."

I have to smile. "Am I?"

"Yes, and I wouldn't miss it, either." He smiles back at me.

"I think you're the interesting one, Nathan. You've conversed with an angel."

"I think you have, too."

"Don't let my Granny hear you say I've been talking to angels. She'd think I abandoned my heritage for sure." I laugh, and he laughs with me.

He lets my hands go with a little squeeze. "I'll see you tomorrow night."

After he leaves, I sit for a moment, staring out the open door into the empty hallway in the quiet building, mostly deserted now. I'm glad the telling is over. I've done my part, delivering the message, without leading or directing anyone. And I think, overall, it didn't go too badly. They didn't run from it. The next time we see each other, we'll all be at the Void. I wonder how many of them know now that they're going to jump. I suspect they all do.

About the Author

Jane Peranteau has worked, written, and lectured in public health, community development, and communication for more than twenty-five years. Jane currently lives and works in Mountainair, New Mexico.

Hampton Roads Publishing Company

. . . for the evolving human spirit

Hampton Roads Publishing Company publishes books
on a variety of subjects, including spirituality, health, and
other related topics.

For a copy of our latest trade catalog, call (978) 465-0504
or visit our distributor's website at *www.redwheelweiser.com*.
You can also sign up for our newsletter and special offers
by going to *www.redwheelweiser.com/newsletter/*.